WOLF'S BITE

MAFIA MONSTERS SERIES

ATLAS ROSE

"Don't come any closer," I warned, my FBI badge useless in the face of this fanged monster. "I'll scratch and bite."

"You'll crawl and beg too." Phantom promised as he strode closer, a glint of desire danced in his eyes. "And that Special Agent...will only be the start of it."

The Costello's were mine.

Mine to corner. Mine to hunt. Mine to bring to their knees.

I've hunted Ruth for years now. Sat outside her house. Tracked every shady deal she'd ever done. She's my ticket to her family, and the entire cesspool they play in. The Costello's are lower than low...they are liars...*they are mobsters.*

They are Mafia.

This is more than a case for me. *This was personal.* The last bullet in my father's ruined policing career. He's a drunk now and alone...and I'm his only visitor—*pathetic huh?*

Only a war erupted. A war which I'm now part of...a war between the beasts that roam west of my city and the powerful Immortals they answer to.

I replayed that night in slow motion. Fangs. Blood...*and* Phantom. The Alpha of the Wolves. The one I saved from a rogue Vampire.

And the one who saved me.

I carry his bite mark on my shoulder...and the memory of what I'd done in his bed.

He might think he has a handle on me...

He might think *this* is more than what it was...

He's about to find out how wrong he is.

BE THE FIRST TO KNOW OF A NEW RELEASE!

Click here to signup for my newsletter.

Like my Facebook Page

Join my Facebook Group

START THE SERIES HERE

Vampire's Kiss
Vampire's Sin
Vampire's Promise

Wolf's Bite

Savage howls of rage tore from the warehouse. I pushed out my Glock, both hands fighting the tension as I stepped inside...and stopped cold. *Jesus.* The place was a bloodbath. Vampires and Wolves everywhere...bits of them, at least. I moved deeper through the open doorway, then jerked backwards as a Vampire tore past me, fangs bared and bloody.

I raised my gun and took aim as the bastard slowed, then stopped, turning his head to set that savage gaze on me. "Don't you fucking even think about it, bloodsucker," I warned, and stepped to the side.

But there was only the wall behind me...the cold, goddamn wall. Panic spiked and a mess of thoughts followed. *Should've called in...fuck what the SAC said.*

"*Mortal,*" the Vampire purred, and licked those bloody fangs. "You smell—"

Squeeze.

Boom.

Squeeze.

Boom.

Squeeze.

Boom.

The inhuman piece of shit stumbled backwards and went down as I licked my lips and croaked, "I do *not* repeat myself."

A Wolf came out of nowhere, lunging across the space to finish the job, taking off the Vampire's head with one unmerciful bite. My gut clenched at the sight as blood sprayed, hitting him in the center of the chest as the beast crouched over the body, strong muscles across his shoulders tensing before he narrowed in on my movement and whipped that terrifying steely gaze to me.

"Easy now, Wolf boy," I urged, and stumbled sideways as a wave of battling Immortals slammed into the warehouse door. The *dong* was soon muffled in howls of agony and piercing screams of fury. I had my gun...a fresh clip, and the desperate need to survive. I prayed it was enough.

A green glow came from the middle of the onslaught. Some kind of towering male moved amongst the glow, cleaving with a huge damn sword as he cut down Wolf after Wolf. I scanned the beasts and the fallen, looking for Ruth's fangers, and couldn't find them anywhere...I couldn't even find her.

But she was here—*I knew it.*

I'd followed her to the alley outside the Jewel, watching as she was attacked by the bloodsuckers. But they didn't kill her. Nothing in my goddamn life could be that easy. I watched as she screamed, drew her gun, and got off a shot before she was hit and slammed into the wall.

Still, the bitch rose in that alley, sneering and bloodthirsty like the deviants she lay with. She might be aligned with the beasts across the river, *but she was still going down.* They all were...every single Costello. If it was the last thing I did.

This was more than a job for me, more than a vendetta. This was justice a repayment for all the nasty shit her family had done...and the destruction they left behind. She had to pay for what she'd done...*they all did.*

I stepped backwards and smacked into something hard.

"Watchit!" A male snarled.

I spun with a mouthful of my own rage on the tip of my tongue, and stared into the unmistakable dark blue eyes of Blane Costello.

"You?" he snarled.

"You!" I spat.

I was lifting my gun before I knew it, justice and retribution burning in my veins, until a shadow rose behind him, and the blood red eyes of a Vampire met mine before it lunged. I couldn't move, not even to fire my gun, as the inhuman beast opened its jaws wide and bit, tearing into Blane's neck.

He stiffened, and then roared, arms flailing as he beat at the beast. Instinct kicked in as I centered the Immortal in my sights and fired.

Boom.

I didn't get to fire again before I was hit and knocked to the floor. My gun flew out of my hand and slid across the concrete floor, beyond my reach.

"Mortal."

I lifted my gaze to the midnight beast bathed in a sea of green. He wasn't Vampire…nor was he Wolf. He was something else…something *other.* I tore my gaze away, searching for my gun, and thrust my heels against the floor, shoving myself backwards.

"You are in the wrong place," he warned, and reached down, grabbing a handful of my shirt before wrenching me up from the floor.

The sound of tearing fabric filled my ears, but I didn't have time to care. I drew on all my training and let my weight fall. My shirt tore even more and cold air slipped in, licking my belly as I fell…before I drove my body upwards, unclenched my fist, and drove the heel of my hand under the bastard's jaw.

His head snapped backwards, not enough to hurt, but enough to bite his fucking tongue.

And it didn't matter how tough you were, that shit hurt.

He grinned as I pulled back, lifted my fists, and readied for the fight of my life.

Black blood slipped over his lips. That green hue around him pulsed with purpose.

"Fuck this," I raged, and lashed out with a fist, catching him on the jaw.

But he didn't fight back, just watched me as I lifted my leg, pivoted, and slammed out my boot, catching him in the side of the knee. He should've gone down…*if he was mortal.*

"You fight like a warrior." He stepped forward and lashed out an arm, grasping the ruins of my shirt. I bucked and punched at his arms, tearing out of his hold and spinning, leaving the ruins behind. Until he lunged once more, moving like a lion, grasping me by the neck.

"I wonder if you'd fuck as ferociously?" he purred in my ear, and lifted me.

My spine bowed as my feet left the floor. Pain dug into my head as he forced me to his will, that pitiless gaze staring into my soul before he clamped his hand over my breast.

Dark words slipped from his lips.

Words that made him smile.

Words that filled me with terror.

When he shoved me away, something stayed with me. My heart hammered, even harder than it had thundered before. I looked down at the deep sparkle of green embedded in my breast.

He smiled. "You'll be mi—"

He was hit from the side by a towering, savage male. Silver eyes of the Wolf glinted as the powerful hunter scanned me, then turned back to the Unseelie. One gnash of his teeth, and the Wolf advanced, hands fisted and bloody...he'd left a wake of destruction behind him.

I tried to look for my gun...but my vision blurred. Something was happening to me, something that made me stumble. Agony roared through my chest and with it came a hunger unlike any I'd felt before. Ravenous. Terrifying. I fought the pain, clawed and yanked my shirt. It was burning this *thing* inside me, tearing through my skin to burrow deep inside.

Unmerciful blows echoed in my ears and the sickening sound of tearing flesh followed. The Wolf howled, and that sound seemed to puncture something inside me...seemed to drive through the wave of terror as the world slammed into me. Senses fired. Adrenaline pounded in my veins until all I could hear

Steel glinted not far from my feet. I lunged toward it, fell, and hit the concrete hard. Agony roared through my knees when I pushed upwards. Teeth and red eyes were all I saw as the Vampire hurtled across the warehouse toward the Wolf.

I tried to cry out...tried to warn him. But nothing emerged but a low moan that burned from the back of my throat. The Vampire lunged, sinking his fangs into the Wolf as he reached for the Fae beast. The Wolf turned and drove a massive tattooed fist into the Vampire's face before turning back to the Unseelie. But he was too late. The Unseelie lashed out, catching the Wolf on the edge of his jaw.

Panic raged in those silver eyes as the Wolf stumbled backwards.

Blood poured from his arm as his eyes glazed over. If he died...then there was no surviving this...not for me. If the damn immortals didn't kill me, then this shit in my chest would. I glanced down at the glowing green fragments embedded in my flesh, fragments that were slowly sinking deeper into my skin. A wave of sickness washed over me as I lifted my gun and took aim. "Get the fuck off him, you filthy fucking vermin." I squeezed the trigger, *Boom,* catching the Vampire in the cheek.

Focus roared back in the Wolf's eyes as I clutched my side and stumbled forward, squeezing the trigger as I went. *Boom. Boom. Boom*...there was nothing but the kick in my hand, nothing but blood and bone blooming. Nothing but the Vampire as he stumbled backwards.

"Kill that *fucking thing, for Christ's sake,*" I roared.

The Wolf snapped to attention. That silver shine in his eyes was both frightening and magnificent. I'd never seen anything like him, not so big...or brutal. He jerked his gazed to the Unseelie monster as I shifted my focus to the Vampire.

"You know what you need, motherfucker?" I asked the cockroach, drawing my gun close and winced as agony slammed into me. I pressed the release on the side and dragged the magazine free. "You need a fresh fucking clip, that's what you need."

The Vampire hissed, its face a bloody, broken mess. I slammed the new magazine into place and pulled back the slide, hearing the *click.* My heart thundered, tearing through my head with a deafening beat...more than panic...more than fear. *Poison.* The thought rushed toward me. *It's poison.*

But there was no time to loose my shit...no time at all, as the Vampire in front of me lunged.

We collided *hard* and went down. My head hit the concrete and bounced. Fangs came for me as it rolled. I drove the muzzle into the thing and squeezed the trigger. The muffled shot was barely audible over the sounds of the Wolf and the shadowed beast fighting.

I fired...again and again...*and again.* The Vampire's hold slipped for a second. I scurried free and shoved against the ground, until I was grabbed and my head yanked upwards.

"Fucking bitch," the Vampire hissed in my ear. His nails dug into the sides of my neck before he slammed my face to the floor.

Stars burst behind my eyelids, blurring the blood splatter on the floor in front of me. I was wrenched upwards again, stunned...barely able to kick. Growing agony spread out through my chest, burning and searing like a brand. Through the distorted shimmer came that midnight beast once more, striding across the warehouse.

"No," I cried out, my arm feeling like lead as I lifted the gun and took aim.

"I'm one of the good guys," the *other* Unseelie snarled, then scowled. "Kinda."

The Vampire dropped me back to the floor as the terrifying beast lunged. I hit the floor, and that's where I stayed. Breathing. Alive. *For now.* The sickening battleground of rage quietened behind me.

Harsh breaths took their place.

"It's a mortal," the kinda-good-guy growled above me.

Shadows swallowed me. I blinked and tried to focus, finding the Wolf instead.

"Saved my fucking life."

"Pussy."

Big hands slid under me.

"Wait till I tell Shrike."

"Eat a dick, Mojin." the Wolf growled, and lifted me. But there was no jerk of my hair, no wrench of my body, nothing but a slow lifting until my side met his warmth.

A wave of agony blasted through me, turning pain into something else...something that howled inside me, something that swept through me like a fever.

"Don't," I whimpered. "Put me down."

"I'm not going to hurt—"

"Poison," I moaned. "I'm poisoned. Don't want you to be..."

He settled that unwavering focus on me, then lowered his gaze. I felt the sweep of his eyes and I quaked in response. "What the fuck?" he snarled, and jerked his head upwards. *"Mojin."*

I felt that hunger move deeper inside me, like glass rubbing against stone. I'd break soon…I'd shatter into a thousand pieces.

Footsteps resounded before the shadowed beast looked at me once more.

"What is that?"

"Fuck me…" the growl deepened with disgust. "She's not going to…"

The world swayed around me, blurring into nothing as his words slipped out of reach. *Scrape…scrape…scrape…*still that glass moved against the stone, wearing and grinding. Movement dragged me to the surface. I tried to force open my eyes.

Steel was all I saw.

Steel and him, the Wolf

He drew me closer, his nostrils flaring as he drew in my scent. "You're going to be okay, mortal."

"Special Ag…." The words were a mumble. He needed to know…*needed to get me to help.* I summoned my last strength. "Special Agent Carina Chase."

He gave a hint of a smile, one that both warmed and chilled me. My body jolted in his arms, pressed against his massive, tattooed chest. He curled his arms, lifting me higher against him as he lowered his head. The sweep of his nose through my hair set that hunger inside me to a fever pitch.

A deep rumble resounded in his chest. "You just saved my life. So, I'm giving you fair warning. I'm not kind," he warned as he walked, carrying me where, I didn't know. "Not even in the slightest. I'm fangs and claws. Sinew and sin. I'm a bad guy…and even badder Wolf." He closed his eyes for a second, and that purr in his chest moved deeper.

There was something utterly terrifying in his eyes when he opened them. He clenched his jaw and bared his teeth for a second, as though he fought a battle for control, then gently licked the blood from my head.

"Fuck me," he snarled, and stared into my soul.

As that glass wall inside me cracked, something pushed to the surface.

Predatory.

Agonizing.

Lust.

2

esire hit me, raw and dangerous, plunging down the back of my throat to fill my lungs. It pulsed and throbbed like a mindless beast. Still, it wasn't enough to occupy my chest. It drove deeper, more ravenous, searching for a way to slide through my body and lick between my thighs.

"Take it away," I growled, and the glass wall inside cracked a little more. "Just...do *something.*"

I closed my eyes with the hunger, clawing his body closer, writhing in the Wolf's arms. Until cold clarity hit me. *This isn't me!* That rational voice inside my head screamed. Still my body strained to get closer, my hands drifted over corded muscles, lips kissed. I even licked a bead of sweat from his skin and shivered.

I heard what I was saying...saw what I was doing...knew what I wanted...*from him.*

I whimpered and shoved, fighting as desperation roared.

This wasn't right.

Wasn't normal.

Panic moved through me like a freight train. My gun...*the Costellos.* I have to get back to them. Have to arrest...a wave of bestial need blasted through me. I moaned and stiffened. Every nerve stung and burned like I was on fire…

He could help me. *"Wolf."* I half growled, half whimpered.

Sweat broke out across my brow. I shivered with a fever. I *craved* this man. Hungered for his power, his control…and that hunger was dangerous. A battle raged. One without guns and claws…one with heat and need. I clenched my jaw, clenching until my head shuddered with the strain.

He glanced down at me as he walked. Silent. *Predatory.* His heat radiated into that punishing throb in my chest. I slid my hand from his arm, caught the bloody marks I left, behind and grasped my breast. "I need you to…" My fingers delved under the edge of my cotton bra to find my taut nipple.

He stopped walking, and lifted me harder against him.

Yes. The hunger crowed.

No! I roared.

One arm slipped free. Orange lights flared in the night before he reached down and yanked open the back door of a car and slid me inside. *"Don't* ruin the leather," he commanded. "It's new."

My own senses assaulted me. Newness. Masculine. The rich, deep, enveloping scent of…*him.*

The car door closed with a *thud.* I was alone.

A whine ripped from me, low, agonizing…*pathetic.* I slammed my eyes closed and felt that pounding in my chest grow stronger. The driver's door opened, my eyes popped wide, and a beast of a man slid behind the wheel. He glanced over his shoulder at me, meeting my gaze before dropping his lower.

My hand was over my breast, the edge of my bra yanked low, exposing my nipple to his gaze. "What's wrong with me?" I forced the words through the desperation and feeling of degradation.

"You've been spelled," he growled and tore his gaze away. "Don't worry, Special Agent. You're safe with me." Still his nostrils flared, that hard draw of breath made him turn back to me. Silver eyes glinted, drifting lower, cataloguing every inch of my body.

Safe.

The sports car started with a thunderous growl. Headlights flicked on, illuminating the street like it was day. Then we were moving, pulling out of the parking space and tearing through the night.

I ripped my hand from under my bra and touched raised red skin.

The sting was instant, blinding...tearing through me like a blast of heat. I moaned and rolled, arching my back before my head slipped and I hit the seat.

Cold leather was thick against the heat. I rolled, lifting my arms, pressing my body to the frigid touch as the car swayed, turning hard into a corner before the motor thrummed into the straight.

"Can't stop..." I whimpered, and slid my leg from the edge of the seat. "Can't stop this."

A growl filled the space.

Carnal and fervid.

I didn't know if it was me...*or him.*

That sound did things to me. I burned hotter, writhed harder. The cracked wall inside me spidered. I was losing control here. "Hospital," I whimpered. "Get me to a *goddamn* hospital."

"I do that, and it's all over. I do that, and I may as well tear out your fucking throat now. You're as good as dead out there... believe me."

I closed my eyes, and dug my bitten nails into the stitching of the leather. *Fuck his seat...and fuck him.* I moaned as we raced through the streets of my city, and I rubbed my crease against the seat edge. Still it wasn't enough. My hand drifted down the soft leather to find my bra. No shirt...*no goddamn shirt.* Exposed. I pinched, rubbed...and moaned.

A sickness raged inside me, making me shiver and shake.

The car skidded sideways as my breaths came harder and my hand drifted lower, over my belly to the button of my cargo pants. Half-lidded eyes closed fully as I bit my lip. I just needed...just *ached.*

"Jesus *fucking* Christ." The snarl came from the front.

For a second, I'd forgotten about him...for a second, I'd given in.

Chink. Fragments of that glass wall gave way. Still that stone was there, pushing against the barrier, waiting for the moment it all came crashing down. *"Please!"* I urged.

I didn't beg...but this was close.

So fucking close.

Tires howled as we skidded and the engine gave a howl before it died. The driver's door opened and closed in an instant. Still I felt him flanking the side of the car. I felt him through steel and glass as he grew closer. Icy night air blasted through the car and me as he yanked open the back door and looked down. I was on my back, my knees bent, fingers almost at the juncture of my thighs.

"Wrap your arms around my neck," he commanded, and climbed inside.

Too close...too goddamn close.

"I can walk, I'm not fucking useless," I snarled and scooted my ass forward, pushing him back. Cool night air lashed against the burn on my chest. Still, I shoved upwards, but as my boots hit the asphalt, I swayed.

Bright lights glittered in front of me. I licked arid lips and tried to focus. I knew this place...*The Hunting Ground,* that's where I was. Panic soared at the barely familiar street. We were across the river. On *their* side of the city. A place every officer knows to stay away from.

"I'm not having you walk through my fucking club trying to hump every fucking male in there."

I jerked my gaze to his. "You don't trust me?" I forced through clenched teeth.

"It's not *you* I don't trust, Special Agent," he barked with a curl of his lips.

It's them. The words raged in his eyes.

An insatiable wave slammed into me, rocking me hard.

I clenched my jaw and closed my eyes. Even now I could feel my breath hitching and my hips aching to thrust. That fire moved deeper, tasting...*claiming* as it went. A bead of sweat ran between my shoulders and slid down my spine, making me shiver and shake. I needed to get this over with...*any way I could.* "It's just fucking sex," I whimpered. "I don't care. I just need it gone."

Thunder rumbled in the back of his throat. "You might regret those words yet, female."

With a blur of movement, he dipped that massive frame, grasped me around the thighs, and hauled me over his shoulder before he turned, pressed the button to lock the car, and strode toward the bright lights.

Music hit me as he punched through the front doors and strode down a flight of stairs. Sensual music, grinding and throbbing, finding that part of me that howled with sickness.

Faint glittering lights bounced and blurred upside down in the pitch-black interior of the club. I caught the wide eyes of patrons as they turned their heads toward me...*was that the fucking Mayor?* I tried to lift my head and narrow my gaze. But we were gone, striding through that deep beat, and through a doorway at the back.

I held on, fingers gripping his biceps, but I couldn't even reach around half of the massive muscles. He walked with predatory grace, his long legs consuming the hallway. My cruel grip eased as that burn in my chest grew bolder. Instead, I flattened my palm and slid along his skin as he shoved open a door at the end of the hallway marked *Private,* and stepped inside.

The place reeked of Wolf. Pungent and enticing, suffocating like a rag down my throat. The place was huge, a kitchen and a living room. A TV was on and blaring somewhere. Still we kept moving, heading down a hallway to a door at the end...and stepped inside.

Bright lights came on before he yanked my thighs, sliding my body down the length of his until my feet hit the floor. I whimpered and dragged my hand up to shield my eyes. The room blurred and tilted. White walls were blinding until the lights softened.

He stood there, staring at me as I shook and shuddered. "You've been spelled," he started, his gaze sliding to my chest. "Fae magic is dark magic. Sometimes it can be used to..." I flinched and dragged that dangerous gaze to mine. "Make a mortal hunger."

"Hunger?" The word was thick in my mouth.

I couldn't feel my lips. Couldn't feel anything but that raging fire inside me.

"You saved my life," he growled, and dragged thick fingers through his short hair. "Back there. Damnedest thing I've ever seen."

I sucked in hard breaths, unable to understand what he was saying. "I feel..." I started, before the room tilted too far and the bright lights dulled...to darkness.

Strong hands caught me. Agony burned at his touch. But it wasn't a normal kind of pain. It was unrelenting and bestial, making an animal of me as I was lifted. He crossed the room in three long strides before I jerked from his hold, and hit the bed. I moved fast, scrambling to the other side of the massive bed, and scanned the room. "Stay...stay the fuck away from me," I warned, jerking my gaze to his once more.

Hard breaths punched me like blows as I searched for a way out of there. Something pinched and burned in my chest. I looked down at the sparkling green fragments that glittered like emeralds in my skin, and lifted my hand.

"I wouldn't do that," he warned.

But I touched them anyway. The burn moved deeper, sickness and frenzied desire drove deeper, making me close my eyes. "Hospital," I mumbled. "I need a hospital."

"And you'd be raped a hundred times by morning."

I flinched as fear stabbed deep. Terror like that changes you. Makes you volatile…*makes you weak.* I opened my eyes to stare at him across the room.

"Easy." He lifted his hands. "I'm not going to hurt you."

I shivered with fever, and my knees trembled, making me double over and grip the corner of the mattress.

"How about I get you some water?"

"No," I growled, and lifted my gaze, finding him through the sweatstained strands of my hair.

He watched me with careful eyes, taking in every tremble and cataloging every twitch.

"This is going to go a lot easier if you just give in."

He stepped on the back of his boot, dragging it free before stepping out of the other. His socks were next, quick sweeps of his hand and he straightened, pulling off his shirt, then reaching for the button of his jeans.

"So, you're going to rape me instead?" I forced out.

I knew the fucking deal. I was here…*alone,* all the way across the river. No backup…not even a call to dispatch. No one knew I was here. I was as good as dead.

"Rape you?" His hands fell from the waistband of his jeans. "I might be a fucking monster…but I'm no rapist. You're sick, female…and you're growing sicker by the second. There's Fae magic in you now. I don't know how long it'll last for, but I've seen the effects of it without someone to protect you. Your scent will change…" his nostrils flared. "I can already taste it. Fervid, carnal. Irresistible to males…especially to males like me. I'm offering you a way out of this."

He reached for the button of his jeans once more.

Brass slid through the denim.

The zipper slipped low.

"I'm offering myself here." His nostrils flared, and something primal moved behind his eyes.

This fever had me by the throat now. Its fangs pressed against my skin, their honed points driving deeper as he pushed his jeans low, sliding them over his hips to reveal thick thighs and the biggest cock I'd ever seen in my life.

"You can use me. It's just sex, isn't that what you said?" A flicker of satisfaction curled the corner of his lips. "Have you ever been serviced?" he murmured, and stepped out of his jeans in all his animalistic glory. Silver shone in his eyes as he took one slow step forward. "I bet you haven't. You've got that hunger inside you, an *ache* that Fae magic has taken over. It can't create what wasn't already there. How has it been for you, Special Agent? A few slobbery kisses, fumbling in the dark until the pathetic excuse for a male shoves it in? Did he pump ferociously, barely making you warm with hunger before he grunted and was done?"

My face burned. "You know nothing about my sex life."

"You're married to your job, aren't you?" He licked his lips. I didn't like the way he looked at me now…*didn't like it at all.* "Leaves no room for a husband. I bet they don't stick around long enough to warm the other side of the bed, do they? The ones you keep in secret…I bet they don't stick around for long at all. You've never been fucked, Carina. Not the kind of fucking that owns your soul. Not the kind you can't run away from. One damn taste and you're a slave."

"Owner of strip clubs and prostitutes, I bet you get all the fucking you can stand."

An image blasted through my head. Him on his back, some random female riding that cock over and over. "I bet you don't even know their names."

He stopped, and that spark of excitement dulled in his eyes. "I don't sleep with the girls. None of my men do. Period."

I've seen the dancers he has here. High class models. The man would have to be blind not to want them.

Emeralds glinted and sparkled in my chest and down my side, casting that sickening green glow across the room.

"Not long now, Special Agent. Once that hits fully...there's no turning back. I can either take care of you...or I can let you leave."

I could smell the sickness wafting from my body. A dark, lush taste that wafted in the air. Heat moved between my thighs, making me shift my stance as I closed my legs tighter. The friction of my cargos making me whimper.

I wouldn't even make the corner...I knew it in my bones.

They'd smell me...and there's no way I could fight. Not like this.

*Use me...*his words rolled through my mind. *It's just sex.*

I licked my lips and tried to find the words. "Shower. Got blood in my hair."

White fangs flashed in the dim light as he smiled. "I don't mind if you don't."

Still, I glanced at the darkened doorway. My heart was thundering, the cracks in the glass wall opening wider, leaving bigger fragments in their wake.

He crossed the room, switched on the bathroom light, and stepped inside. The hiss of the shower was so loud, it made me flinch. I wanted it, wanted to wash this shit off me...wanted to wash it all away. I shoved against the mattress and stumbled around the side of the bed.

He was waiting for me as I entered, leaning against the vanity, his rippled body like a god's.

"Don't stand there like that," I bit.

"How would you like me?" He shoved forward, towering over me as I gripped the edge of the door. "You want me on my knees, Carina? I can do that...On my knees. You on your knees. I don't give a fuck how this happens...as long as it happens."

I nudged off my boots and reached behind me for the clasp of my bra before I stopped. His voice was deeper, guttural and strange. There was a beast in his eyes...and that beast watched every inch of me as I worked the metal hooks and let the garment fall.

That guttural growl mingled with the hiss of the shower.

The same sound that had filled the car.

"Careful, Wolf," I cautioned. "Your fangs are showing."

I shoved down my jeans, taking my panties with them. I didn't give a fuck about being naked in front of him. Couldn't have cared less that his gaze followed me as I stepped into the spray and moaned.

My hands spread out against the shower walls. The heat moved down the length of my back, until rivulets slipped into the crack of my ass. A touch against my side made me flinch before the sweet scent of soap stung my nose.

He was gentle. Gentler than those big hands should've allowed. Still that fire inside me was moving, shifting and rolling, pressing against my skin...*or was it my soul that writhed in desperation?*

I was lost in the feel of his hands as he reached around me, fingers sliding over my breasts, wide palms following. My hips rocked forward with the sensation...a slow, unfulfilled thrust.

One brush as he swept my hair to the side and reached for my chin, tilting my face upwards, my hair falling under the spray. He left for a second, before those fingers delved into the strands to find my scalp.

He washed me, cared for me. The strange sensation made

me flinch. I'd never had this before. Not this kind of attention... or trust.

No trust, no way.

Trust only got you into trouble.

Trust got you killed.

The creamy feel of the conditioner moved through my hair before he was sliding lower. His warm breath melted against my skin as I pushed backwards and moved out of the spray. His hands ran upwards, across the scar at my calf, and reached higher, sliding between my thighs.

The brush of his thumb along my crease had me whimpering.

"I'm gonna take real good care of you," that fierce, bestial tone promised.

Then he was rising, running his fingers through my hair until the strands squeaked, then the spray ended. He was gone from the shower before I turned. Grabbing a towel to hand to me, using another to run across his body. I dried, shivering and shaking. My eyes were drawn to those fingers, those hands. "Why?" I jerked my gaze to his. "Why do this?"

There was a twitch in the corner of his eye. I swore I saw panic for a second before he smothered it with a lazy, seductive smile. "It's just sex, remember?" he murmured.

But even as I rubbed the soft cotton against my skin, I knew he was lying.

Call it a cop's instinct.

Call it a woman's intuition.

Call it anything you damn well wanted.

The hunger in me didn't care, not even when he closed the distance between us and took the towel from my hands, leaving it to drop to the floor. "Now, about that itch, Special Agent."

My knees trembled and that shit in my chest glowed as he grabbed me around the waist and carried me from the bathroom.

My spine hit the bed, wet strands of my hair flung onto the pillows. He rose above me, the dim light catching a scar on his cheek. I was so mesmerized by his eyes, I hadn't noticed it before. I lifted my hand, my fingers tracing the edges. *Alpha.* The word raged. "I don't even know your name," I murmured.

He grinned, those eyes sparkling. "Phantom."

"Phantom." I moved against him, my legs still hooked around his waist…until I stiffened.

That fever was moving like a freight train through my veins.

"Easy now," he murmured, and lowered his head to my breast.

Warm lips. Warmer breath.

He took the hard peak of my nipple and that ravenous need howled inside me. My hips bucked against his belly. His face was illuminated by that sickening green as it ebbed and glowed.

His fingers traced the grooves of my ribs as he moved lower, breaking the hold of my ankles, his hands spreading out against my belly. I knew what Wolves were like, knew how they killed their prey—he kissed my stomach—they took the soft organs first.

Canines scraped against my skin, making me lift my head. *Fuck me, his fangs were huge.*

His nostrils flared as he moved lower, his hands sliding to the backs of my calves before he lifted my feet to the edge of the mattress, drawing my knees higher, the size of his body splaying them wide…as he looked down.

He closed his eyes for an instant, that internal battle raging once more.

"What is it?" I moaned.

"*Nothing,*" he forced the word through clenched teeth before he opened his eyes and lifted his gaze. Silver shine was all I saw. But it wasn't the man staring back at me. *It was the beast.* The hunter. *The Wolf.*

With a low, throaty growl of hunger, he lifted his hand to

spread my lips wide. One lick of his tongue, and I closed my eyes and threw my head back, howling my own desperation.

The air shuddered.

The walls shook.

The tip of his cock danced around the sensitive flesh of my clit, making me whimper. My hips bucked, but still he took his fucking time. The heat inside me was an inferno.

This was no fucking sex…

This was goddamn torture.

"Stick it in for fuck's sake," I pleaded, hands fisting the sheets on either side of me.

"Stick it in?" he repeated.

I traced every brush of that swollen, sensitive nub, my legs spreading wider. I looked down at the glistening core of me, weeping…*aching.*

He lifted that unmerciful gaze to mine and moved deeper, dragging his finger along the center, only to dance around my core…until his beast let out a savage, unmistakable warning, and he clamped his mouth over me, his tongue delving deep.

I screamed with the pleasure, bucking and thrashing. My hands fell to the back of his head as I climaxed. The wave was sudden, consuming, leaving me breathless as he dragged his tongue along my slit, taking in every part of me…over and over.

"I licked it." That bestial snarl of thunder came as he looked up from between my legs. "So it's mine."

3

I *licked it...so it's mine.*

I sucked in hard breaths. "Just fucking sex, *remember?*" I growled.

That hunger didn't ease, it rolled through my body and tore apart my resolve. I moaned and dropped my head backwards to slam against the bed. A hot, savage blast of rage filled the air. A storm raged inside me. One that had no plan on easing.

"Just. Fucking. Sex." He repeated each word a stab of his tongue.

I rocked my hips upwards, that sick Fae power still rising inside me.

"Just sex," he growled against my belly as that heady, aromatic scent bloomed deeper in the air.

He grabbed my hand and lifted it, pinning it outwards on the bed. "Just lust. Nothing more than *fucking*." He grabbed my other wrist and slid the back of my hand out to the other side.

My legs lifted and wrapped around his hips, heels digging into his ass as he thrust against me. The swollen head of his cock pushed in, making me bite my lip. God, I'd never felt anything like him.

Nothing so primal.

Nothing so raw.

"Yes!" I screamed and arched my spine from the bed.

His tongue raced across my nipple, and his fangs dragged across sensitive skin. I clawed his body, desperate for that bulbous head to slide all the way inside. But he didn't, he slid back out…then in again—leaving me aching—a tortured existence.

He curled my hands higher, elbow digging in the bed as he stared into my eyes. This was a man who knew how to fuck, how to torture…how to kill. I met that steely gaze with my own, and even as the heat of the Fae's power rode me, something else bloomed inside.

A flower opened.

A whisper released to the wind.

An alteration in my subconscious. One I felt in the marrow of my bones. That heady, masculine scent filled my nose and plunged deep inside. I clamped my lips closed, drawing it in deeper, letting it spread through my lungs. I didn't know what I wanted more…that scent or the languid thrusts of his cock as he worked himself in deeper.

"More," I cried, and ground my teeth.

"More fucking," he growled, and thrusted in deep. "As you command."

My eyes widened, and my breath caught. He stretched me, filled me, stoked that hunger inside. I curled my fingers around his as heat turned to rage. *"Harder."*

His gaze shifted with a curl of his lips, unfocused… unbridled. He slammed his hips against mine and I was lost in the brutal ecstasy of him. In the power…*in the strength.*

For a second…just one blinding second, I imagined him as *mine.* My lover…my Wolf. My defender…my partner—before I ripped the illusion away.

He wasn't mine…and never would be.

Wrong side of the river…for both of us.

The orgasm barreled down on me, filling my ears with thunder…sending tremors quaking through my body and sparks of lightning behind my eyes.

He stilled, hilt deep, his warmth spreading inside me. Still I rocked with the motion, desperate for every inch…and every drop of him. Hard breaths filled me as he lowered his head to the side. I turned my face into the side of his neck.

And as the pain of what *might've been* lashed with a cutting sting, I pressed my lips to the pulsing vein in his neck and kissed him. He stiffened, and a low growl rose before it was swallowed.

"Do that again…" he murmured.

I dragged my nose against his neck, drawing in that seductive scent of his skin. One tiny lick of my tongue against the pulse and he shivered. I kissed his neck…small, tender kisses. When that green pulsing shit flared again in my side and I stiffened and moaned, he grew hard inside me and settled into that rhythm once more.

He moved lower, kissing my breasts, pulling that thick, throbbing, delicious length free to slide his fingers inside me.

"Come for me, Carina," he murmured, his thumb circling my clit. "Come."

I bucked and howled, digging in my heels to drive my body down harder. Splayed thighs, throbbing pussy. He stared down at me with singleminded focus, the slick fingers of his other hand pressed down on my abdomen as he locked me in place.

He fucked me with his fingers.

He fucked me with his tongue.

And when that agony eased inside me…I finally closed my eyes. Hard breaths eased…and carried me away into darkness.

I slept, plunging into terror once more. Red glowing eyes waited for me.

You fight like a warrior…

It's just sex.

Dreams haunted me. Agony mingled with lust. I cracked my eyes open, my body aching and sore.

"I'm right here." That voice from my dream was beside me.

His hand on my hip rolled me onto my side. A massive thigh pushed between mine. I whimpered as he slid against my entrance. I was burning up inside, aching and throbbing. My whole body was one giant pulse of need.

I barely had enough strength to lift my arm over my head, but he was there. The scratch of a beard that wasn't there before, and the faint sound of voices somewhere outside. The door opened.

"Not now," my lover growled.

A dream. It had to be a dream. A sinful, erotic dream. The door closed once more and it was just us again, thrusting... needing. That heavenly scent moving deeper inside me, making me push back against him.

"More," I murmured, my voice thick with sleep.

"Deeper?" he asked.

"That smell," I answered. "I want more."

A deep growl against my throat and it was there, heavy and ripe in the air. He moved between my legs, his finger finding my clit, circling and claiming, drawing deep shudders from my soul. I lifted my knee, wanting him everywhere.

I couldn't get enough. Even when I quaked...even when I came.

Thick tears slid down my cheeks. I never cried.

I never cried.

He slipped from me and curled his body against my back.

I drifted once more into the darkness....and this time there were no Vampires waiting.

This time there was only him.

Phantom.

4

———

PHANTOM

She's mine. The hunter staked his claim. *I want to keep her.* "No," I commanded as I stood beside the bed, watching her chest rise and fall. He just snarled, bared his teeth, and pawed at the ground.

No? he said finally. That one defiant sound said all I needed to know. This was going to be a battle for the fucking ages...I could feel it in my bones.

"No," I answered. "She doesn't want us."

Then fucking make her want us, he demanded.

I turned away from the sight of her, the thin sheet draped over her body and crumpled at her waist. The mating scent was thick and fucking choking. *What the hell have I done?*

One glance over my shoulder and I was tearing myself away, turning the handle and striding from the room. Voices roared, filling the hallway from the other side of the house. I opened the door of the bedroom next to mine and strode to the closet.

"Your marking stench is stinking up the place." The growl came from behind me.

I grabbed a pair of sweats before stepping into them and yanked on a shirt.

"What's up with that?" Church leaned against the doorway.

"None of your fucking business…that's what."

There was a twitch at the corner of his lips. A raw nerve, stabbed and flailing…he knew better than to push it anymore.

"The fallout?" I demanded.

"It's bad," he said with a shrug.

"Justice?"

"Alive…for now."

I stilled at the words. *For now. That* didn't sound good. "Set up a meeting with the Fae…make that Mojin. Here."

"Here?" his voice rose. "You sure that's wise?"

"No." I turned to him. "You want to tell me how to run the pack and take care of business?"

He backed down. "Here it is."

"We need eyes and ears watching Finis. I want to know his every fucking move. I need to know where he goes, who he sees. I need every communication, Church."

"I know, brother."

I jerked my gaze to his. Panic crowded in. I couldn't let it. Not panic. Not fear. It had no place in my world…it was hunt or be hunted, kill or be killed. But still it was there, at the edges of my mind…like a scream, trapped…*frozen.* One gut-wrenching, terrifying sound. *A woman's scream.* Howling. Soul-shattering. But I wouldn't allow that scream in. I wouldn't turn my attention to it…*not yet.*

"The girls?" Church asked.

"If need be, we torch the files."

"We do that and we lose track of them…every one of them," my enforcer warned.

A sinking feeling filled me. I drank it down deep. Every hurt and every pain…every woman's name that'd crossed my desk. "So be it. The pack needs to be ready to run…" my focus drifted to my bedroom. "But not yet."

"She's gonna be a problem, that one. Has a hard on for the Costellos a mile long. Heard she's tough…it's in her blood."

"Isn't it always?"

First the Costellos…and now the goddamn FBI. That's all we needed with the Inner Circle breathing down our necks. "Did the Feds get everything?"

"Every fucking fiber. They're having a goddamn field day. You know they're looking for her, right?" He didn't need to jerk his head, but he did…just to aggravate me.

"They can keep on fucking looking. I can make her disappear faster than they can blink."

"You sure you want to do that?"

If she was gone…then she was gone. There'd be no coming back.

No, I wasn't sure…not about anything when it came to her it seemed. Two days she'd been out. Two days, and still that mark on her side clung tight. I'd seen shit like that once. A dark Fae warrior taking a human as a sex slave. That shit kept her pliable…that shit kept her on him every second of the day.

The thought rose inside me. A sick, twisted thought. A raging hunger. One I shoved away. No, I wouldn't do that…still, I turned my head and sniffed myself. That unmistakable scent was stronger than before.

Want her, the beast urged.

Silver eyes shining in the darkness of my soul. "Keep wanting. She's not ours to take."

"The men are ready when you are. I'll make the call and summon the Genie."

"Keep calling him that and he'll give you three wishes that'll terrify you," I warned.

The bastard smiled before he turned.

"Church."

He stopped at the doorway to his bedroom and looked over his shoulder.

"She's different."

His nostrils flared. Hunger moved behind his eyes. He felt her, too...I knew it. His jaw clenched and his muscles bulged. Even his fists were tight. "I know," he answered before he went into his room and firmly closed the door.

I know. I closed my eyes for a second. Maybe I wasn't the only one totally fucked in the head? Maybe I wasn't the only one who felt her hunger like a furnace? I lifted my hand and pressed it to my chest. A goddamn ache burned there, blue flames burning the hottest. The woman was going to set my entire world on fire. I could just feel it.

I want her. The beast didn't give a fuck. He wanted what he wanted, and took with savage need...*The only thing was...he'd never wanted until her.*

Never demanded.

Never raged.

But now he paced. Claws extended. Fangs bared. *Yeah, he wanted alright.*

I strode out of the bedroom, and lingered at my door, senses searching, finding her breaths steady, her pulse slow before I made my way along the hallway to the others. Two days they'd been holed up here, hiding, *healing.* The cops knew better than to descend on this side of the river without bringing everything they had. But they'd come...sniffing around, *if only for her.*

The heady scent of eggs and bacon wafted in the air. Feeding time was six meals a day in our house. We all took turns at cooking and cleaning, even me.

But they never said a word when I strode into the kitchen. Just sly glances at me, and at each other. I didn't give a fuck. I'd killed more than my fair share that night. Saved more than one of their asses...and they knew it.

I grabbed a plate and moved to the heavy skillet. Only the best pieces, crunchy on the outside, thick and meaty in the middle. The smell of cure and salt made my mouth water. Still, I took my time, touching each piece, laying the bacon out flat before I hunted through the wreckage of what was left behind for another.

The hairs on the nape of my neck rose, then settled.

Eggs were next. I grabbed the spoon and carved through the fluffy scramble, searching for fragments of shell… then placed it to the side. "Tomato?"

"Didn't cook it."

My top lip curled with a flash of anger before I reached for the smaller frying pan. Knobs were turned, and hungry flames lit, heating up the surface before I reached for the refrigerator door. I grabbed the butter and the best tomato I could find, then straightened. I sliced the ends and through the middle, placed a blob of butter in the searing hot pan, then the tomato on one side, sizzling and growing softer.

"You okay?" Vitold asked.

"Fine," I answered and turned, meeting his gaze.

"Is she…" the Wolf started before he licked his lips.

Ready? Is that what the bastard was asking?

"Healing," he finished. "The Fae sickness."

"A little," I answered and turned, grabbing the edges of the tomato and flipping it. But my subconscious rose like a wave. "Shouldn't have brought her here."

"Where else were you going to take her? She saved your ass, right?" The Wolf shoved off from the counter and stepped closer.

The others were in the living room…listening.

"She saved your ass, so you're indebted. That's all. Heal her up, and send her on her way. Simple."

Was that a warning…or a nice solid word of advice?

Either way, I swallowed it like a fucking stone.

One nod and I turned, grasped the handle of the pan, and slid the tomato onto the plate.

"You *are* gonna send her on her way, aren't you, brother?"

Vitold urged.

"Yes," I forced through clenched teeth, that seething rage punching higher until it was all the way to the surface. "Yes, I'll send her on her goddamn way."

He was satisfied. It was all about the operation anyway, wasn't it? Can't have the Feds showing up here...can't have the bastards sniffing around at all. What was gone must stay gone...*forever.*

"The money?"

"All taken care of. Hurrow flew down. Ruin took care of the rest. The girls are working...everything is running like clockwork," he answered softly. "Can I see her?"

"She's asleep."

"Can I see her?"

I jerked my gaze to his. Inside, my Wolf went quiet and still, scenting...*careful now.* Hackles itching, a tremble in his lips. My gaze shifted from the Wolf's gaze to his throat before I licked my lips and gave a slow nod. "Do not wake her."

Part of the pack. What belonged to the Alpha...belongs to the pack.

Didn't mean I had to like it.

I wasn't like the fucking Vampires.

He never took his gaze from mine as the Wolf stepped backwards, turned a little, and left. I closed my eyes, sensing him as he headed along the hallway, each step toward her like a fist against the cage of my chest.

Hard breaths. Her food was cooling by the second. I tore my gaze away, fighting every fucking urge to lunge like the damn beast I was and take the enforcer to the floor, my fangs against his neck and that warning growl tearing through my throat. *Back the fuck off.*

I was moving before I knew it, long strides gaining speed. Church raised his head, following the movement, before he turned back to whatever was on TV.

The door to my bedroom was open…

The Wolf was inside.

A *crack* tore through my jaw as I clenched tight and strode through. Vitold stood against the bed, staring down at her, his hands in the pockets of his hoodie, not touching her…*not yet.*

She was naked, the sheet tossed aside, her firm breasts rising with each breath with the Unseelie mark marring it, her belly caving with the movement. That hunger inside me rose, and my cock twitched against the soft lining of my shorts.

Her legs were bent, her dark thatch of hair glistening and wet.

Fuck me, she looked good.

Honest.

Raw.

Mine, my Wolf demanded.

"She's…beautiful." Vitold murmured and turned away, those dark eyes filled with need. His jaw was clenched tight, his hands fisted and pressed against his sides.

There was a flash of anger before that need turned to panic.

He felt her.

He saw her…*the real her.*

The woman she was becoming.

All that fucking potential…right in front of us.

And fuck me if the enforcer wasn't hard for her as well. But it didn't matter. None of this did. I had businesses waiting for me, and once that shit in her side stopped humming, she'd run a goddamn mile to get away—*I would.*

Vitold lowered his gaze, then his head. The submissive stance howled like thunder. He wanted her…but he wouldn't step a foot wrong where she was concerned. He'd chosen which side he wanted…and he'd chosen right.

The fetid scent of Unseelie hit me. Rage made the hairs on my arms stand on end. That same sick energy that came from the shit in her side…now carved through the air.

The dark one was here…

"Bring Mojin to me," I commanded.

A nod of his head and the Wolf glanced at her once more, nostrils flaring wide with the scent of sex and lust…*and her.* He left, closing the door behind him…

Too soon.

The thought filled me. Too soon to see her. Too soon to touch her. I closed the space between us in an instant, lifted the sheet, and covered her body. Her tight nipples peaked under the covering. Fuck, I wanted them in my mouth. I chased the thought with the slide of my tongue across my lips. I wanted everything in my mouth. I lowered my gaze to the soft hair between her thighs.

Owner of strip clubs and prostitutes, I bet you get all the fucking you can stand. Her words roared back to me. If she only fucking knew…

The door opened behind me and the dark one strode in.

"Wolf."

"Dickhead."

I caught the small smile at the corner of his mouth before he stepped closer to the bed. A vibration was in the back of my throat. I couldn't help it.

"Easy brother, just gonna move the sheet at her side, okay?"

That warning eased. Still the tension was there, wound fucking tight, like I was about to snap when he lifted the middle of the sheet and dragged it from her side.

He touched her, pressing his fingers against her belly, then her breast, and I fucking hated every second of it. He said nothing as he fixed the sheet and straightened.

Those cold eyes grew even colder. There was a clench of his jaw and a curl of his lips. Panic filled me for a second as he jerked his head toward the doorway. We left her then, covered, sleeping, lost in a world I wanted to know. I was falling…hard. Desperate. *Driven.*

The door closed gently behind me before I was grabbed, my shirt fisted, and I was hauled into Church's room.

"You were supposed to take care of her, *not fucking bond to her*," Mojin snarled, eyes dark and wild, teeth bared and savage.

"You think I meant for this to happen?" I punched his hold from my fucking shirt and turned to pace.

"You know what this will do to her, right? And I'm not talking like a few days of under the goddamn weather sickness. I'm talking about *life fucking altering*."

Panicked, I glanced at the open door behind Mojin...my door was closed, and she was asleep.

Still, that didn't change the fact I was a selfish sonofabitch.

"She'll forget me."

"Like *hell* she will. No chance on that. You decided that the minute you let your beast claim her."

"You think I meant for this?" I forced the words between clenched teeth. "If I could've controlled the beast, I would've."

"That's the fucking problem with you Wolves...you're all goddamn hot-blooded. Doesn't change the fact she's now *your* problem...judging by the scars and the way she fought, you've got your work cut out for you...*good luck with that.*"

The Unseelie turned, and shadows grew along the wall around him.

"Can you change it? Take it out...*break the bond?*"

Mojin stopped. "Carve out her fucking soul while I'm at it?" he snarled over his shoulder. "May as well kill her now. She'd be as good as dead."

He left then. His heavy steps echoing all the way until the front door of the club closed with a *slam!*

"Fuck me," I snarled, and sighed.

Her food.

It was getting cold.

Jesus, what had I become?

Still, I lifted my head. This bonding shit was a double-edged sword...or a double-ended dildo, whichever way you looked at it—we were both about to be fucked.

5

Life fucking altering.

Panic filled me as I scanned the room and yanked the damn sheet against my chest. *Fuck!* My gun. My clothes. I jerked my gaze to the door. The words slipped through the cracks in the door.

*He'd bonded with me. Changed me...*I looked down as the sheet pooled in my lap. Emeralds still glinted and ebbed, embedded in my skin. *He'd claimed me...somehow.* I lifted my hand, tried to dig my nail underneath. Pain and hunger roared instantly, rippling and carving through my chest. My pulse boomed like thunder and that sickening glow throbbed.

Part of me wanted to go to him, wanted to get down on hands and knees and beg for release...and other part...was fucking disgusted. *Get a goddamn grip, Chase.*

I yanked my hand away, rolled, and stumbled for the bathroom. Acid rose in the back of my throat. I gripped the vanity and clung tight. Hard breaths slowed the panic...and the agony ebbed away.

He'd done something to me. I lifted my gaze to my reflection in the mirror. Hard brown eyes stared back. I looked the same—

I lowered my gaze to the sparkle in the swell of my breast —*apart from that shit.*

I lowered my head, eased the tap on, and drank from my cupped hand. Cold water hit my belly, but before it had a chance to warm, I reached to the floor and gathered what was left of my clothes.

Splatters of blood had dried. My bra was filthy.

Touch me. The words rose from my memory. That's what I'd said to him…that's what I'd begged for him to do. He hadn't then…he'd carried me, protected me. *It's just sex.* That sounded like a fucking joke now, didn't it? I scrambled, yanking on my cargos and shoving my bare feet into my boots, leaving my underwear and socks behind. I needed a shirt…*and a fucking gun.*

Then I was out of here.

I had enough shit and drama in my life without adding this freakshow to the mix. Glowy shit or no glowy shit, I was done.

I strode to the door, gripped the handle with both hands and cracked open the door. The faint smell of bacon made my damn mouth water. But the place was silent. *Maybe he was gone?* I stepped out, rolling my heels as I moved, glanced into the bedroom next to this one, and stared at the open closet.

I hurried, making as little sound as I could, and yanked out a black t-shirt five sizes too big and slipped it on. Steel shimmered on the shelf. A shiny brand new Sig. It's wasn't a Glock…but it'd do. I pressed the release, checked the loaded magazine, and quietly pushed it back into place. One check of the slide and a round was there.

I headed for the door as the deep growl of an argument spilled along the hallway.

But there was only one voice…*the Alpha…Phantom.*

I lifted the firearm in front of me and stepped out of the hallway, scanning a sunken living room before I turned to the towering male standing in the middle of the kitchen…arguing to a plate of bacon and eggs.

He stiffened, then slowly turned his head. Eyes widened, but it wasn't because of the gun in my hand…it was because of me.

"You're awake." He searched my eyes, then swept his gaze down, stilling on the shirt I wore.

Those damn nostrils flared, and his lip curled for a second. Anger, pure hot-blooded anger. He didn't like me wearing it. But he swallowed that fire, his voice growing cold. "How long?"

"Long enough to know you did something to me. Made me want you…"

He shook his head. "No, that was the spell."

"Then it was something else," I bit back, the gun steady in my hand. "Either way, you took advantage."

Fuck me, he was spectacular. He straightened, rising to his full height. Memories invaded, low moans of desire, the tangle of our limbs. My cries of *more…harder.* That ache never satisfied. Still he didn't demand, didn't take, only offered himself time and time again. "I gave more than I ever took."

"I don't think so, *buddy.*" I took a step toward the door.

"You like to fuck…and you like to fuck me. Your body likes it, too," his voice deepened into that seductive purr that made my knees tremble as he took a step closer. "Deny it all you want but it wasn't just the spell was it Special Agent? It was you toward the end. You who wanted all the carnal things I did to you. Why fight it?"

"Because liking it and wanting it are two different things." I forced steel into my tone and met his gaze. "Now, *back the fuck off* before I do something I'll regret."

"I thought we did that already."

There it was…that cold hard shine in his eyes. A beast waiting. Pain was hard in him. Just as it was hard in me. Stone cold steel.

"Carina, put it down," he muttered, and that hard tone grew

harder as he stepped closer, flanking me until he stood between me and the door. "In case you've forgotten you have a chest full of Unseelie desire. You might feel strong now, but I guarantee it'll come back. It'll hit you in waves that you can't control. It's dangerous out there for you." That glint in his eyes hardened. "Other males won't be so kind. Stay here. Stay and I can protect you."

"I warned you." I sucked in hard breaths, fighting that shake in my voice. "Get the fuck out of my way, Wolf. Let me go."

"That's not going to happen." He gave a shake of his head, his own chest rising hard. "You know that...*I know that.* Put down the gun and stop being childish."

Childish? I lifted the muzzle slowly, past his knee. The idea of hobbling him appealed, slow the big fucker down. Then I moved to his thigh...and higher, lingering on his balls long enough to see him pale...just slightly, but it was there. "Now I'm walking out that door...and you're not going to move. Promise me."

He smiled, his fangs showing. "I'll do no such thing."

"Then I have no choice." I lifted the gun, center of body mass.

"You wouldn't dare..." he started.

Until I squeezed the trigger.

Boom!

He rocked backwards.

Blood trickled from his chest.

My heart hammered. *NO!* That shrill sound roared in my head. But underneath the rage, I was seized by the movement as he stumbled backwards and lowered his gaze.

He was Immortal...

He was Immortal.

That means I can't kill him...*right?*

Panic filled me as blood trickled from the wound. But before I could stumble toward him, slam my hand over the wound, and scream for help, I ran like the fucking coward I was. I launched toward the door, clawed the handle, and shoved through.

Darkness swallowed me along the black painted hallway. I blinked and stumbled, wrenching my gaze over my shoulder to the open door I'd left behind. Silence made my steps slow. *Go back,* that urgency filled me.

Under the black t-shirt the Wolf hated…my body started to throb and glow. Heat moved through me. That sickening hunger. That ravenous need. Even now, I wanted him. His touch, his eyes, *his goddamn fury, for that matter.*

I wrenched my gaze forward, caught the glint of steel, and grabbed the handle. One twist and I was out, stumbling into the quiet darkness, the bright backlight of the bar the only illumination. I blinked and lifted my hand. Sun washed through the glass doors at the front of the club.

It was daylight.

How long have I been gone?

I smacked into a table and pain roared through my side, that blinding agony turning into a dark, rutting need. I gotta get the fuck out of here. Away from the smell of him. I lowered my face, yanked open the neckline of my shirt and inhaled.

He was everywhere, that deep, seductive voice calling. Jesus. I gripped the railing and hauled myself up the stairs. The doors were unlocked. Steel howled against steel as I yanked the handle and stepped out into the air. A Jeep was at the front of the club, a guy bent over the open driver's door, rummaging around inside. I gripped the gun and rushed forward.

"FBI. I'm commandeering your vehicle," I ordered.

The guy straightened, clutching a Victoria's Secret bag filled to the brim. Dark hair, gleaming leather jacket, quick eyes, and a quicker smile. "Just like that, huh? No first date…not even a damn kiss. Just take your goddamn car, may as well take my wallet, too."

I flinched, then scowled. What the fuck was this guy talking about? I stepped closer, lifted the gun a little higher. "I'm FBI, *buddy*. And I need your goddamn car."

"I need a fucking day off from crazy-ass women, but do I get one? No. I don't." His gaze narrowed as he glanced behind me to the open door of the club. Something changed then, something *shifted* in his eyes. His nostrils flared.

"No," I commanded with a shake of my head. "No, don't you do that." I glanced at the vehicle. "No sniffing me, no saying a fucking word."

"You were supposed to be out for a week," he murmured, and stepped closer.

"Careful," I warned. "I shot your damn Alpha, and I'll shoot you."

He froze then, fear sparking in his eyes. "You shot Phantom?"

"I just need your damn car and I'll leave." I stepped sideways. "Don't make me hurt you."

He didn't move, only pivoted to watch me when I yanked open the door.

"The keys are in it...just don't burn it." He growled. "I fucking love this car."

"I'm not going to..." I answered, and slid into the car. "I just need to get away."

He watched me, not moving an inch as I turned the key and started the four-wheel drive. I stomped on the clutch and shoved the Jeep into gear, and as I pulled away, I caught movement in the side mirror. The Wolf lunged toward the open doorway and disappeared inside. To the Alpha I'd shot...

The one who'd protected me.

The one who'd kept me alive.

The one who done things to me no man had ever done.

I burned and ached for him, even now. My hands were slick against the wheel as I turned the Jeep toward the on-ramp of the bridge. I'd never been so thankful to smell the fresh breeze from the river, or the sun on my skin. Still, I had to clench my fists around the wheel to stop from turning around.

You wouldn't dare. The words haunted me, as did his face as he rose over me on the bed, and his eyes as he stared up at me from between my legs. *I licked it...so it's mine.*

I shuddered and fixed my gaze on the off-ramp up ahead. The sun wasn't as warm now, cool river air not as clean. My soul was stained with him, his touch, his scent...his focus.

A whimper ripped from the back of my throat as I hit the off-ramp. I signaled, slipped into a side street, and pulled over. My hands were shaking, my body trembling. I yanked open the neckline, but that strange green glow was dulled and less painful. Something else was affecting me. Something he'd done to me. *Something he changed in me.*

I was broken before.

Now I felt...*shattered.*

Shards and holes all that was left.

Tears slipped down my cheeks. *What the fuck was I crying for?* I sucked in hard breaths and tried to still the shaking. "Get your shit together, Chase." I stared at the hood of the Jeep until the shudders eased.

I could do this. I could get home...get cleaned up. Call Harlan and receive an ass-chewing of the century. But I'd be back. I'd be alive. I'd be ready to get to work...and hunt Ruth down.

I winced. Heartsore and tired, I felt like I'd lived a hundred years. Still, I shoved the Jeep into gear and pulled into the road. Keeping to the back streets, staying low...my gaze was divided between the mirrors and the street ahead until I turned into my neighborhood. The sound of a siren was a backdrop for the cheap housing. I'd lived here my entire life. This was a working class part of the city, where rich bitches like Ruth Costello feared to tread.

But that wasn't why I hunted her...

No, that wasn't why I hunted her at all.

I pulled up and parked outside the small clapboard home. The grass was up to my ankle. Overflowing trashcans sat out the front. *Fuck, I'd forgotten garbage day...*the place was old and worn, last year's attempt at a garden was now nothing more than weeds gone to seed. I lifted my gaze to the darkened windows and closed front door before I rolled the windows up, hauled my ass out of the Jeep, and locked the doors.

The locals wouldn't steal it, not when it was parked here. But every now and then you got a newbie to the lower-middleclass grandeur that was River Heights and they trespassed where they shouldn't and took what wasn't theirs to take. I had enough paperwork on my desk to last me a fucking lifetime. I didn't need some Wolf's commandeered Jeep to go missing.

Harlan would have a goddamn stroke.

If he hadn't had one already.

It was midafternoon sometime, as I walked along the side of the house, shoved through the gate, and climbed the three rickety steps to the back door of the house.

The TV was on, voices slipping through the dim interior. It didn't mean anything though, if you were counting Dad as awake. He was, or he wasn't. But still that TV ran night and day. I stepped inside, letting the back door slam. "Pops," I called.

I didn't wait for a response...I knew better than that. I stepped into the kitchen, where the faded linoleum on the floor was cracked and puckered in patches. Just one more job on the list. Next year. *Yeah, next year...*

I yanked open the refrigerator and winced at the stench. "Jesus, that's ripe." I grabbed a beer and shoved the door closed before lifting the icy can to the back of my neck.

Do that again... His voice invaded as I closed my eyes, rolling the icy touch across my skin. One lick of my lips and I was drawn to the memory of my lips on the throb of his vein.

Gotta stop thinking about him. Gotta get myself under control.

I popped the can open and lifted the rim to my lips. Long gulps turned consuming until I broke away, sucking in air, then swiped my mouth dry. Still the TV sounded, one stupid fucking show after another.

"Pops, you awake in there?" I strode from the kitchen to the entrance of the living room and the lone recliner chair. A figure sat there, silent, staring at the screen. "Oh, you're alive, Carina," I muttered. "I was so fucking worried when you didn't come home…for days."

I stepped closer, my eyes dropping to the two bottles beside the chair. Empty. Of course.

Three pictures sat in darkness on the wall…and not one of them was my mother, or me, for that matter. Not that I cared. Gleaming smiles, brass plaques. Crisp blue uniform of a police lieutenant. My father had been decorated, saluted…and then destroyed. All because of one man…and one man alone. *Denzel Costello.* The beginning of the end for my family.

"Dad." I sighed and stepped closer, sniffing the stale foulness in the air. "Come on, buddy, it's time to shower."

He grunted when I grabbed him, lifted his hand and swiped the air, but he'd long ago lost his aim, and his strength. Once, he was fit, vibrant, and healthy. Now he was bedsores and a bulbous red nose, and reeked of alcohol.

I hauled him from the chair and forced him, grumbling and cursing, toward the bathroom. He knew better than to refuse to shower. I'd done it once, and I'd do it again, even if it'd been traumatic for both of us. While the shower was running, I found him clean clothes, threw his clothed into the dirty hamper for Mrs. Killjoy to wash, then went back to the kitchen and scraped together a sandwich. God knew when he'd eaten last.

He stumbled out of the bathroom, hair still damp, eyes bloodshot. One look at me. "You look like hell," he grumbled.

"And you're a picture of fucking health. There's a sandwich." I nodded to the food.

"Not hungry."

I gave him one of those stink-eye stares Mom used to give and held his gaze until he yanked out the chair with a grumble and grabbed one half with a trembling hand.

I tried to not let it get to me.

Tried to forget the past.

But when the past was sitting in front of you, pissing the rest of his life away, it was a little hard for it to go unnoticed. "Eat up, Dad, then try and get some sleep."

I turned then, grabbed the rest of my beer, and strode out the back door and into the backyard. The grass was higher here, rustling midway along my legs. But I found the worn path...one that took me to the gaping fence. I gripped the wire, ducked under, and kept on walking, all the way up to the two-story place that was in a little better condition at least, and climbed the stairs.

I tossed the can over my shoulder, not even bothering to aim for the trash. Five years I'd lived here...and still didn't have a goddamn key.

I had a gun, that was enough...and years of pent up rage.

Enough to keep me warm in the winters...

For the rest of my fucking life.

I kicked the door closed behind me, and stepped out of my boots on my way to my bedroom. I couldn't even care about a shower. Not yet. I tore off the shirt that had offended the Alpha and unbuttoned my cargos. I stepped into the bedroom, opened a drawer, and grabbed clean panties, stepping into them before I slid on an old FBI training shirt.

My knees buckled two steps in. I sank to the mattress and shoved aside the sheets. That hunger flared in my side, dark and demanding, making me moan as I rolled. I slipped my hand down between my thighs and rubbed.

You like to fuck...and you like to fuck me. Your body likes it, too. I hated his words. Hated his voice. Hated his stare. Hated that he was right. Even now I'd go to him, swollen and exhausted. I'd drop to my knees for him, let him fuck me raw. *And there wasn't a damn thing I could do to stop it.*

I looked down feeling that hunger seething in my chest. I didn't know if this was the spell, or what the Wolf did to me, either way it didn't matter.

For the first time in my fucking life, I felt something more than hate and desperation.

I felt wanted.

I felt used.

I felt *incredible.*

6

The piercing blast of a car alarm wrenched me awake. I surfaced just a little, moaned, and dragged my knees to my chest. "Imma shoot whoever has that fucking car." I mumbled. "Motherfuckers."

Still it wailed and howled, shattering the last fragments of my sleep. I clenched my jaw and nudged the pillow with my face until I buried my ear deep.

Fucking car alarm.

Fucking car.

Jeep. Black. *I'm commandeering your vehicle.* I wrenched my eyes open, the past few day descending like an avalanche. *"Fuck!"*

I shoved upwards, stumbled, and swayed. For a second, I was in a white room with a massive bed, my heart thudding hard against my chest, the dark spice of sex and hunger intoxicating in the room. Until the shattering alarm ended...and so did the vision.

Someone was breaking into my car!

I lunged, scrambled for my gun, and snatched it from the floor. Five blurry steps and I was yanking open the back door to the house. My training took over, driving me harder, faster. I was the hunter—*and there was no way they were getting away.*

That siren wailed and howled, growing louder as I scrambled down the stairs, raced through my yard, vaulted the fence, and threw myself toward the side of Dad's house. I was out in the open before I knew it, lifting the gun, to the street kids as they laughed and jumped on the hood of the damn thing.

"Whoa, Miss Carina." The first kid froze and lifted his hands, staring at me as I stood in an old training shirt and my damn underwear, gripping a shiny silver Sig in my hand. Blue eyes widened on the snot-nosed pain in my ass that lived across the street as Davie gasped. "Didn't know this sweet ride was yours."

I stared at them, just kids…just goddamn kids.

They slipped from the gleaming black hood, never once taking their eyes off me. I sucked in hard breaths and scanned the street. "Davie…and the rest of you." I looked each one in the eye. "Stay the fuck away from my goddamn car."

They backed away and headed across the street where the ruins of a house remained. One Davie and his druggy mom, Claire, lived in. I knew them, knew them the moment they moved in five years ago. "And get your asses home. You should be in fucking school."

Kids. Jesus, I swayed on my feet, adrenaline thundering in my veins.

I turned, took one last glance at them over my shoulder, and made my way back to my place. I climbed through the fence, then marched through the backyard before I made it up the stairs. I was inside before I knew it, with the uneven floorboards and faded, chipped paint, my life and responsibilities crashing down around me. Agony pinched in my side, drawing my focus to the grind in my chest and the fire between my thighs. *Unseelie magic.* That's what the Wolf had said.

Dark Fae magic.

That's right…I was royally fucked.

I licked my lips and stumbled to the bathroom. Damn Wolf got under my skin, found the cracks…forced his way in. I gripped the sink, still feeling that thick length between my thighs. Christ, I'd never had anything so goddamn ferocious. So *primal.* So fucking perfect. I dragged my teeth across my lip as a memory slipped in.

Those big hands cupping my breast, hard muscles rippling underneath me. His focus on the juncture where we became one. I could still feel him inside me, stretching, rubbing, slick as he slowly thrusted, drawing out every shudder.

More. My damn knees trembled. I needed more, needed him harder…needed him riding me just like this sickness was riding me. I lifted my gaze to the pitted mirror. Lips parted, brown eyes almost black, skin pasty white. Sweat glistened on my brow. I was sick…that's all, just sick. I'd worked through the flu, worked through countless colds. Hell, I'd worked with a broken rib and a fractured cheekbone. I could work through this.

I unhooked my bra and shoved my panties down, leaving the Sig balanced on the corner of the sink. I stepped over the edge of the bathtub, pulled the curtain closed, twisted the handle, and waited for the pipes to stop howling and the blast of hot water to come through.

He'd been gentle.

The words slipped in as I stepped into the spray, then cursed and fumbled with the heat. He'd been so fucking gentle, washing my hair…rubbing in conditioner. Jesus, I could still feel those big hands running over me.

No. Not gonna think about that.

"Get it together, for fuck's sake, you got a case to close, remember?" I shoved my face into the spray, keeping my hair out, and grabbed the bar of soap, hurrying to wash. Delving that ache between my legs until I shoved out a hand and braced myself against the wall.

There wasn't time…no, *there was always fucking time.*

But not like that. Not when the hunger was riding me, not when his face, his smell…his fucking *everything* waited in the darkness, desperate to invade my world once more. I shoved backwards and twisted the handle, squealing as the savage rush of ice-cold water hit me.

I shivered as I turned off the spray and stepped out, taking one glance in the mirror at the shit still in my breast. He'd said it was a spell…a Fae spell…*You fight like a warrior. I wonder if you'd fuck as ferociously?*

Those words slammed into me. Blood. Death. Red eyes waiting for me in the dark. I swallowed hard when the thunder in my chest filled my head. Can't lose my shit. Not now…*no way.*

I knew better than to press against the mark in my breast, knew better than to touch the shit in my chest. I knew better than to let myself be taken back there, to that night…to the fight. It was all over.

I was alive.

So was Ruth Costello.

That's all that mattered.

She and I had a history. She and I had a future. One where she was behind bars…and I could walk into that fucking house and say the words I've longed to say. *"I got her, Dad. I got the lot of them. They're gonna give you that pension now. Gonna give you everything they took."*

I yanked a towel from the rack, dragging it over my face and down my body. That day was coming. I could feel it in my bones. I strode out of the bathroom and headed for the dresser, grabbing cotton underwear and thick-soled socks before I went to the closet.

Black pants, white collared shirt. I walked out of the bedroom, grabbed my boots, and headed to the kitchen. My old phone was around here somewhere. Same SIM, same contacts.

Just my gun that was missing. Goddamn SAC was going to have a field day.

I rummaged around under a pile of paperwork and found the thing upside down, a crack across the screen. It'd have to do. I pressed the button and waited for it to fire up, grateful it was still charged, then turned to the fridge as a howl of hunger roared through me.

My hands shook, my jaw ached. That burn in my chest flared deeper, all the way to between my thighs. "Eat. That I can do." I yanked open the refrigerator and pulled out stale bread, butter, sausage, and cheese. I'd eat all damn day if I had to, until my ass no longer fit in my jeans.

I carried the food to the counter, slathered the bread with butter, meat, and cheese before lifting it to my mouth. I chewed and swallowed, then stabbed the screen and waited for the red light to stop flashing. Five more minutes. I tossed the food back into the fridge, chased the sandwich down with a couple of gulps of juice, and finally picked up the phone...and made the call I was dreading.

Harlan's phone rang eight times before he answered. "What? *Wait...*Chase? *Is that you?"*

"It's me, call off the damn search party."

"Where the *fuck* have you been?" he snapped, then sucked in a hard breath, his voice rowing deeper. "We've had the entire Crown City police force out looking for you."

"I was knocked out, woke up in some fucking alley. Took me a while to come around."

"Two goddamn days. Two goddamn days and you couldn't have called me before?"

"I'm calling you now."

"You better get your ass into the office. I want a fucking explanation why I've had my ass handed to me this morning by not only the AD, but also the AEAD. They're holding me personally responsible for what went down in that fucking warehouse, I hope you understand that…and you know what happens when it comes down from the top?"

"Shit rolls downhill," I answered.

"Damn right, and right about now…you're neckdeep in the stuff. Your gun, Chase…your fucking gun, of all the goddamn things to leave behind."

"I know." I shoved my hair from my face and winced as the butter on my thumb smeared onto my forehead. "I know…but sir…I've got something that's gonna set everything straight."

"You better, Chase. That's all I'm gonna say…" he growled and hung up.

I leaned against the counter and tried to remember how to breathe. *I got her…that's my ace in the hole, Ruth fucking Costello on camera, right there for the entire city to see.*

I thought about it…the reaction…the high fives and fist bumps. After all these years of pissing off the SAIC and going rogue, it came down to this. I smiled, flicked off the butter from my face, and popped my finger in my mouth.

I shoved forward, grabbed my old phone, and walked back into the bedroom. I found the keys to the Jeep in the pocket of my cargos. I'd get one of the boys from the PD to call the Wolves to come get it…damned if I was gonna be within a mile of that side of the city, or the Immortals, again.

I winced, remembering the look on the Alpha's face when I'd pulled the trigger.

My heart thundered…panic raced.

I whirled and ran to the bathroom, grabbing the gun I'd left on the edge of the sink.

I'd shot him…almost point blank.

If he was alive, he'd be pissed. I would be.

I lifted the weapon and my ID, then walked to the closet. Six digits in, and I shoved the firearm into my safe. That, I'd deal with later…and the Alpha, for that matter. Agony sank fangs into my side, making me clutch the doorjamb…and moan. The throb was nauseating, making me lean my weight on my arms.

Hunger roared. I clenched my jaw and took the punishment until my knees trembled and sweat broke out along the nape of my neck. I swallowed air until I could finally breathe, then I grabbed my shoulder holster, gripped the key to the Jeep, and marched to the back door of the house.

My boots were loud as they thudded on the stairs. The sunlight was too goddamn bright. I shielded my eyes and carved through the jungle to the house I grew up in. The TV noise drifted through the open back door. Dad was awake…or asleep, who the hell knew. The Jeep was still there…which was a damn bonus.

I jumped in the damn thing and started the engine. It roared to life with a growl as I shoved it into gear and spun the wheel. Top down, wind blowing my hair, it was easy to see why the Wolf liked it. I drove through the streets stopped at the small corner fresh fruit market and grabbed two containers of fresh, blood-red strawberries before making my way to the other side of Crown City. The streets were wider here. Towering trees shaded the footpath and every block had its own park equipped with kids swing sets and expansive green grass perfect to run and play. The kind of place we might've lived in…if things had been different.

I pulled up in front of a low-set house with its white picket fence and mass of bright colored petunias along the front. I'd been coming here for close to two years now and each time the place made me sad. If only things had've been different—*for all of us.*

I climbed out of the Jeep, walked along the pavement to the small gate before I unlatched the bolt and stepped through. The small ramp led to the verandah. I pressed the doorbell and held the strawberries up for Heather to see as the door cracked open. "A gift cause I fucked up."

The feminine chuckle slipped out before the door closed again and the chain rattled. "Carina, you never fuck up, child. Come on in. Lenny will be pleased you came."

I stepped into the quaint, tidy house with it stark white walls and furniture and bright paintings of flowers hanging on the walls. "I remembered he liked them." I smiled, stepped forward and gave Heather a hug.

"He does, thank you." She squeezed me tight and took the berries.

Every month I came here. At first it was for answers, and then it was guilt. It should've been me giving *them* answers. It should've been me saying the words we all wanted to hear. *We got them, we got them good.* But it wasn't…not yet at least. "You doing okay?"

Heather gave a nod and a smile, and as always it didn't quite reach her eyes. "Some days are better than others. You're lucky, today's a good day."

I glanced over my shoulder to the slow-mechanical hiss that came from the living room. The TV was on, the volume low so she could hear Lenny if he struggled…lately that was all the time.

"Why don't you sit with him while I put these away?"

It was my turn to give her a smile. I made for the wide doorway and stepped onto the mottled brown carpet that was all the rage back in the 60's and glanced at the pictures that lined the walls. They were almost the same as dad's…*almost.* Only these weren't shrouded in shadows and stained with the stench of piss and fear.

Lenny and dad stood alongside each other, arms over each other's shoulders. A grinned from ear to ear. It was the two of them celebrating, holding up up shining medals. For all to see. If only it stayed like that.

Hiss…thump. Hiss…thump.

I turned my attention to the man in the chair. A man who

looked nothing like the photo. This man was frail. This man was weak. This man breathed through a tube connected to his lungs, and was fed with a plunger into his stomach.

"Uncle Lenny." I came close, bent and kissed him on the cheek. He gave no response. Just stared at the TV across the room. The constant drone seemed to quieten him. "I've had quite the week." I started. "Crazy fucking things happening. Which is why I wasn't here yesterday. But I brought you those strawberries you liked. You're going to enjoy them. They're fresh too."

I reached up, brushed the wayward strand of his hair, my eyes drifting to the scarred mess of his scalp, one that covered the metal plate that replaced his skull.

I tried to keep it together, tried to focus on all the reasons why it was better to be alive than it was dead. But the truth was this man I'd known most of my life was dead, and he'd been dead for a long time, ever since they found him with a bullet hole the size of my fist in his skull.

Dad was fired three days later…

There were rumors, lots of them. Dad shot Lenny and was cornered. But I knew that just wasn't true. They were best friends, loved each other like brothers.

"Warehouse downtown. We're bringing you exclusive news of this horrendous story. Jerry Costello, brother to the late, Denzel Costello was found dead at the scene."

I glanced to the TV as Jerry's face filled the screen, and then turned to Lenny. I didn't need another damn reminder of that night. Lenny's eyes widened and that *hiss…thud,* stopped cold.

There was nothing but fear.

Nothing but terrifying fear as I glanced to the image of Denzel Costello on the screen.

"Lenny?" Helen called from the kitchen.

Hiss…thud. Hiss…thud. The ventilator kicked back in and that rhythmic sound filled the living room once more. Helen peeked her head around the doorway. "Everything okay?"

I glanced at the machine, and then Lenny as that cold fist of fate clenched around my heart. "Yeah, we're all good here."

Denzel Costello. It all came back to him. Everything. His wife. His daughter. Helen disappeared once more.

"It was him wasn't it?" I murmured and stared into the unflinching eyes of someone who'd never walk or talk again. "It was Denzel Costello that did this to you."

And for the first time since the accident…my father's best friend and partner turned his head and met my gaze. I didn't need a nod. Didn't need a damn word. I saw it all the shine of his eyes.

My damn heart lunged as I reached for his hand. "I'm going to get them, Uncle Lenny. I'm going to find out what they did to the both of you, and the whole world will know once and for all."

I shoved up from the lounge, turned and hurried from the living room, stopping long enough to give Helen a hug.

"You going already?" Surprise filled her face.

I was burning with purpose. "Yeah, sorry. I'll make sure to stay longer next time. Take care, and call me if you need anything." I gushed and headed for the door.

I was outside and climbing back into the Jeep second later, and then hauled ass for the FBI offices downtown. The traffic was busy, slowing to a crawl. By the time I turned into the underground parking that panicked feeling calmed to a stone-cold determination once more. and pulled into the government building drive. I pulled up hard at the first checkpoint guardhouse. One scan of the four-wheel drive and the guard's brows rose.

"Don't give me attitude, Beth-Anne. I'm not in the mood for it," I grumbled.

"Honey, when are you *ever* in the mood. All I'm gonna say is,

I want me some fancy FBI badge so I can drive around in a sweet ride like this all damn day."

"It's not mine," I started and winced. "I took it…"

"Mhhmmm. Honey, my advice is, just don't give it back. Sexy, that's how you look…damn sexy," she threw over her shoulder as she reached for the button to raise the boom gate.

A man's roar cut through the parking lot, the sound drawing my gaze as the lone guy strode across the front of the parking lot and screamed at the top of his lungs. *"Is ANYONE LISTENING TO ME? They have my wife! They kidnapped her. They fucking sold her. Do you care more about the fucking monsters than you do about us?"*

"What the hell's going on with that?" I cut her a glance.

"Pain in my ass, that's what." Beth-Anne muttered. "Fucker's been at it for days, hootin' and hollerin'. Something about his wife being taken by the Immortals. I told him a thousand times he needs to file a missing persons report with the police. But *nooo*…he just wants to scream at the top of his lungs and give me grief."

"You should have his ass arrested, maybe then he'd find the right guys to listen to him."

Beth-Anne barked out a laugh and glanced my way. "I threatened that exact same thing. That's why he's out there and I'm in here. Won't step a foot across that painted line."

I chuckled and eased the vehicle forward, pulling under the shelter at the rear of the lot… near the elevator. I checked the mirrors as I killed the engine and scanned the other cars, stopping at the dark gray Focus further along. Shit.

I yanked the keys free, shoved open the driver's door, and locked the damn thing before I hurried to the elevator. The keys were in my hand, the jagged edges nestled between my fingers in a clenched fist. I hurried, keeping my head down at the sound of a car door opening.

"Hey, Chase!" came the call as I stabbed the buttons on the elevator. *"Chase, hold up!"*

The elevator doors opened. I was inside in an instant. The thunderous sound of heavy boots echoed through the space, jacking my pulse as I jabbed at the close-door symbol.

Murphy's face came into view as the doors began to close. Hate raged in his eyes, cold, jilted hate. I stepped backwards until my spine hit the wall and let out a pent-up breath on a shudder.

The shine on the floor was always the first thing I noticed about this place. Shiny and sleek, and neat as a pin. But the open glass doors off the hallway hinted at anything but. Chaos waited for me in there. Chaos and photocopiers and a desk piled with paperwork. Maybe if I buried myself in there, no one would actually come near me. Give Harlan the shock of his damn life.

I marched out of the elevator and made my way along the hallway to the fifth door down, turned the handle, and stepped inside. Old carpet, older magazines still stacked neatly in the corner.

"Carina." Harlan's receptionist peeked up from her desk.

"He's expecting me, Trace."

"Tracey," she corrected. "And isn't he always, but hey, look…at least today you showed up." Her eyes sparkled as they shot wide. The fake smile on her face was almost as fake as her personality.

"Fuck you very much," I chimed back, smiling wide, and walked to the closed door marked *Harlan Beneford, Special Agent in Charge.*

One twist of the handle and I stepped into world war three.

"Yes, sir. I understand, sir." Harlan's solemn voice filled the room. "I want you to know I'm personally looking—Yes, sir. Yes…I understand. She just stepped into my office. I will, sir. I'll make her fully aware of the position we're in."

He stopped, exhaled what sounded too much like a moan,

hung up, and lowered his hand. He looked at me...and swallowed. "That was the third call I've had this morning."

"Harlan—"

"Aaah..." He shot a hand up to stop me. "I don't want to hear it. I don't want you to speak. I don't even want you to breathe. Can you sit there and not breathe?" he snarled.

"I can try," I offered.

His brow furrowed, and his lips curled. He just stared at me, one of those murderous, *I'm gonna wring your damn neck* stares. I get those a lot.

"I have her," I murmured, pushing my damn luck and sliding my ass to the edge of the seat. "Ruth Costello."

He let out a tortured moan.

I shot upwards, grasping his hand. "I'm not bullshitting you, Harlan. I have her. Pick up the phone, make the call...ask for the camera footage of that warehouse."

"I already have," he muttered. "Are you now going to tell me how to do my damn job?"

"Have you looked at it?"

"Have I looked at it?" His eye twitched as he snarled. "Of course I haven't looked at it! I've been too busy being assfucked. *Do you know how much I love being assfucked, Chase? Go on...have a guess."*

I wasn't game to answer.

He just huffed and twitched...until finally he picked up the phone. "Romero. Have you got the footage from the warehouse? Send it to me. *Thank you."* He ended the call and replaced the phone. "See what happens when agents are at their desks, *actually doing their fucking jobs?"*

I waited.

His gaze slipped to the screen, lips working as he mumbled under his breath. I've had worse chew outs from Harlan...a lot worse, but this one was different. This one was a catalyst. He clicked the file, gaze narrowing as he stared at the screen. Five minutes in and he stabbed the mouse, rewinding. He watched again…and rewound. "What the fuck?" he sighed.

I sat back in my seat and waited.

"Is that?" he shot me a look.

"Ruth Costello…back from the dead, it seems."

"Jesus fucking Christ," he muttered. *"Jesus fucking Christ.* Do you know what this means?"

I just smiled and nodded. Costello Corporation was no more. It'd been hacked up and sold off. The sole beneficiary of Denzel Costello was filthy rich…even richer with the company now in pieces.

"If we could find her and prove she set up the whole dissolution and payout from her death to get out of paying taxes, then…" He tapered off, eyes growing wider. "We could use that as a back door into *all* their dealings."

"Every single one of them," I urged. "All we'd need is an order from a judge, and we can go back as far as the courts allow."

"We've got them…the whole family." Excitement raged in his eyes. "We *got* them."

Purpose made him still. I could almost hear the cogs churning. "We need to get on this. *All of this.*"

"I agree."

"I want you to hand over every file you have. Montey will head the operation."

Montey? "Wait…*what?* No fucking way." I shot forward and winced at the flare of pain in my side. But I didn't care about that now. Didn't care at all. "This is *my* case, Harlan…*my fucking case.* I worked on this on my own. *I busted my fucking ass.* Almost got myself—" I pulled up short.

"Almost got yourself what? Special Agent?"

Goddamn killed. Spelled. Murdered and left for dead halfway across the river. The words swept through my mind. I'd hugged the entrance to the warehouse that night as soon as I caught sight of the cameras. I wouldn't be in view…mostly. "This has been my whole life, sir." Desperation deepened my tone. "Don't take this away from me."

This wasn't how I'd imagined this would go.

Kicked out of the operation.

Files ripped from my desk.

My name nowhere to be found on the arrest.

"How bad do you want this?" Harlan leaned forward as the door opened behind me.

"As much as my next fucking breath." I held his gaze and answered.

"Then you'll be working with a partner." Harlan's words chilled me to the bone. I swallowed and lifted my gaze, looking to the agent standing beside my chair. Murphy's eyes were hard…*dangerous.*

"It's this or you're out," Harlan forced the issue. "You're a loose cannon, Chase. We don't do loose cannons here. Murphy's a good agent, one of the best we have. You need to learn to work with others, Chase. This isn't a solo operation."

The terror of the past three years rose inside me. All the careful rejections…all the brutal ones, too. Still, he never took no for an answer. He came back twice as hard. Harder, colder…

"I was calling you before." Murphy lowered his gaze to my open collar. There was only skin…nothing else to see. I knew better. "Didn't you hear me?"

I heard you, mutherfucker. "No," I lied. "Got a lot on my mind, must've missed it."

"No loose cannons, Chase. From now on, Murphy's your goddamn shadow."

7

My shadow smiled, then grinned. "Partners," he said, staring into my eyes.

"Partners," I repeated. "On the job, Murphy. I think we need to set some boundaries here—"

"I think we need to do damn well whatever the fuck *I* say, Chase," he bit back, low and threatening, too low for others to hear. I glanced behind him as he leaned on my desk and towered over me. But Stash was on the phone behind him…and everyone else was too far away.

"This is work, Murphy." I lowered my tone as that sinking feeling spread through me. "We work together, that's all."

"Sure it is," he lied. "Now, first things first. I want a timeline of everything that happened from when you first noticed Ruth Costello to the events that took place in the warehouse. Just verbally, mind you…on our way to the morgue."

"The morgue?" I jerked.

"The morgue," he repeated. "I'm driving."

Which meant I had no transport and no way out of this. "I gotta go to supplies first." I shoved my chair backwards and rose. "I'll meet you downstairs in thirty."

"Make it twenty," he ordered, and straightened, looking down at me, his eyes lingering on my chest. "And Chase...you owe me fucking lunch."

He turned his back then. I shoved up, grabbed the jacket I left at the office draped over the back of my chair, and hurried from the room. Frantic thoughts swam around my mind as I yanked on the suit jacket and buttoned it up, focusing on each step. *No fucking way...no way Harlan was making me work with him.*

It was a bad dream...it had to be.

The sonofabitch knew about Murphy. He knew about the calls to my cell phone late at night. The ones I'd traced back to Murphy's personal phone. He knew about the repeated harassment, the catcalls, the constant asking me out on dates... had even roared at me to put in a complaint. *Put up or shut up, Chase.* Isn't that what he'd said?

Was this me putting up now...or shutting up?

My boots resounded as I stepped into the elevator and smashed the button. I didn't need this now...not now. Not when everything was finally clicking into place. Not now when I finally had a chance to crack this thing wide open...and spill Ruth Costello's lies and shady dealings all over the place. I'd expose her...and her so-called family.

Blane Costellos face roared back into my mind as the elevator sank. His shock...his blood. The savage way the Vamp had struck. There was no way he'd survived that. No goddamn way. So we were dealing with one dead Costello...and a runaway...*again.*

Fragments of that night slipped back to me. The terror...the blood. *You fight like a warrior...*I flinched at the words and exhaled hard. Numbers flashed above me in the elevator's display...until they stopped on the first basement level where the supplies store was located.

The doors opened, and silence greeted me. I made my way

along the darkened hallway where the lights flickered and buzzed. I hardly ever came down here…I doubted many did, unless they wanted something. There were two sub-levels to this place and four levels above. I had no idea what was below us, not much according to Stash. Rooms filled with furniture from the sixties, and empty bathrooms no one ever visited.

The faint sound of off-key singing…made me grit my teeth. I stepped around the end of the safe room, saw SSA Grove's back, and slowed my steps. He was old school…like back in my-dad's-day old school. I sighed, just get this over with.

I stepped up to the counter and pressed the bell.

Still the singing continued.

I pressed the bell once more…and held the fucker on.

"Okay!" Grove barked. "I fucking hear you. I'm not deaf!"

"Tone deaf maybe?" I mumbled. "On account of your singing."

He flashed me a snarly look, scanned my face, and that snarl turned into downright cold anger. "Yes?"

"I'm here for my new gun."

"And where's your old one?"

"Evidence." Not that I had to explain a fucking thing to him.

He crossed his arms. "You got the right paperwork?"

So, it's gonna be like that, is it? I gave a nod toward the desk behind him. "I'm guessing that's it right there, the one marked Chase?" Tracey might be a bitch but she was damn good at her job. Government issue anything was her domain, so I knew without a doubt she was all over it.

"You getting smart with me, Chase?"

"No, sir." I answered. "Just helping you locate the correct paperwork, sir."

"Fucking traitors," he muttered under his breath as he turned to the desk.

My face burned and that burn burrowed deep into my chest. "What was that?" Cold anger deepened my tone. Still the bastard ignored me, slipping his earphones on as he reached for the whole stack of paperwork instead of mine on top.

Fuck you.

That burn blasted into agony, making me catch my breath and grab the counter. Pain brightened the lights above me, until the blinding white was all I could see. I tried to breathe...tried to hold on. Heat moved through me...heat and lust and *fire*.

"Not now," I pleaded. "Jesus Christ, please not now."

Sweat broke out along my brow as the SSA stiffened and slowly lifted his head. He yanked at his collar, and cleared his throat before turning on his heel to face me.

"What the fuck is that?" he barked.

I pushed the agony down, buried it under all the fucking years of putting up with this kind of shit. *Traitors. Liars. Pathetic. Not good enough for the shield...*and the worst one. *Corrupt.*

Grove yanked the earphones from his ears. "Answer me, *Special Agent.*"

"*I. Don't. Know.*" I forced the words. But even standing on one side of a barred window, I could see the effect I had on him.

His breathing deepened and his nostrils flared. His lips parted, sucking in my scent. *You're sick, female.* The Wolf's warning rose like a goddamn tsunami. *And you're growing sicker by the second. Your scent will change. Fervid, carnal. Irresistible to males...especially to males like me.*

Irresistible...that's what he'd said.

Grove slapped the paperwork on the counter, stumbled to the side, and all but threw a pen at me. "Sign it," he commanded. He walked over to the desk and picked up the weapon, a new magazine, and a box of ammunition before putting it all on the counter. Excitement and rage mingled in his eyes. "Use the safety barrel at the end of the hall to check and load. Now get the fuck away from me."

I grabbed the weapon and the ammunition, my steps a blur as I hurried to the end of the hall. *Gotta get it together...breathe.*

Just fucking breathe. I could feel that hunger and taste the anger, like blood down the back of my throat.

Warm blood...

Hot and heavy. I ground my teeth. I felt *predatory.*

Footsteps cracked along the hallway far behind me, then the scrape and *whoosh* of the elevator doors. I ignored those sounds and stopped at the safety barrel at the end of the hall, then pointed the muzzle into the opening, checked the slide, fired, and slipped it into my holster against my breast. One touch, and that ache came alive once more, digging and clawing along my side.

Five minutes, and I was hurrying back to the elevator with my weapon and a spare mag locked in place, and my damn head in turmoil. I had to get it under control, had to keep whatever was happening to me...from happening.

The elevator doors opened with a *ding.* I stepped inside and waited for the doors to close before I braced one hand on the wall and shuddered. My whole world was unravelling, coming apart at the edges. First this...goddamn Unseelie shit, and now Murphy. I closed my eyes as the elevator rose. But all that stuff paled to compare to the low throb inside me...the one that had me by the throat, fangs pressed to my skin...

The Alpha waited in the desperation and the need. His face, his body...*You've never been fucked, Carina. Not the kind of fucking that owns your soul. Not the kind you can't run away from. One damn taste and you're a slave.*

I'd never been fucked...before. Not like that. But I felt fucked now....in every sense of the word. I was hungry. I was aching. *I was a slave.* It wasn't just the fucking, either. It was him...the Alpha...*the Wolf.*

The elevator shuddered to a stop at the ground floor and the doors slid open. I went outside and waited. Murphy would be waiting for me in his car, hands on the wheel, determined to get me alone, wanting me vulnerable. A shiver raced deep. I was backed into a corner, with no place to go. One step out of line and I'd be pulled from the case.

Everything I worked for would be gone in an instant...and Murphy knew that. I took a step into view, head down...moving quiet and fast. I speared my fingers into my pocket and yanked out the keys. A partner was one thing...but fuck if I was spending a second more with him than I had to.

I climbed back into the Jeep, feeling a pang of regret. I should've had this taken back by now. Or the owner called, at least. One look over my shoulder to the shadow behind the wheel of the Focus, and I started the four-wheel drive, snapped the seatbelt shut, and backed out of the space.

I caught the jerk of Murphy's head when I shot past him with a wave. He'd be pissed...no, he'd be downright fucking furious. But there was no goddamn way I was spending a second more trapped with him *anywhere*. They wanted me at the morgue...then that's where I'd go.

I gave Beth-Anne a nod as I slowed and went past, but all she did was smile and shake her head. Like she knew me...or the trouble I was neckdeep in. Trouble I didn't want...but trouble that seemed to find me anyway, no matter where I went.

I turned into the city traffic, working the gears. I really was starting to enjoy this car. A lot. Too bad my money didn't stretch beyond the damn necessities, even with me cutting out my heat in the winter. Between topping up Dad's measly government pension and my own pathetic existence, there just wasn't enough left.

But there would've been if Dad hadn't been kicked off the force and his entire future ripped away from him. *Traitors,* Grove's snarl rang inside my head as I turned the car. Traitors indeed. I tried to piece together the events that had surrounded my father's spectacular fall from a highly decorated officer to the one now broken and ashamed.

I knew the official version...dismissed from duty without

pension. But the records were sealed, and no one was talking…*not even Dad.* I'd only found one name when I dug into Dad's private things. An entry in a journal with most of the pages removed. But on the last blank page, I found an impression of his familiar scrawl.

I'd used the side of a pencil lead to shade in the writing… only to find a name that filled me with rage. *Cassandra Costello.* A date and time had been scribbled next to it. The exact date and time she'd run her car off the side of the road and straight into a power pole.

There'd been whispers of an affair. But I knew that wasn't true. But what was true was that no one was talking. Whatever was inside that caused the sealing of the case file had been enough to shatter his life…and mine along with it.

Mom left not long after the drinking started. I didn't blame her…not many did. It was hard to envision a future when your entire world was one big shit show…just like mine was now. I glanced into the rear-view mirror and turned the Jeep into the back streets that'd eventually bring me out to the Crown City morgue. But the closer I came…the more that growing sense of ominous darkness rose.

I'd not only have to deal with Murphy…but this sickness inside me, one I had no control over.

One that had control over me.

The sad gray concrete building rose in front of me. Ten floors of the Crown City Public Hospital loomed like a monolithic, ancient structure. I pulled the Jeep onto the graveled back road and swung the wheel, pulling up onto the grassy area at the business side of the morgue. Four white vans had been reversed outside the mammoth garage doors. I glanced at the neat black letters on the sides, *Crown City Medical Examiner,* and tried to ready myself for this.

"You can do this," I murmured. "Just keep it together for a few more hours, that's all you have to do."

I lowered my gaze to my hands on the wheel. Who the fuck was I kidding?

Something glinted in the corner of my eye, metal of some kind. I reached down in the compartment beside the seat and pulled the thing free. It was a tooth…*no*, not a tooth. *It was a fang, on a leather thong.* It was long and curled, thick at the base and tapered to a hard, barely rounded point. Not as sharp as the Alpha's I'd seen, but older in a way…more yellowed.

I clenched my grip around the fang and closed my eyes. A tremor raced through me, like a shiver of something settling into place. I opened my eyes at the sound of a car growing near, and did something I'd never done in my life.

I took something that wasn't mine. "Borrowing it," I urged myself, and slipped the leather thong over my head. I didn't understand the need inside me, not for the necklace…or to take what wasn't mine to take.

Still, the second the fang settled against my skin, I felt that tremor inside me…that *calling* to something deeper than flesh and bone. I felt *him*…the Alpha. I touch of him, anyway.

I shoved the door open, climbed out, and was striding across the dirt road as Murphy called out. *"Hey! Don't you walk away from me!"*

The heavy thud of boots sounded beside me as I hit the locked double doors. I pressed the red bell for assistance as Murphy grabbed my arm.

"Don't *fuck* with me, Chase." His hand clenched tight, fingers digging in, gripping my arm like a vise.

I jerked my gaze to his, leveled him with a savage stare, and tried to jerk my arm from his hold. "I'm *not* fucking with you, Murphy. Boundaries, remember? Get your *goddamn* hand off me."

My heart was thundering. The icy touch of fear brushed along my spine as hate and lust moved behind his eyes. He looked down at his hold, scowled for a second, and dropped his hand. Behind us, the door to the morgue opened with a *beep*.

"IDs, please," the clerk said.

I reached into my pocket and handed mine over as Murphy relinquished his.

My arm hurt, the pain throbbing and gnawing, pressing into bone. A nod from the clerk and he turned and shoved the door open, leaving us to step into the building. The sharp scent of antiseptic mingled with the bitter cold. I swallowed a shiver as Murphy followed, his heavy steps following me as I cut past the waiting area…to hunt down the dead.

8

PHANTOM

Christ, that stung. I moaned as the sound of her steps receded along the hallway that led to the club. *She fucking shot me?* I looked down at the bullet hole in my chest. She did… she fucking shot me!

Go after her, the beast snarled, nostrils flaring as he drew in her scent.

"No," I answered as I probed the small wound and drew my fingers away. The tips glistened crimson and the raw smell of my own blood plunged into my nose.

The beast sniffed deeper, scenting, tasting. *She doesn't want us.*

"Gee," I growled. "Whatever gave you that idea?"

White fangs shone in the darkness as my beast bared his teeth. Midnight eyes glimmered, growing brighter as the sound of booming steps barreled our way.

"Phantom!" my enforcer roared.

My beast let out a snarl, a warning, hackles rising a little. He was one of ours. Still the animal inside me struggled to care. Pack. Loyalty. *Home* Those things didn't come easily to him. They made him pace, made him cautious…made him *dangerous.*

"Fuck me!" Arran barked as he lunged inside, then froze, his gaze stopping on the goddamn hole in my chest. "She fucking *shot* you?"

"She fucking shot me," I repeated.

Even as I said the words, I wanted her again. She'd been savage in that moment. A magnificent hunter, ready to pull the trigger on anything that stood in her way. Pride burned in my veins. There was no stopping the desire that raged inside me, even if it did come with a healthy dose of agony.

"I'm fine," I growled as the beta yanked out his phone and punched icons. "No need for the others." But he ignored my comment, just like the pain in my ass always did.

"Arran," I growled, and the thunder of purpose quaked through the air. He stiffened, turned, and fixed his gaze on me. I had his full attention now. His *undivided* fucking focus. "Where is she?"

"Gone," he growled. "Stole my damn car, can you believe that? I fucking love that car."

"Let her have it." I turned my focus to her. "Take the Camaro instead."

"The Red Eye?" he muttered, his eyes opening wide. "You love that car."

I have him a nod, then turned away with a wince. "I'll be in my damn room when nurse Church gets here."

I staggered along the hallway, and slowed at the entrance to Church's room. She had on his shirt, had his gun, too, but I didn't care about that. She had on *his* goddamn shirt.

Not ours, the beast snarled. *Not our smell. Not our scent. Not us she wanted.* He pressed his snout to the floor, marking and scenting as I tore my gaze away and pushed open the door to my bedroom...and was slammed with the essence of her.

She was everywhere, on the sheets, in the air. *Poison,* she whimpered inside my head. *I'm poison. Don't want you to be...*

Hurt. She didn't want me to be hurt. Not from the markings

on her skin. Even as she suffered, she'd put my damn well-being before her own. What kind of woman does that? I unbuttoned my jeans, slid between the sheets, and stretched out. *Tink.* My body trembled as the bullet hit the floor.

*Stick it in for fuck's sake...*her cries echoed inside my head.

I'd stick it in alright...and it wasn't just my cock I'd bury deep. I wanted that mortal woman. Wanted her in ways that both terrified and exhilarated me. She was prey, and not the kind of prey I wanted to tear apart. I wanted to play with her, tease, taste...

I wanted to fight for control, and relinquish. I wanted to feel her power. I dropped my hand to my chest, maybe just next time without a gun in her hand. The woman was Alpha in so many fucking ways she set my blood on fire.

Footsteps echoed along the hall. My bedroom door cracked open.

"You're alive," Church growled.

"No thanks to you." I stretched my arm upwards and rested my head on my hand. "Your new Sig isn't so new anymore."

He glanced at the deep purple bruise that was spreading out from the wound and winced. "Lucky it wasn't the new rounds then."

"That's all you got to say?" I growled...*she wore* his *fucking shirt.*

"You want me to kiss it better?" Church took a step forward.

I met that hard fucking gaze, knowing he would if I wanted it. Church enjoyed all kinds of fucking, men, women...variety, he called it. That was his thing, it sure wasn't mine. And he damn well knew it. Anger gave way to a deep throaty chuckle that spilled from my chest.

He was a hard bastard. Ruthless and savage when I needed him to be, caring and thoughtful when I fucking didn't. I shoved upwards, letting the sheet that had covered her body just minutes ago spill into my lap.

Vitold and Arran stepped into the room behind him. My pack...my hunters. I met Vitold's gaze. "Find her, watch her. She's not to be harmed. I just want..."

"To protect," the beta answered for me.

To protect her. I gave a nod and met his gaze. The Wolf's eyes sparked with urgency. He'd watched her sleeping naked, smelled her scent, and seen her vulnerable. He'd watch her back, that I trusted. I leaned forward and climbed from the bed, my fingers sweeping the floor until I found what I wanted. I crossed the room in an instant, bare and bruised, and pressed that bloody bullet into the Wolf's hand. Vitold turned, his boots smacking the floor as he left.

"We have a problem at Wild," Church informed me as I sat back on the bed. "Harmony's husband is at it again, coming to the club, harassing the other girls."

"Does he know where she is?" A twitch caught my lip.

"No, but he's talking about going to the media."

I stood from the bed. "Then I'll pay him a visit, shall I?"

This was pack business...*my fucking business.* The last thing I wanted was another pain in my ass all over social media, bring more goddamn attention to my bars. After last night, the fucking mortals were sure to descend with their cameras and their goddamn warrants.

"Everything is hidden, right? No leads to the girls, or anything else, for that matter?"

"Locked down tight. We even had the Mayor call to assure us he'll do everything he can to tone down the heat. Can't let his favorite club get closed down and all."

Discretion was trade.

Sex was the end product.

They wanted it and we provided.

Hardcore, BDSM, bondage.

Strippers and lap dancers.

But that wasn't all we traded in…and the Mayor of the city knew it. "I want to see the girls at Wild first."

"I'll get them ready."

I strode for the shower and bit back a snarl. It'd do no good to look at them and smell the Special Agent all over my fucking cock…no, no good at all.

But still I hated stepping into the water…I fucking *loathed* washing her from my skin. "She'll be back," I growled to my beast, and braced my hands against the wall, letting the heat travel down my spine. "And when she does, she'll never want to leave us again."

I washed as that thought clung to me, then dried and dressed, yanking on dark blue denim and a leather vest before lacing up my boots. Five seconds later and I was leaving the back door of The Hunting Ground and climbing onto my Harley.

The bike started with a throaty growl. Arran could use the Red Eye until she returned his Jeep. I licked my lips, fighting the urge to visit her myself under the pretense of retrieving what was mine…*and the female was mine, whether she knew it or not.* Fuck the four-wheel drive. I'd buy her a new one if it came to that. I'd buy the woman anything…as long as she slept in my bed.

I knocked the bike into gear and eased the throttle, pulling out of the dirt parking lot and into the street. Wild was one of the clubs on the other side of the city. The mortal side…where shit could get complicated real goddamn fast.

Like last night. I fucking blame myself for that…

He needs us. My own growl rang in my head. I'd reached out to Maxim, who had ties to the Vampire Forllen. Apparently Elithien had turned the bastard down when he tried to get Elithien to betray us.

Not just turned him down…but threatened the greedy bastard's life. Forllen was furious, tearing home with his tail between his fucking legs. No doubt he'd be back. He wanted the Inner Circle gone more than anyone. But it wasn't going to be by Elithien's hand.

The Vampire was just too fucking honest.

By the time I found that out, it was almost too late.

I'd grabbed Shrike, Mojin, and the rest of our packs and followed the Unseelie to the warehouse in time to stop them all from being slaughtered. We were almost too late. I opened up the bike on the bridge, letting the wind slap against my skin. Still, I blamed myself for Justice. I blamed myself for it all.

But if I hadn't gotten there...not only would the Vampires be dead...*so would Carina.* That thought rolled through me like thunder. I felt that anger now...harder than any gunshot to my chest. I felt it in that dark pit inside me. My untapped potential for violence. My *animal rage.*

The Harley lunged harder, booming through the air, making little kids clamp their hands over their ears...and their parents wince. There was a cruelness inside me. One I wasn't proud of...still, it was there just the same. A cutting edge I honed my fangs on, and sharpened my nails.

That vile part of me was always ready.

Born from weakness.

Honed from pain.

I'd never go back there. I'd never stop hunting, never stop searching.

Never stop filling that pit of savagery inside me...

It was a Wolf eat Wolf world...and I was fucking starving.

I eased onto the off-ramp and took the shadowed streets of Crown City all the way to the quiet night streets of the Sapphire Section, where the place came alive after dark. Cars were parked along the curb, so I slowed the bike and eased it into the narrow lane along the side, pulling into a parking space at the back.

I knew what people thought of me, knew what they

expected, as well—from this kind of job, to the girls. They expected cheap, they expected dollar bills, and the girls to drive around in rusted-out pieces of shit. But there were no faded Ford Lasers and barely running Camrys here.

Audis and Lexuses filled the space, and it looked like Britt had even gotten herself that Explorer she'd been wanting. These were high-end girls who were paid well indeed. Which is why I needed another boyfriend bitching and raising hell like a hole in the fucking head...I already had one in my damn chest.

I killed the bike's engine and climbed off, leaving it parked at the rear entrance. The door's coded lock waited. I punched in the code and pushed the door wide. Perky, upbeat music greeted me. The girls' music...not working music. The kind where they could laugh and be normal, for a little while at least. I strode along the hallway, and turned at the end, where right would take me to the smaller living quarters the pack used, left took me right to the girls.

It was Halsey today, and her 11 Minutes with Yungblud who spilled out from under the closed door labeled *Females Only - No entry.* I raised my knuckles and gave a hard rap against the door before I counted to ten and turned the handle, cracking the door open. "Everyone decent?"

Laughter came, some low and chortling, others giggled and called out. "Never fucking decent, Phantom. But you can enter at your own damn risk!"

I grinned and pushed the door opened, then was smacked in the face with the heady scent of perfume and dry shampoo. My beast coughed, sneezed, and shook his head until he whimpered. I breathed through my mouth and tried to stop the burn in my eyes. "Jesus, ladies, you alone are gonna destroy the damn ozone layer."

"But we're gonna look fabulous doing it!" Jace cried...at least I think it was Jace. I couldn't quite see through the damn tears as my eyes watered.

"You okay, Alpha?" Dark eyes flashed close to me. The touch of a hand, a thumb swiped a tear from my cheek.

"I'm good." I flashed Riley a smile and gave her a nod. "Not so tough am I, when a can of Chanel No. 5 takes me down."

"You need a woman who smells like blood and gunpowder," Jace countered.

I swallowed hard as Carina blazed to life in my mind.

Fuck me if my heart didn't start pounding.

"Yeah, I do." I gave a small smile.

Riley didn't like that at all. I needed to be gentle with that one, careful of my words and my actions. She'd called my personal cell phone a number of times, needing help...I always sent one of the others, knowing exactly what kind of help she wanted.

I didn't sleep with the dancers.

None of us did. It was an unspoken rule.

We protect...we don't take advantage.

"I hear we've had some trouble," I started.

"James again," Britt explained with a careful stare. "He came around last night and wouldn't leave. He says he's going to go to the police, says he has proof she's been abducted and says it's all you, Phantom. That you were the one who took her. You were the one who traded her to the Immortals."

"Is that so?" I murmured, my voice hardening to stone. "And did he say what that proof was?"

She gave a shake of her head. "No, but he was pretty adamant about it. But you said Harmony left him."

It wasn't a question, so I didn't answer. Offer nothing and give little away.

"And you don't know where she is exactly?" Britt prodded.

They all looked to Britt...she was tougher than the others. Harder, more tempered by her shitty childhood, and smart as a fucking fox.

"No, I don't know where she is," I answered. That last part

was the truth. "I want you to be careful." I met every gaze. "I don't want you talking to him, not here or at home. He's dangerous."

So are you, Britt's gaze echoed back.

If she only fucking knew.

"I'm going to have extra security at the doors for the next few nights. If you need an escort home, my men will be available. And ladies, if you have any problems…"

"We come to the Pack," Riley answered, her gaze a little too dreamy for my liking. "We know the drill."

A nod of my head and I left. "Have a good night tonight. Make a lot of money."

"Oh, we will," Riley called. "We *always* do."

But Britt didn't smile as I nodded. She just looked at me with those hard eyes. I'd keep watch over them…while they worked and in their personal lives. I'd hate for them to go missing, too.

I left them and closed the door behind me before I made my way to the offices at the back. A light was on, shadows moving around from inside, the smell of sex, grunting in desperation. I cleared my throat and waited. "Wry, when you have a moment."

There was a scramble inside. A few choice words were muttered. The low-level Wolf hurried to make himself presentable and yanked open the manager's door. I caught the flash of a boob before I turned my head. "Respect your damn female, beta. Don't be a fucking asshole."

"Sorry," he almost whimpered.

I tried to tune out their voices as she snapped at the Wolf. He deserved it…didn't the damn fool understand by now, *women always come first?*

He cleared his throat. I stepped to the side, meeting her gaze for a second as she smiled, her face burning before she slipped away. Her steps were light and fast. I tracked her to the connecting door of the bar and across the quiet dance floor to the exit. "How many is that this week?" I asked, turning my attention to the red-faced Wolf.

"Lost count, to be honest. But that one." His gaze drifted to the door. "That one I like."

"You said the same thing last week. This is a business, Wry. Treat it as such."

He gave a nod. "Yes, sir."

"I'll be calling in additional security for the girls and the club."

One brow rose. "Something happening?"

"Nothing you need to be concerned about...for now. I'll let you know when they arrive. And Wry...those Wolves are *not* our pack." The warning was loud and clear.

No funny business...or the young pup might just find himself on the end of their wrath. And that was never a good place to be. When you messed with the Breeds, you weren't just messing with one...you were messing with the entire damn platoon of packs, and covens, and dens...every single goddamn Immortal you could think of was there. Ruthless. *Unstoppable.* Goddamn terrifying, if you asked me.

I left him then, hoping to god he got the message. But I doubted it...pups like him never did. I strode along the hallway and shoved through the back door of the building. Barely a heartbeat later, and the bike was snarling between my legs as I peeled out of the parking lot and headed for one of the quiet new suburban developments of the city...where Harmony and her husband lived.

I didn't need a map, didn't need company files.

I knew exactly where she lived.

The twinge came in my chest as I turned into her street. Sunlight gleamed off the shiny new Tesla in the driveway. I glanced at the license plate *Eriks Rde.* "Nice," I muttered, and killed the engine.

The two-story house was nice. Large tree ferns out front,

deep rich wood layered over slate marble on the facade. The place was expensive, and that's putting it mildly.

The door opened as I walked up the drive. Anger and rage filled the doorway.

"Unless you've come to tell me where my fucking wife is, then you need to get off *my* property."

I lifted my gaze to the male standing in the doorway. Clear brown eyes stared back at me.

"I understand you're concerned—" I started.

"Concerned? How about downright frantic?" He dragged his fingers through his hair. "I haven't heard from Harmony in almost a week now. I want to know where the fuck *my wife* is."

"I have no idea," I answered. "And neither do the other girls. I suggest you focus on the search. Help the police with any information you might have." *Which is absolutely nothing.* "I'll do the same. I've already had a meeting with the detective handling the case, and I'll make sure to follow up with Marksen for another. We're all concerned about Harmony's well-being," I added, meeting those clear brown eyes. "She is a valuable employee and a good friend to many of the other women. I want you to be clear. I'm dedicated to Harmony's safety, so much that I'm offering a half a million reward to anyone who has actionable information."

Those clear eyes widened. "Half a million?"

"Yes," I answered, watching the fire in his eyes extinguish. "To *anyone* who has any definitive information on her whereabouts."

"Company money, probably insurance…"

"From my own account," I clarified. "This has nothing to do with the company. She went missing on my watch. I take that personally…*very personally.*" He grew quiet. "If you find out anything, I'm sure the police would be only too happy to investigate. Now…if you'll excuse me, Erik. I have others to check on."

"I love her," he murmured. "I need her back."

"I know you do," I responded, and turned before striding away.

I took one last look at that shiny new Tesla. Must've cost a fortune…not bad for someone who didn't work, for someone who whored his wife out at any opportunity outside of club hours. Not bad for someone who turned a blind eye when one of his friends left her hurt and bleeding for the last fucking time. Not bad at all…

9

Murphy's steps followed me, smacking loudly on the hard morgue floor as we made our way from reception to the room where the drawers were. I shivered and tried to focus on the stark white walls and not the growing fear that welled in my gut, or the nauseating stench of formaldehyde.

Just do your job and get the hell out of here.

Harlan wanted a complete inventory of the dead...*all* the dead, even the ones who were supposed to be unkillable. Moments of that night tried to press into my mind. I shoved them away, pushing them to the edges, where they snarled and waited.

They could keep fucking waiting for all I cared.

I never wanted to go back there again.

My arm ached and throbbed. I could feel the bruise settling deep, tiny punctures in the shape of his fingers. I swallowed air and fought the urge to retch.

"Where do you want to start?" the clerk asked, turning to me.

For a second, I couldn't answer. My heart thudded hard as

panic crept in. I licked my dry lips as Murphy answered behind me. "We'll start with the beasts."

A nod, and the clerk led us to the drawers on the far side of the room. "We retrieved nine in total, but you can only view five."

"Why?" Murphy barked. "I have full fucking justification here. If they wanted to go to war in *my* goddamn city, I have the full fucking right to pick their dead apart."

The clerked stopped somewhere toward the far end of the wall of stainless steel doors and turned to face him. "You want to do that...pick their dead apart?" The take-no shit scrawny guy muttered before he moved to the closest drawer and yanked the cold steel handle.

I flinched at the sound, my pulse ratcheting that little bit faster as, with one yank, the drawer slid free, with a lumpy black plastic body bag on the tray inside.

"Go ahead." The clerk's voice never wavered, nor did his deadpan stare. "Pick away."

The hairs on my arms rose as Murphy cut me a savage stare, eyes bright, lips curled, and reached for the zipper on the body bag. Hunger pressed against me, making that ache in my arm throb harder. Fluorescent lights buzzed and hummed, the lights piercing, nearly blinding. Flashes behind my eyes came light gunshots. I reached out, touched the cold chill of the metal drawers, and wrenched my hand away.

The dead were in there...cold, *waiting*.

You fight like a warrior. The words pushed into my mind as Murphy gripped the zipper and tugged it down low.

The side of the bag flopped open...and fine black ash spilled like powder from the opening to fall to the floor.

"Nice one" The clerk glared. "You've just spilled Vampire all over my floor. Do you have any idea how hard that stuff is to get out of the cracks?"

Vampire.

Red glowing eyes.

Fangs dripping blood.

Screams in my head. Unmerciful screams as the creature sank its fangs into Blane Costello.

"What the fuck!" Murphy roared and stumbled backwards, smacking into me. Hate raged in his eyes…hate that burn even hotter when he fixed on me. "Get the fuck out of my way, Chase."

He was my senior, and the SAC's brown-nosing bitch. I bit my tongue until I tasted blood. It was either that or ruin my day and my damn career in one perfect remark. Instead, I ground my teeth and stepped out of his way.

"You should've warned me," he snapped at the clerk, and stabbed the air with a finger.

"And *you* should've let me finish what I was trying to say. I swear, you cops are all the damn same." He shot me a glance and winced. "Most of you, anyway. Always so eager to throw your damn weight around, especially where it's not needed. *So, as I was saying.* You can only view five of the Immortal dead, seeing as how we only have five bodies to view. The rest are…" He lifted a hand to the mess. "Quite literally gone."

Murphy just bent and smashed his hand across his trousers before slamming the toes of his boots on the morgue floor, dislodging the fine black ash. "Then give me something I can damn well view."

With an audible sigh, the clerk stepped forward and carefully zipped up the Vamp's body bag.

"You just going to stand there, Chase?" Murphy turned that searing fire on me.

"What exactly do you want me to do, Murphy?" I ground out the words.

"How about *your fucking job?"* he spat.

The steel drawer closed with a *slam!* One quick glance my way from the clerk, and he gave a tiny jerk with his head. I swallowed the flare of anger and the tiny tremble of fear and stepped around my piece-of-shit partner.

"Lycanthrope." The clerk glanced at me and pulled open the drawer. "Cause of death...well, I'll let you be the judge of that." He stepped to the side.

*Do that again...*The Wolf's voice slipped back to me.

In a second, I was back there, with the hard thud of his pulse against my lips. I was desperate for the scent of him, deep, hungry, *alive.*

The clerk's lips moved as he cast quick glances my way. But I didn't hear a damn thing.

I wasn't here, in the cold and cruelty. I wasn't here, surrounded by death.

The clerked stilled, his fingers wrapped around the tab of the zipper. He gave me a scowl, before he dropped his hand and stepped away. "I'll just give you some time on your own then?"

That hunger spilled through me, tearing along my side, making my breaths deepen.

"Well?" Murphy growled. "You heard the clerk, start the inventory."

I couldn't move, nailed to the spot as agony cut across my chest.

"What the fuck is wrong with you?" A hard shove at my shoulder made me stumble forward until I smacked into the pulled-out steel table.

"Don't fucking touch me," I growled.

Hunger shifted under my skin, coiling...writhing.

"What did you say to me?" He pressed his body against me, wedging me in.

I could feel he was hard. His cock was digging into the top of my ass.

"You want to push me right now?" Murphy snarled.

He was different from the Alpha, colder, crueler. My stomach clenched at the feel of him. I gripped the cold steel and shoved backwards before I turned. I let that hate roll through me as I stared into his eyes. "I said, *don't fucking touch me.*"

He leaned down, making himself feel taller...did he feel more like a man when I was frightened?

Yes. I think he did.

"Everything okay here?" The low snarl slipped through the air...and my heart leaped at the sound.

A male came into view as he stepped around Murphy. Quick eyes met mine, something shimmering in them. I knew instantly...*he was Wolf.*

He glanced at Murphy leaning over me, took in his stance. His lips twisted as he found the tented hardness in Murphy's pants. "Sorry for interrupting." He glanced at me.

There was something about his voice that nagged me. An accent, just slightly...Russian maybe

She's...beautiful. The words swept through me. That same accent...that same *scent.* Heat, and pure brutality washed over me.

"Vitold." The Wolf held out his hand and stepped closer, his gaze never once wavering from mine.

"Carina Chase." I gripped his hand...warmth closed around me and that heat raced through me like a shockwave.

"What the fuck are you doing here?" Murphy snapped, shattering the hold. "This is a restricted area."

Only then did the Wolf turn his attention to Murphy and drop my hand. Those dark eyes shimmered with pure savagery. "I've come to claim what's mine."

My breaths stilled...pulse stuttering.

Part of me thrummed with excitement. *Yes...*the word was on the tip of my tongue as the Wolf shifted his gaze behind me. "When you've completed your investigation, of course, I'd like to take my brother home."

"So you can tear him up and eat his fucking body, I suppose." Disgust filled Murphy's tone.

"No." Vitold turned to him, his lip curled in warning. "We prefer to eat our prey kicking and screaming."

The Wolf took a step closer and Murphy moved backwards, his hand dropping to his holster. "Don't bother, Special Agent." Vitold said to Murphy, then turned his head to stare into my eyes. "Your bullets can't kill us."

His nostrils flared for a moment as he pretended to lean over the body in the drawer, and his arm brushed mine as he reached forward, feigning to look at the name tag on the body before he pulled backwards. "Carina," he murmured and stepped away.

He moved with the grace of a predator, all sleek muscles and savage gaze that he swept over Murphy before he turned and strode from the room.

The thud of his footsteps made my body tremble. I wanted to race after him, wanted to feel his warmth and his touch…I wanted to lower my face to his neck and smell his Alpha.

"You know that fucking punk?" Murphy snapped at me.

"No," I answered, unable to tear my gaze from the open doorway as the thud of Vitold's boots faded.

"Sure seemed like he knew you. Goddamn fucking animals. They should all be put down."

"Why?" I jerked my gaze to his. There was no backing down now…no cowering, no…*giving in.* Career or no goddamn career, I was done with taking Murphy's shit. "Because he's different from you? Who knows…maybe *we're the fucking animals, Murphy.* Ever thought about that?"

Heat bloomed in his cheeks. Confusion flared as he met my gaze. "What the hell are you talking about? What the fuck has gotten into you? Do the fucking inspection your goddamn self, *Special Agent.* I want the file complete and on my desk first thing in the morning or you're off the goddamn case. And if you think I don't have the power to make it happen, just fucking try me."

He spun on his heel, took two long strides and all but ran for the fucking door. I sighed as his steps resounded. Hate and desperation mingled with the agony in my chest until I was a pit of seething rage. I turned, gripped the zipper, and yanked it down.

Clouded white eyes stared back at me, pale lips now shrunken to reveal long, bloody teeth. His chest was a massive fucking hole where his heart had once been. I related, a little too close for my liking. "I'm sorry," I whispered as I touched his cold face. "That was a brutal fucking night."

I tried to maintain some distance, yanking my phone free and pressing the record icon. I detailed body after body, cataloging every detail I could find, until there were no more Wolves to look at and only the mortals left.

Four soldiers and two civilians.

Those two civilians were Costellos.

I searched for that burn as I yanked the zipper down and stared into the vacant blue eyes of Jerry Costello. But all I saw was an old man with a massive hole in his chest. Gone. Just like that. A flicker of heat raced at the thought of all the truths this fucker took with him.

The kind of truths that'd set my dad free.

But no, Jerry Costello had to go and get himself killed.

I found that burn then, that deep, seething hatred of retribution, and by the time I turned to the last body bag, I was shaking with anger.

Blane Costello was exactly how I thought he'd look. Bloody, sickening...and very, *very* dead.

I took my notes, mumbling into my phone, and took a step backwards.

Movement came from the corner of my eye. A young man stood there, his eyes wide...a camera in his hand. I knew what he was in an instant. A vulture, a paparazzo. The scum that exploited other people's pain.

"You've no right to be here," I growled. "I should arrest you this second."

His eyes were impossibly wide, looking from the open body bag to me. "I-is that...t-that's...B-Blane Costello, isn't it?"

Hate and honor collided in an instant. The cruel savage hands of justice were wrapped around my throat, strangling me, as I stared into the cameraman's gaze and answered. "Yes."

"Jesus...Jesus, that's him." He licked his lips.

I had a choice to make here...do the right thing for them *or for me*.

The burn settled deep inside me, turning cold as the howling December winds. All these years, I'd hated. All these years, I'd craved justice. But this...this didn't feel like justice—and as the paparazzo lifted his camera and took aim, I heard myself say. "No. Get the fuck out of here."

His finger pressed, shots were taken as fast as the shutter could work. I lunged forward, grabbed him by the shirt, and hauled him through the open door to the morgue and along the hallway.

The clerk looked up from behind the counter, a pen poised in his hand.

"You let this fucking piece of shit in here?" I roared. "What kind of fucking security do you have here?"

I shoved the bastard backwards, watching as he clutched that camera to his chest as that cold rage spilled through me. My fists clenched and a rumble sounded in my throat. In that moment I was more animal than I was human.

It felt good...it felt pure. "I see you around here again and I'm going to make it my personal mission to make your life a fucking hell."

The asshole stumbled backwards, through the door and out into the open. I just stood there, strangling nothing, when all I wanted to do was scream. The clerk rushed forward, his eyes wide as he looked at the swinging double doors, then at me.

"What happened?" he cried.

"The news is what happened," I barked. "That fucker just got the headline of his damn career."

I turned away then and made my way back to the exposed body of Blane Costello. My fingers trembled as I yanked the zipper closed and shoved the drawer back in place with a *thud*. I wanted out of here. Out of this place and out of this anger…

The thought made me stop still. I wanted out of the anger. Out of the rage. Out of the pain.

Out of this…*neverending loneliness.*

"I f-filed a complaint," the clerk stuttered behind me.

"Good for you."

"He shouldn't have been here, must've slipped through somehow. I could lose my job for this."

"Probably." I shoved past him and couldn't summon the strength to give a shit.

I should've smashed the camera, fuck whatever assault charges came my way. I should've done a great many things, the main one was leaving this fucking place when I had the chance.

I pushed through the doors and strode toward the gleaming midnight Jeep. Sunlight glinted, bouncing off the chrome. One press of a button and I climbed inside, pulling the door closed behind me.

I saw it the moment I turned my head.

Sitting on the dashboard.

One gleaming spent cartridge…*covered in blood.*

It was a sign. I jerked my gaze to the rear-view mirror, then scanned the parking lot. I knew in an instant whose it was…and who had put it there.

What the fuck are you doing here? Murphy's voice invaded…

As did the Wolf's response.

I've come to claim what's mine.

10

PHANTOM

"Did you hear what I said?" Vitold paced the floor in front of me, his focus like a shark that smelled blood in the water…if there wasn't any yet, there soon would be.

"I heard," I replied. "But I want you to tell me again…every *fucking detail.*"

"I smelled her before I got through the door, Phantom," he snarled, then turned on his heel and kept walking, head down, lip curled. "She was fucking shaking, and that bastard…had her pushed against the table. I could smell what he wanted…what he *enjoyed*. He liked her scared, liked her *alone.*"

Vitold froze, boring a hole in the wall with his gaze. "He was hard for her. That piece of fucking shit was ready to cum right there. I could smell her pain…and it wasn't just the Unseelie marking that hurt her. I tasted sharp pain, new pain." His eyes glazed, losing focus as he reached up and cupped his bicep. "Fingers digging in, leaving bruises."

A murderous sound vibrated in the middle of my chest. The warning spilled outwards and filled the room. "What was his name?"

"Murphy, she called him."

"Murphy." I let the name roll over my tongue.

I didn't mess in the affairs of mortals. I made it my fucking life's mission to stay right away from their special brands of torture and pain. But on this occasion…I might just make a fucking exception.

"And you left her the message?" I lifted my gaze to the Wolf.

He gave a nod. "She can't miss it." Doubt flared in his eyes. "Will she come to us?"

I froze, my heart clenching tight. I didn't know…didn't understand why she hadn't given in to me by now. Anyone else would be crawling…*begging,* but not her. Not this stubborn, goddamn, mortal *female.* No, she had to have the grit of a fucking lion. I sucked in hard breaths.

But even lions get hungry…

Even lions need to mate.

I licked my lips and turned my focus to Vitold. "She is to be protected…at all costs."

One nod of his head, and the Wolf's eyes sparkled with ravenous hunger. I stood up from the chair and turned to Arran, standing in the doorway. "I want to find out who this *fucker,* Murphy, is…I want to know every goddamn thing about him."

"And my car?" Arran looked at Vitold hopefully.

"Not a fucking scratch on it." Vitold's lips curled as the Wolf sagged against the doorway.

"You know," I took a step toward him, "I worry about your unhealthy obsession with that thing."

There was a scowl…teeth bared, before a smile came that could light up a room. "She's my baby."

I left them in the manager's office of The Hunting Ground and made my way back to the living quarters. The place was starting to feel a little too closed in, a little too familiar. But fuck me, I couldn't leave…not when the memory of her was here.

Why won't she come? the beast pawed the floor and sniffed the air.

"Because," I answered as the memory of the warehouse roared back to me, and that rush of excitement ripped through my veins. "She's a fucking warrior."

Warrior or not, she was marked by an Unseelie…that made any male around her a fucking adversary.

I grabbed my leather jacket and made my way out to the empty living room. Church and the others were overseeing the girls and our new muscle.

I wanted new blood…dangerous blood. There was none more dangerous than Pathfinder and his men. A dangerous breed of Wolves…the words filled me. A dangerous Breed indeed.

He worked for The Company.

A secret organization that controlled the Breeds.

A team of Immortals specially trained…and boosted with synthetic DNA.

The same type of shit that now coursed through Justice's veins—if the Vampire was still alive, that was. I strode past the empty living room and snatched the keys to the Camaro from the counter. Breed or no Breed, I needed to do a little hunting of my own.

I grabbed my phone and headed for the parking lot. I needed someone with connections…someone who wasn't above breaking the law, someone who wasn't afraid to get a little…*dangerous.* I hit the button, and the Red Eye unlocked with a flash of crimson in the headlights before I approached the midnight beast.

The heady scent of brand new leather filled my nose as I pulled open the door and sank into the racing seat. Exhilaration, that's what this car was. I lifted my gaze to the rear-view mirror.

Can't stop…can't stop this. Her voice filled my head as I stabbed the button and started the engine. I shoved the car into gear, rolled out of the driveway, and turned left. It wasn't the city I wanted…not yet.

The sleek Camaro hugged the corners and hunkered down on the straights as I punched the accelerator. I was slowing before momentum kicked in, down-shifting, turning into the gate. Razor wire glinted in the sunlight. I scanned the warehouse, and the shadows that clung to the walls.

The place was a front really, nothing more than rooms filled with piles and piles of money. Money we delivered on a nightly basis to the Fae, who controlled the power. It wasn't just any power. It was Fae Magic. Corrupt Unseelie dreams...stained with green.

The warehouse backed on to a dead part of the city. A part no one went to...no one who wasn't Fae, that was. Abandoned, perpetually dark, like night had fallen on the streets behind the warehouse this side of the city, and never rose again.

Creatures lived there...like the infernal monster, Kapre...I winced as the gate rolled backwards, then shoved the car into gear and gave it just enough to roll the vehicle through as I tried not to think about what they'd done to the bodyguard.

The torture. The pain. Fuck me, the male didn't even know what he was capable of. But one day he'd find out...and when he did—I lifted my gaze to the warehouse—I wanted to be as far away as fucking possible. That was between him, the Vamps, and the Dark Ones. The Wolves had enough shit of their own.

I killed the engine and climbed out, closing the door behind me. This place was quiet, a little *too quiet*. The sun beamed down on this side of the warehouse and birds were chirping somewhere behind me. I edged to the corner of the towering building and pressed my hand against the steel.

Something was brewing inside. Malignant. Dark...Deadly. I jerked my hand away. Not my problem...not my fight. Fae magic bled into the steel bones of this place and breathed life into the air like a heartbeat. I could almost feel the throb from here.

I stayed away from the walls and headed for the door. The

damn thing was ajar when I reached it, and damn if I didn't hesitate, hand outstretched, fingers hovering above the handle before I gave a snarl and wrenched the damn door open.

Shadows waited inside, crowding the doorway even as I pulled the damn door wide. Sunlight didn't invade here, nor warmth or brightness. This was the kind of place most feared to tread. The hungry waited here. The vile torturers. The Unseelie Fae.

I lowered my gaze and stepped inside. The thud of my boots resounded in the dark as I scanned the parking area inside the warehouse and the steel vaults locked up tight. No one would be stupid enough to come here, no one would dare risk the wrath of the Crown City Immortals.

"Mutt." The low growl came from my right.

The hairs rose on the nape of my neck. There was a hardness in the Unseelie's tone, like the scrape of a blade against my skin. I dragged in the cold, and waited for the edge to come. "Brother…everything okay?"

"Why wouldn't it be?" That blunt answer made me fucking cautious.

"No reason." I kept my voice calm.

A green glow spilled out from the darkness under the stairs. The same green glow that pulsed from the Special Agent's chest. Something was happening in the portal to the Unseelie world. Something that hadn't happened before.

"Anything you need help with, Mojin?"

"Not unless you'd like an afternoon of torture."

A frigid touch swept through me. My breath caught and my mind raced. "You caught him."

White teeth shone in the dark. The Unseelie shouldn't smile at me like that…*ever*.

"Why are you here, Wolf?"

I licked my lips. "I came for information. I need…a full name. FBI and two addresses."

"Hmmm. What have you got?"

"Murphy, last name or first, I'm not sure. He's working the warehouse crime scene with Carina Chase."

"The mortal…so she has a name."

"Yeah," I reached up and rubbed the back of my neck. For some reason, I didn't like him knowing her, not her name…or where she lived. But trust was hard to come by, hard in mortals…even harder amongst beasts.

I'd lay down my life for this Immortal. I'd fought side by side with him and his damn host. He might not be the Unseelie leader, but he was pretty damn close.

"You have an interest in this…*Murphy?*"

"Yeah," I answered, my own growl bleeding through. "You could say that."

"Consider it done." Mojin stepped backwards, blending into the shadows once more. A scream tore through the air, coming from that pulsing green glow. Howling and terrifying, a male reduced to his baser instincts, those of an animal. "You want to leave now, Wolf…and whatever you do…*don't look back.*"

My heart punched into the back of my throat as Mojin disappeared from the warehouse. There was no life, no heartbeat…no fucking time to give a shit. I kept my gaze low, scanning the floor as I turned and rushed to the door.

That demented howl only grew louder, shaking the walls as I lunged through the doorway and out into the sunlight. My damn hands were shaking as I hit the unlock and climbed into my car. I sat there, staring at the looming steel walls and tried to get my shit together.

I'd battled Vampires.

Even gone up against a demon or two.

But the Unseelie scared the shit out of me.

I stabbed the button, started the car, and turned the wheel. The gate was already open as I nosed the Camaro toward the street. A nice little *get the fuck out of here.* They didn't need to worry. I was as good as gone. As the tires hit asphalt, I shifted gears and punched the accelerator. I couldn't get away fast enough.

I sped past the club and headed back toward the city. Pathfinder and his men would be descending on Wild any second, and I wanted to be there. An Alpha that didn't prowl his territory was no Alpha at all. I knew every inch of this city. Every club and motel where the girls…and guys worked.

I knew what mortals wanted.

They wanted both sides of the spectrum.

The weak and vulnerable.

And the strong and deadly.

I catered well to those wants.

Fifteen minutes later, I was pulling up alongside Wild. The front door opened, and Wry strode toward me as I climbed out of the car, concern etched all over his face. "Alpha, when you said protection…I didn't think you meant *the Breeds*."

"No one's going to bother you or the girls." I shifted my gaze as the massive Alpha Wolf filled the doorway.

"How long?" Wry asked.

I didn't answer, just gave him a pat on the shoulder and left, striding through the open door of the bar and shook the outstretched hand of the biggest, baddest motherfucker I knew.

"You bring me here for tits and pussy?" The male dragged fingers through his fiery red hair.

"I brought you here to protect those tits and pussy," I replied. "With your fucking life."

One brow rose. "Something going down we should know about?"

Yes, that desperation snarled inside me. "Mortals causing problems."

Path took a step closer, keeping his voice low. "You dragged my ass here for mortals? I don't think so, buddy. Word on the street is some bad shit's gone down here in Crown City. No one's talking though...*not even the Vamp, Caedes.*" He gave me a stare. "Not talking, brother, cause the Vamp hasn't been seen."

"Mortals are the targets." I licked my lips and met that savage stare. "You watch the bar, and the girls. Escort them home if they need. No funny business, they aren't just pieces of ass here...they're to be protected." My tone hardened.

The Wolf gave a nod. He understood my rules. This wasn't our first dance together...not by a long shot. I called the Wolf brother, and he called me fucking crazy.

"And Finis?" he asked cautiously.

"You just let me worry about him." I answered and stepped away. "Watch the girls' asses."

He scratched his stubble. "Oh, don't you worry about that. I plan on watching every fucking inch."

I gave a small smile as my phone *beeped.* I grabbed the phone and stared at the screen.

Chap Murphy, 1356 Riledsway, Bullyard.

Carina Chase, 8898 Salt Street, River Heights.

River Heights? That was a hard neighborhood, low-income housing, kids running the streets. What the hell was a Fed on a decent income doing living in a place like that? My mind wanted to wander. Still, I stared at the two lines of text.

No note? No fucking warning? *Mojin must be busy.* The Immortal was usually a pain in my ass about staying away from mortals, not that I needed the damn advice. By the time I slid behind the wheel of the Camaro, the afternoon was closing in. But I didn't want to go home, wherever home was...four walls and a fuckton of problems. All of that could wait.

I wanted her. To see her, even if from a distance.

I started the engine and pulled away from the curb, catching sight of the young beta and the war-torn Wolf standing nose to nose and not in the romantic way. There was potential in the young beta, but he needed to sharpen his fangs on someone hard, someone tough...someone who wasn't me.

He owed no loyalty to the Breed, and that would give him enough rope...so long as he didn't hang himself...which was damn likely.

I turned the Camaro to the other side of Crown City's beating heart. The side where concrete government offices crowded the skyline and most of the traffic was the Feds. *Chap Murphy.* The bastard's name rolled through my head as I slowed the Camaro past the Fed Building, then kept on going.

I wanted to not just see her...I wanted to *know her.*

Know where she lived...where she breathed.

What moved her.

River Heights. It was a bad neighborhood and a place I hadn't been to in forever. None of the girls lived there...and I sure as hell wasn't keen on a leisurely drive past burned-out cars and boarded-up crack houses.

No place for a cop...certainly not one like her. The further I drove, the more I wanted to know. What made a woman like Carina Chase hard as fucking nails? More importantly...what the hell was she doing in that warehouse in the middle of a goddamn Immortal war?

I turned the corners, downshifting and tearing past the more lavish suburbs, to the ragged outskirts of the city...where River Heights waited. Sirens were the soundtrack here, cars pulled over on the side of the road, red and blue flashing lights behind them. I kept on driving, winding my way further from the river to the brown lawns and old rambling buildings, until I pulled over.

I yanked my phone free, scanned the address one more time, and pulled up a map. The address the Unseelie had given me was five streets over. Red and blue flashed in my rear-view mirror before a marked cop car sped past, followed by another and another.

Five more streets of this? What the fuck was this?

I waited for the special forces SUV that followed, then pulled out onto the street behind them. Who knew where they were headed? I followed the map, pulling into a quieter street and easing along until I stopped outside a decrepit, faded lime green clapboard house.

I winced and glanced back down at the address Mojin had sent me, then to the map on my phone. This was the place. Movement caught my eye. A kid...ten or so, raced across the street behind the car. I leaned forward before I knew what I was doing and killed the engine.

The sound of faint screams greeted me as I climbed out of the Camaro and scanned the houses around me. The kid was there, peeking out from the corner of a rusty old trailer. I narrowed my gaze as he stepped out and jerked his head in greeting.

I placed one hand on the car and curled my lip, baring my fangs long enough for him to get the message, *don't touch the goddamn car.*

His eyes widened, but he didn't move, just watched as I turned back to the ugly green house with its weeds and cracked driveway. The old carport housed a fifteen-year-old Chevy that'd seen better days. Faded navy blue paintwork and pitted chrome. I reached out, dragged my finger through the inch-thick dust, and dragged in the air.

Her scent was here, faded...but growing stronger the further I walked along the side of the house. I breathed in the sharp sting of urine and alcohol, and winced. *What the fuck?*

One slide of my tongue across my lips and I glanced over my shoulder, scanning the houses and the street. This wasn't my business...wasn't my place. But fuck if the beast inside wasn't insistent, pressing his nose to the trace of her, dragging in everything he could and making me step around the corner of the building to the rear of the house.

The wooden door was open. Darkness and answers waited inside. A buckled screen door was the only thing between me and her goddamn smell. I reached up, clenching my fist before I gripped the handle of the door. Hinges howled with a vengeance as it opened. I froze, wincing at the shrill goddamn sound and moved more slowly, opening an inch at a time until I slipped inside.

Cracked linoleum, and a foul, musty stench that filled my nose. This wasn't what I'd imagined…no, not at all. A soft snore drifted through the doorway, and the pungent odor of alcohol grew stronger…*as did the stink of male.*

I stepped around the opening, scanned the musty shadows that clung to the corners of the room, and lowered my gaze to the male slumped in the old recliner. He mumbled, and snored, His pale lips quivering with the sudden draw of breath. There was a faint resemblance to the Special Agent. A strong jaw, full lips, but that was where it ended. There were two empty bottles wedged between his leg and the chair…and two more lying on their sides on the floor. But not one drop had been spilled…not one drop had been wasted. Carina Chase's father was a drunk.

He mumbled something, curling his lips on a snarl as a car drove past, a glint of light shining through the filthy windows and bouncing off the picture on the wall.

Three pictures, actually. The darkened hue of a man in a cop's uniform. One that drew me closer. I was soundless as I stepped in front of him and made my way to the wall of pride. He'd been a police lieutenant, with a chest of medals he wore with pride. Harry Chase, the name plaque said. Harry Chase, once a decorated police officer and now a drunken bum.

A nagging feeling wormed its way inside my head. Shadows shifted, coming clearer…a glimpse of something much bigger than I'd expected. There was a reason for this…for the past and the present. A reason that drove a lone female agent with no goddamn backup into a brutal Immortal attack.

A reason she fought like she did.

A reason she'd saved my goddamn life.

I wanted to know what that reason was...

I made my way through the rest of the house. Her scent was faint, not soaked into the walls and the floor as I'd expect if she lived here. I left the house, making my way quietly out the back door, before a faint breeze picked up and I found her scent again.

I followed that scent through a thick, unmown lawn and a buckled fence before I stepped into the backyard of a neat two-story house. The closer I came, the stronger she was, making me lengthen my stride and glance at the small heap of empty beer cans as I smiled.

She was here...her scent as heady as a goddamn pine forest, making the beast sniff and paw the ground. I climbed the stairs to the back door of the house and stopped. Part of me wanted to respect her privacy and back away. Who the fuck knew...maybe a man lived there.

A man who fucked her...who lay with her., fed her food he prepared from his fingers and kissed every drop of water in the shower from her skin. A bestial sound trembled in the back of my throat at the thoughts.

A man she didn't want...

A man she didn't need.

Not when she had me.

I gripped the handle, expecting to tear the fucking thing from the lock, and twisted before it pushed in. "Doesn't anyone lock their damn door around here?"

I stepped inside, to the perfect scent of her, and that snarl in my chest grew louder. *More,* the beast urged. *More...*

The kitchen was spare, although brighter than her father's. Cheap appliances—I yanked open the fridge and stared at the shriveled package of lunch meat and the half a loaf of bread on the otherwise empty shelves—and goddamn food.

The place was hollow. I made my way along the hallway to the bedroom, where her smell lingered the strongest, and stared at the mattress on the floor. She lived like a damn pauper, no fucking food, no goddamn belongings.

I glanced over my shoulder at the two suits and small pile of clothes in the open closet and felt that urgency rising, desperate to know...to understand...*to fucking fix*. "What the hell happened to you, Carina?"

11

My hands were shaking as I reached for the bloody bullet on the dashboard of the Jeep. Not a warning, no...*a calling.* I knew where it came from without even thinking. Instinct raged as I closed my fingers around the cold slug and gripped it tight.

That ache raced through my chest to well in my heart. *Go to him,* the words raged as sweat broke out along the nape of my neck. *Go to him...to the one who can help you. The one who can protect you.*

The one who can save you.

As if I needed saving. I lifted my gaze to the stark gray walls of the Crown City morgue and felt my world sink away.

Fight.

I closed my eyes and gripped the wheel. *You can fight this.*

But the harder I pushed against that growing need, the more I burned inside. Flames licked hotter, reaching between my thighs. I wanted the Wolf, wanted his fingers on my skin and the heat of his gaze. I wanted that savagery, that strength...*I needed the Wolf.*

I ground my teeth and dragged up the only thing I knew

that'd kill that hunger inside me...*my goddamn reality.* Home. Bills. *Dad...drunk on the couch.* I opened my eyes and glanced at the time. It was getting late. Murphy wanted this information on his desk by morning.

Five Immortals and six humans. By the time I got through typing all that up, it'd be close to midnight as it was. Fuck going back to the office. I slipped the slug into the pocket of my jeans, leaned forward, and started the engine. I felt the bullet there, pushing and prodding, drawing my focus as I shoved the Jeep into gear and pulled out of the dirt parking lot and along the worn track.

Black and whites tore past on their way to the latest damn incident. It seemed like there was always something happening. Some shootout or hostage situation—or damn war breaking out in the warehouse behind the Jewel.

Even with the beasts all west of the river, we still had problems here. Territories became a battlefield, and not just on the streets. Immortals were pushing into all levels of mortal strongholds, not even the government was safe. My thoughts turned to the Vampire Prince who'd run for Senator and ended up beheaded, probably murdered by his own kind.

I thought of the Wolf...*of Phantom,* hurt like that. Betrayed, abandoned. My fists strangled the steering wheel and that vicious sound slipped from my throat. I'd protect him, hide him. Bring him into my miserable world...until he left, that was... until he found the real me. There'd be no pretense then, no lies. It'd all be there in every sickening detail.

My life of burden.

I turned the wheel and worked my way through the city streets as the sun slowly sank to the horizon. By the time I pulled up outside Dad's place, the vibrant splash of a pink sunset glimmered in the rear-view mirror. I grabbed my phone and climbed out, locking the Jeep behind me.

"Miss Carina!"

I groaned internally, not bothering to look as Davie stepped out from the corner of his trailer. "What is it, Davie?"

He seemed hesitant, stepping closer before he scanned the houses around us and rushed forward. "Had a visitor today, Miss Carina."

I narrowed my gaze on his, finding the smear of dirt across his cheek, and a thick trail of yellow snot from his nose. "That so?"

"Big, black flash car—"

The hairs on my arms rose.

"He looked at me funny."

"How?" Panic pushed in...making my pulse race. "How did he look at you?"

The kid curled his top lip, baring yellowed teeth crusted with plaque. "Ike thish," he mumbled, keeping his lips drawn back as far as he could.

A chill raced down my spine. I was already turning. "Did he go inside the house, Davie?"

"Think so, Miss Carina."

I lunged from the driveway, boots slamming on the ground. "Dad? *Dad!*" I roared, tearing past the carport and pivoting at the corner. The screen door howled as I yanked it open. I was inside in an instant, hurtling through the kitchen and into the living room. His head was tilted to the side. I scanned for blood and stepped closer. "Dad?"

A snore tore through the room, low, muffled by the thick, flabby muscles of his throat.

"Jesus fucking Christ," I gasped, and sucked in hard breaths. "I thought...I thought you were dead."

He never answered, just kept on sleeping in his intoxicated slumber. I glanced at all the bottles. "No more fucking deliveries. How many times do I have to call those idiots and threaten them?"

It didn't matter how many refused to deliver to him, my

father, the drunk, would always find a way to get what he wanted. He always did. "'Cause who cares about anyone else, hey Dad?"

A snore answered me.

I stepped closer. There was no way he was waking any time soon and damned if I wanted to fight with him to shower tonight. I glanced around the living room, settling on the pictures on the wall before I turned and walked through the house. There wasn't a damn thing out of place.

I turned my head and glanced at the backyard of my place.

He wouldn't have gone there...*would he?*

The thought of Phantom in my house didn't terrify me like it should've.

I shoved through the back door of Dad's house and made my way into the backyard, then climbed the steep rise to the stairs of my house. The door was closed—I tried to feel him, sense him somehow—but couldn't. I stopped at the top stair, twisted the handle, and stepped inside. There was nothing out of place, not in the kitchen, or in my bedroom. "What the hell are you playing at, Wolf?"

The urgency filled me. I never backed down. Not from a fight...or a promise, and this was one helluva calling card. I turned and made my way back down the stairs and through the yard to where the Jeep sat outside.

Splashes of deep crimson replaced the pink as night grew closer. I forgot about Murphy and his reports, forgot about Dad and the empty bottles lying at his side. I forgot all about Carina, the Special Agent with the FBI, as I climbed back into the four-wheel drive.

Davie was nowhere to be seen as I started the car, turned the wheel, and drove out of River Heights, making my way back toward the river...and the bridge. Tension rippled through me. It wasn't excitement that filled me...it wasn't that at all.

I licked my lips and pressed the accelerator hard.

No, not excitement.

Christ, my body was on fire.

Lights sparkled across the river as I drove toward The Hunting Ground. The speedometer crept higher the closer I got. "Get out of my fucking way," I snarled, and overtook a minivan.

By the time I exited the bridge and turned down the brightly lit street filled with sex clubs, I could hardly breathe. My chest tightened and my heart clenched. I slowed the Jeep and pulled into the parking lot marked *Private*. The Camaro sat amongst the others, gleaming...*gorgeous.*

That was the car...rich leather seats.

The throaty growl of the engine.

The kind of car I could only dream of.

The slug in my pocket dug into my hip as I killed the engine and climbed out. I had no idea what I was going to say to him, or how to act. I dragged my gaze from the Camaro and turned to the seductive lights of the strip club.

I'm not having you walk through my fucking club trying to hump every fucking male in there. His voice boomed inside my head.

I was back there in an instance, that searing anger tearing through me as I snapped, *You don't trust me?*

But his answer stopped me cold. *It's not you I don't trust, Special Agent.*

It was everyone else he didn't trust. Not when the Unseelie mark was fresh on my skin. It moved in me now...*still.* Although not as savage. I didn't dare touch the emerald green stones embedded in my skin, not now...not when I was about to walk into the Wolf's den.

I strode forward, leaving the Jeep behind. Night was settling in, darkening the city to that sullen twilight hue. I yanked open the door and jerked my head toward the massive bouncer sitting on a stool against the wall. "Don't bother getting up." I reached for my badge, flipped open the leather case, and held it up.

He just scowled, then glanced at my ID and at me. "What the fuck do the Feds want here?"

"None of your damn business, how's that?" I muttered.

"She's fine, Squash," came a low growl in front of me.

I jerked my gaze toward the sound. A Wolf came toward me, climbing the stairs with lethal prowess and lifted clear green eyes to mine. He was...an Adonis. Sandy blond hair, the most perfect, hardest jaw. The kind of body most mortals spend years sculpting, but somehow, I knew he barely trained at all.

"Special Agent," he murmured.

I was transfixed by those lips. "What?"

He just smiled. "Business or pleasure?"

Dear God, that bass in his voice rumbled through me like thunder. "Bleasure," I muttered. "I mean Pusiness." *Shit.* "The Wolf. I want to see him."

That smile only grew wider, showing perfect white teeth. "You're gonna need to be a little bit more specific here."

He knows who I mean...he's playing with me. "Phantom," I forced his name. "I want to see Phantom."

But the blond-haired Wolf god never moved, just stood in the middle of the stairs, barring the way. "Is he expecting you? He can be kinda busy."

"Listen." I stepped down, until I was one stair above him, so close I could stare into his eyes. "You know damn well he's expecting me. Now are you going to take me to him, or am I gonna have to start waving my badge around and demanding he come out and see me?"

Adonis just straightened, met my gaze, and leaned closer. The second we touched, that fire ripped through me like a damn inferno. His blue eyes sparkled that little bit colder...*or was it crueler?* Like a damn Arctic wind.

He leaned in, his lips hovering dangerously close to my ear. His low growl sent shivers along my spine. "You start waving *anything* around, Special Agent, and I'm gonna have to take you to the floor. Something tells me I'd enjoy that very much."

He was cold this one, *chilling*. Hoarfrost in the dead of winter. The cutting blade of an arctic headwind, tearing through me in an instant and plunging into my soul. I shivered under his gaze, breath trapped, eyes locked.

In that moment, under the spotlight of his gaze, I saw us...*together*. Like a glimpse of the future. We were inseparable. Honest and raw. *Unbreakable.* I stiffened as the image rolled through my mind. His gaze narrowed and his focus grew sharper. "Let me take you to him," he said finally, and that heady sense of forever drifted away.

Music throbbed inside the club. Hard, grinding, making my pulse race as the Wolf in front of me turned and made his way back down the stairs. Long, sleek strides cut through the club. Not once did the male turn his head and look at the entertainment...and there was plenty to look at.

Two women danced on a stage at my right, both brunette and gorgeous. One lithe and perky with tight natural breasts that jiggled and bounced, the other fuller, with thick thighs and a nice round ass, wearing barely more than a piece of string. She was beautiful, model beautiful, working everything she had as she sank to the floor, knees parted, hips thrusting into the faces of three men as they watched her. She liked to be watched, I could tell.

Heat rushed through me, welling between my thighs and burning in my cheeks. I'd seen it all in my line of work; the best of mortals...and the worst. I'd seen girls who were far worse off than this, forced to sell their bodies for some piece of scum who they thought was worth saving. They weren't, they never really were...and then there were the girls who disappeared completely. Who left behind nothing more than photographs and a faint memory of someone who saw them at a party one night, and they were never seen again.

Yeah, those stuck with you, long after the case was closed.

But they were nothing. Another stripped at my right, a gorgeous blonde with the kind of body that most women would kill for.

But the magnificent male in front of me never even glanced at her as she writhed in a plush midnight chaise lounge in front of a group of men. I caught the flick of her eyes toward him as he cut through the dance floor and headed to the bar, and for a second, I thought I saw wanting there, needing, an urgency that screamed *look at me.*

But he didn't look at her, or any of them, not once, like he was totally oblivious to their presence.

A slurred bark roared through the club. The Wolf jerked his gaze toward the sound. He was on it in an instant, striding toward the messy fucking male with his tie skewed and the neckline of his shirt open as he gripped the bar and swayed on his feet.

"Problem here?" The Wolf towered over the poor inebriated schmuck.

"Problem?" the asshole slurred, and tried to whip his gaze to the male towering over him. "I'll tell you what your problem is…"

The Wolf waited, brows narrowing, until he looked at the bartender. "Where's Arran?"

"Here" The mutter came from behind me.

I turned and met the Wolf's gaze. He was spunky, cocky, and walking with a swagger. His gaze instantly brightened as he met mine, his lips curling into a smile. "Hey there, Special Agent." He greeted me like a long lost friend. "Here to bring me my car?"

"No," I answered.

The smile died. "No?" He glanced at the blond. *"What the fuck?"*

"Not now," the Adonis commanded with a jerk of his head. "Get this idiot out of here."

"Hey!" the idiot slurred as he narrowed his gaze on me. "She's hot..." One lick of his lips and he stumbled toward me. "I'd bang her."

A growl came from behind me, low...*threatening,* making the hairs on my arms stand on end. I knew who it was even before I turned. *I felt him...*like a river rushing through me. Like the draw on the tide from the moon...and I turned.

Silver sparkled under the overhead lights of the club, cutting through me like steel.

"Special Agent," he murmured, never once taking his eyes from me.

Phantom...the Alpha of their pack, took a step closer, drawn by the pounding in my chest.

I had his complete, undivided attention in this moment.

Like I stood in the cross-hairs of a sniper.

An *exceptionally* dangerous sniper. One whose lip curled as he moved against me, and stared down. I craned my neck, lifting my gaze—until he was all I could see...all I could feel... and *all I wanted...*

12

They affected me...*these Wolves.* It was more than that green pulsing power in my chest. More than the heady rush of being prey to this predator...and I *was* prey, I was under no illusions about that.

They were superior in every sense of the word; faster, stronger. *Hungrier.* The only thing we mortals had on our side was our sheer exhausting numbers.

"Wolf," I responded.

A flicker of something danced in his eyes at my answer. A smirk twitched at the corners of his lips.

"I want her, on her fucking knees," the drunk slurred, and stumbled forward. "This *bitch* right here. I bet she fucks like a wildcat."

Phantom moved faster than I knew was possible. He lunged forward, eyes wild, teeth bared, to tower over the drunk. *"Speak to her again...and you'll have no fucking throat. You understand me?"*

The drunk just looked up at Phantom and swayed. "Jesus, man...it's just a joke."

"Get this *pile of crap out of my club before I end his miserable life."* Phantom jerked that hostile gaze to Arran, and the smaller Wolf moved...*fast.*

"Let's go, schmuck." He grabbed the asshole by the collar and dragged him from the bar toward a side entrance. "Just gotta piss off the Alpha, don'cha?"

Though smaller than Phantom, the cocky Wolf was imposing. Corded muscles tightened as he moved, bulging under the skintight black shirt Arran wore. Nice ass, too, firm and tight in those black jeans, not that I was looking. *Who the fuck was I kidding?*

"Like what you see?" The low snarl filled my ear, half inquisitive and *all* fucking dangerous.

I turned my head, and my body followed as I stared into the eyes of a hunter. *Yes,* the memory of those lips came roaring back to me. *Very much so.* "I'm not here for that," I lied.

"No?" Both brows rose. *Liar,* he said with his eyes.

I swallowed hard. "No."

"You mind telling me exactly why you've come here, then? If it's not to be naked in my fucking bed, I've got limited time."

I stiffened, heart stuttering...heat rushing. "You got time to fuck me, but no time to talk to me?"

"Female..." Nostrils flared as he drew in my scent. "I've got all the time in the world for you, but you come in here waving *your...*" the muscles clenched in his jaw, *"everything* around. You rile the clientele. You rile them, and they stop drinking...they stop drinking, and they stop paying. So tell me what you want from me, and leave."

Leave?

Heat rushed to my cheeks with what felt like a slap.

*I'm offering myself here...*the memory pushed to the surface. *Use me...It's just sex.*

He was pissed at me, snarling and feral, licking his wounds before he lashed out in pain and anger. This is what this was, wasn't it? *Pain and anger.*

"You came to my house today." I kept my voice controlled.

"Did I?"

He knew damn well he had, and he knew I'd find out, too, *and* I'd be pissed...enough to come and face him.

"You want to know something about me, Wolf?" I kept my voice calm and took a step closer. "Then ask me."

He reacted...like I knew he would. His laser focus bored into mine as his chest rose with a harsh breath. This *battleground* between us raged, nether giving an inch before he leaned closer, that deep rumble in the back of his throat as he commanded, "Out back, *now.*"

I thought about fighting him about not budging a fucking inch until I had it out with him. But the grinding music around me grew bolder...and eyes watched me from around the room. Not my scene in the slightest.

Movement came from the corner of my eye as I pushed off from the bar. The Wolf, *Arran,* just watched me with interest. I caught his stare before he gave me a wink and nodded his head toward the door at the back of the room.

Go to him, the motion said and damn if that hunger inside me didn't howl with purpose. I strode forward, leaving the sleazy stares of the patrons behind, followed the Wolf along the gleaming bar, and shoved through the door marked *Private.*

He wanted to keep this between us...well, he'd better be ready for a battle of the fucking ages. My footsteps echoed in the hallway as I headed to the private quarters out back. Each step felt like destiny, drawing me back to something that felt like *home.* But this wasn't my home, and nor was the male waiting for me as I twisted the handle of the Wolf's quarters and stepped inside.

Hazel eyes flashed silver from the living room. The Wolf, *Vitold,* sat there, bare chested, with one arm extended across the back of a sofa. "Special Agent," he greeted, his gaze searching my face, then my body, lingering on my arm where he'd seen Murphy grab me.

But it was the towering giant I searched for, the one who'd lured me here…like prey to a predator. The kitchen was empty and, apart from Vitold, so was the living room. I shifted my gaze to the hallway, the one which led to the stark white bedroom. *His bedroom.*

He was there…*waiting.*

The air rippled with his energy, *trembling* like foreshocks of a quake.

That agony flared deep, like a fist driving into my chest. I felt that fist, knuckles grazing my ribs, fingers curling around my heart. I took a step, and another, drawn by something far deeper than anger…or pain. Something I'd never felt before, and as that fist clenched tight, squeezing life into my veins, that heady sense of purpose took flight.

I was meant to be here. In this place in this moment.

In this power.

I strode along the hallway, my gaze fixed on the cracked open door of his bedroom. Stark white walls called me. I stepped inside, finding him leaning against the bathroom doorway, his massive arms crossed. His gaze fixed on mine the moment I stepped inside.

Instinct raged as I closed the door behind me. For a second, I didn't know why. But he did…the Wolf whose eyes shone silver, whose nostrils flared, drawing my scent in deeper as I crossed the room to stand in front of him.

Silence filled the space. There were no words needed. Not when every look…every breath…*every thought danced across his gaze.* He wanted me. Wanted me so much he could barely breathe. Fear flickered. I wondered what that felt like to him… something so alien as fear.

Had he ever felt that before? Or was this all so damn mortally new?

"You came to my house," I said finally. "I want to know why."

His hands slipped on his arms, sliding down the rock-hard biceps. "You know why."

My heart beat faster. But I didn't give him an inch. Instead, I drew on every ounce of my training. "Why don't you tell me?"

"Because *you*, Special Agent, are a fucking menace."

I tried to smother the flinch.

"You want to know why? Want me to explain it in terms you can understand?" He shoved off the doorway and took a step, flanking my side before stepping behind me.

Panic filled me. But this time I didn't reach for my gun...*it wasn't that type of panic.*

My heart was racing, my mouth was dry. His breath came on the nape of my neck. "Stubborn," he growled. "Pushy. Invading *my* territory."

I lowered my gaze to the floor and looked behind me. "You invaded mine first, remember? Wrong side of the fucking river and all."

The chuckle that followed was dangerous... then it ended. "Take your clothes off, Carina," he murmured against my ear. "I'm not fucking around anymore."

A shiver raced down my spine.

But I didn't move.

Not even when he pressed against me.

Warmth bled into my body. The back of his finger grazed down my arm. "I'm not playing."

"I never thought you were." My breaths raced.

He reached around, cupped my chin, and turned my head toward him. "Clothes *off*," he ordered. "Now."

My hands lifted on their own as that pulsing ache spilled through my body. Green glow spilled through my shirt to kiss my hands as they worked the buttons.

"I can feel your hunger, feel it against my mouth, sliding

down my goddamn throat. Welling in my fucking chest, and gripping my cock. Feel it like I've felt no other."

Heat moved through me, tight and punishing between my legs. This wasn't what I came for...this wasn't what I needed. *Lies.* They were all lies. Lies I tried to tell myself. Lies I wanted to tell him. I closed my eyes as they faded away.

"Tell me you want this as much as I do." His growl was in my ear.

I dragged in the scent of him, animalistic, *savage.* "Would it make this any easier?" I ground out the words. "You know I can't resist."

The chuckle was there in an instant, deep and rumbling. A storm at my back...threatening and wild, all that power desperate to be unleashed.

I lowered my head. The way he commanded me...the way he pushed me. I was so fucking weak with him, weaker than I'd ever been in my life. Unable to resist him. *Helpless.* I unbuttoned my jacket and slid it free. The shoulder holster was next, sliding down my arms until my gun hit the floor with a *thud.*

He stepped away from me then. Cool air pressed against my skin as that bestial need roared inside me. I felt him, his savagery filling the air, standing the hairs on the nape of my neck.

But it wasn't just *his* energy that danced across my skin. It was all of them.

The blond.

The cocky bartender.

The Russian with his intense eyes...

Fuck me. The clasp released and my bra hit the floor. I turned then, finding his brutal stare, and shook my head. "No...this isn't me. This isn't what I came for."

"Lies," he forced through clenched teeth.

I clenched my jaw, my heart thundering. Their feral energy

pulsed against me…not just one, but the entire pack. "This isn't me. None of this."

His eyes flashed silver. "It is and you fucking know it. You've never wanted anything more in your goddamn life. You fucking need this…all of this. You need the heat and the power. You need the hunger like it's ripped out your fucking throat. You need to feel *alive.* That's what I make you feel, Carina. *Alive. Powerful. Desired. All of it.*"

His words slammed into me. Driving deeper than skin and bone.

All the way to my soul.

"Don't come any closer," I warned, my FBI badge useless in the face of this fanged monster. "I'll scratch and bite."

"You'll crawl and beg, too," Phantom promised as he strode closer, a glint of desire dancing in his eyes. "And that, Special Agent…will only be the start of it. Now take off your clothes before I rip them off, and get on the fucking bed."

Tremors tore through me, but I worked the buttons of my shirt until it fell away, crumpling into a heap on the floor, and I reached for my bra. "Fuck you," I whispered, kicking off one boot, then the other.

He stiffened in an instant. The heavy thud of his steps boomed as he closed the distance between us. The back of his fingers brushed my arm at the throbbing ache.

"He did this to you?" His voice was stone fucking cold. "The male you work with."

I froze, then slowly looked down. The red indentations of Murphy's fingers were already darkening where blood vessels had burst, blood pooling under the skin.

"Answer me, Carina. Did he hurt you?"

"It doesn't matter," I deflected.

One low snarl, and my breath caught. "It matters to me."

I turned then, meeting his gaze. "I can handle myself. *You of all people should know that.*"

He smiled then, that chilling, terrifying smile. "You can," he murmured, and dropped his hand, stealing the warmth of his fingers from my skin. "Of course you can."

I waited for a *but*. Because that *but* welled in his gaze, unspoken…and menacing. A warning no one ever sees coming. But he didn't say the word, he didn't say a thing, just lifted his gaze from the bruise around my arm to my eyes.

"You push me more than anyone has ever fucking pushed, Carina. You make the beast in me come alive…and that's a *very* dangerous thing," the Alpha growled. "He wants you…wanted you from the first time he saw you, covered in blood, ready to fight and kill…an animal hiding in a mortal's skin."

My hands went to the button of my pants as my heart thundered.

That's what I'd felt like my entire life.

I was different.

I was *more like them,* always savage, always hungry…and the hunger never went away. I flinched with the thought. How far? How far do I push this? That throb in my side punched higher, and the fist clenched tighter around my heart. How far do I dance with the beast?

Just this once…

The words were shaky in my head.

Just this once and we're done.

The glow in my chest burned hotter as I slipped my pants down and stepped out of them. Socks were next, leaving my badge and my gun on the floor. "Just this once." I snarled and lifted my gaze to his. "And no more."

He smiled then, all teeth and unmerciful glint. *I don't care how this fucking happens…*

His words raced through my head as I slid my fingers under the elastic of my panties and pushed them down. The Alpha's gaze tracked the movement, lingering at the juncture between my thighs.

That glint shone brighter as he met my gaze. I knew now… knew who it was who stared back at me…*his beast…his Wolf.* The hunter in a man's skin. I made my way toward the bed as the air cracked with wild need.

"Kneel," he commanded, his voice deeper than it was before, more guttural and rawer. "Hands on the wall…do not fucking mark it."

My damn knees trembled as I buckled and sank to the edge of the large mattress. I leaned over, splayed my hands on the bed, and crawled toward the headboard.

"Eyes front," he commanded. "Do not turn around."

My fingers curled and my nails scratched the paintwork as I flattened my palms against the cold wall. I stared at the white wall…but my senses were on fire, tracking his every move as he stepped close, the slide of fabric against his skin, falling to hit the floor.

There was nothing but the pounding of my heart.

Nothing but the whisper of a zipper.

My pulse jacked as the mattress sank at the edge. A whimper tore free.

Still, there was nothing but silence between us…and anything but emptiness.

The room was filled to overflowing…and it was all *him.*

This man who made me both weak and strong. Both powerful and helpless. Both wanted and used at the same time. I was at war with my body. A hostile takeover raged within me, guns were drawn…demands given.

I dropped my head at the trail of those callused fingers down my spine. They were toughened from fighting, blood-stained… death-delivering, not kind…not in the fucking slightest. Utterly *Alpha.*

"You think because you carry a badge you can bust down my door…and invade my fucking life? You think you can make that dead thing in my chest come alive? I killed it long ago, Special Agent, tore it out and swallowed it whole."

A shudder tore through me in answer. His heart...that's what he meant. His fucking heart.

"You need to understand who you're playing with, Special Agent." His hands gripped my hips. Jesus, just that deep, graveled voice made me wet.

One draw of a breath and I knew he scented me...the low rumble in the back of his throat was all fucking promise.

"I..." I started.

"I?"

Thick knees pushed between my splayed thighs. Powerful thighs opened, making my knees spread outwards. *Hands on the hood...legs out wide.* I could hear my own commands come back to me. How many times had I said that in the field?

My legs were out wide, pushing wider the more he moved.

"I'm gonna show you just what I think of you waving your fucking gun around," he growled. "I'm gonna punish you for shooting me in the fucking chest. Are you ready, Special Agent?"

He yanked my hips backwards, and my splayed hands slid down the wall, until the tip of his cock danced at my entrance. "Oh my God." My eyes fluttered closed.

My body was on *fire.*

My focus was on that touch...on that brush of the most sensitive part of me...the belly of the flame burned when he thrusted, sliding the head of his massive cock inside me. I bit my lip, head lowered, nails scratching the walls...*must not mark the walls.*

"You fucking shot me," he growled, hands closing around my hips like a fucking vise, pulling me backwards, then pushing up. I couldn't have gotten away even if I'd wanted to. Grinding, dipping, stretching me wider until my pussy clamped down... and then he pulled free.

"Fuck you," I whimpered. "Give me a gun and I'll shoot you again."

A deep rumble of laughter spilled across my bare skin. His thighs flexed, driving his body upwards until his hard chest pressed against my back. "I have no doubt about that," he murmured against my neck. "No doubt whatsoever. But right now...you're mine, Carina Chase. I *own you*, pussy, tits...and soul."

I whimpered at the words, bearing down, desperate for an inch more...and he had plenty to give. *More than I'd ever had before.*

"Look down, Carina." His hand was gentle and yet forceful against the back of my head. "Watch while I fuck you, and when I finish fucking you, then you'll know who you belong to. You'll know whose pack is yours. Pro tip. It's not the one with the shiny badges and the goddamn mortal rules. You belong to *us. You are owned by us.*"

"No..." I started as his cock pushed in deep, filling me up, sliding all the way inside until I lost control of myself. Not him. Not *us.* Not any of them. Not owned...*not owned...*

Something slick slid down my cheek, warm and wet, dancing on the tip of my chin before it fell. I'd known it the moment I ran from this place, known it before I pulled the trigger. Part of me remained there when I left and it wasn't in the bricks and mortar. It was in *him.* This Wolf, this world...this *connection.*

Slow. Hard. The thrusts dragged me from my own soul, and left me in the dirt and the mud...in the primal yearning of what I'd always longed for.

Family.

Purpose.

Love.

He claimed me...deeper than any bite ever could. I pushed back and met his thrusts driving down...hard flesh slapped on flesh, that fire stoked inside me, rising up as I did until he pressed his thumb against my ass.

"Open up for me," he demanded. "Open up and I'll show you how a real man takes care of what he owns."

My muscles clenched, my breaths came hard and fast. But his hand never moved from the back of my head, his fingers stayed tangled in my hair. I watched his cock slide out of me, pink skin glistening from my own savage need. That pressure against the ring of muscle pushed harder...until it pushed inside, fucking me...with his thumb and his cock.

"I'm going to own this," he growled and thrusted his hips harder. "I'm going to own it all."

That urgency grew inside me, making me clench deep inside, drawing a savage sound from the Wolf. "Do that again and see what happens."

I couldn't stop it. The hunger, that savage, *unmerciful hunger*. My body clenched as I watched him push inside me. His cock glistened as he slid free, my release slick and white over his skin, stretching over the tip as I shuddered. My body hummed, pulse frantic, as the energy in the room seemed to change.

Hungry...

So fucking hungry.

He kept that thumb pushing into my ass and slipped two fingers from his other hand inside my pussy. "You want to come?" he growled.

I trembled, fighting the truth that I already had. Still, those low shudders tore through me as he stroked his fingers higher, making me lift my head.

"You don't come, Special Agent" he ordered. I grew slicker with the snarl. "You don't get to come at all, you understand me?"

I bit my lip and squeezed my eyes closed. Something was changing in the air around me, something feral and dangerous.

Something that slipped across my mind. A touch. A sniff…a warning snarl in my ears, rumbling and brutal.

I let out a whimper as his fingers slipped free. Darkness crowded all around me. Darkness and death.

"Do you want to be ours?" he murmured in that strange, savage tone.

My heart stuttered and the agony in my side roared. Still the white room grew darker, as though the sun was dying…leaving us behind. I didn't care…not about the sun, or the moon, not about my job, or my father.

All I cared about was him, him and what he claimed. His cock pushed in deeper, thicker than before, stretching me wider until something thick and hard pushed against my opening.

"Do you want to be claimed by a Wolf?"

*Ours…*the word raced through me as that pressure at my opening grew bolder. Slick sounds followed. I stretched my thighs even further apart and lowered my head, finding that pulsing vein that ran along his cock, then froze.

The thick base was bulbous, hard as a rock, stretching me thin as he thrusted. That burn came at my opening as the knot drove inside me, and slipped out. Jesus Christ. I grew wetter… burned hotter, as I pushed against his thumb and whimpered, "Yes."

The room grew darker in an instant, leaving shadows and sin behind. That burn filled me, driving deeper as he wiggled his thumb inside my ass. "I can feel myself inside you, feel your body reacting, clamping down around me, milking me. Fuck me, Carina. I've never wanted this before…never wanted the beast to…"

A threatening sound filled the air, low, chilling. There was a rush of cold air all around me, something brushed my arm.

"Tell me you want us," he demanded. "*All* of us."

"I…want you." I whimpered as that heat inside me burned. "Fuck me, I want you."

The green glow from my chest pulsed against the wall, throwing shadows in the darkened room. Shadows slipped and moved against the wall, more of them...more and more and more. My vision blurred. Phantom became another, then another...and another. Energy pulsed as he gripped my ribs and pulled me against his chest. His hand slid around my throat, that bulbous cock pushed in deep, until it was all I could feel, wedged tight inside me. Throbbing with power.

Fingers grazed my arm, lips kissed my thigh. That savage growl came at my ear and a sharp sting sank into my shoulder. The metallic scent of blood slipped into my nose. My own blood, bitter and sweet.

"I can't stop myself." That guttural voice said. "Can't stop."

I clamped my eyes closed as pain flared hot and tight, making me buck against him as I came. The stinging on my shoulder was gone in an instant. There was only him, only pain...only the brush on my clit, of fingers sliding down my slit.

"Come in her." That thick Russian accent filled my ears as Phantom bucked once more.

Hard breaths gripped me, just like his big hand was around my throat. My body was on fire, he was still hard and wedged inside me. Heat bloomed as Phantom let out a savage snarl and came.

Fingers, lips. Warm breaths and soft lips worked their way up my shoulder.

"Need to stay like this," Phantom grunted. "Inside you...just for a bit."

He cradled me, lowering me to the bed. Someone brushed my hair from my face and pushed a pillow under my head. Warm lips claimed mine. The kiss was different, softer.

"You're safe here," someone else murmured as I closed my eyes and tried to breathe.

"Wolf from the bar?" I whispered.

"Arran," he answered.

"Ours." Phantom nuzzled against my back as exhaustion rose up inside me.

Warmth pressed against my back, and my front. Someone wrapped their arms around me. Panic flared for an instant. They were everywhere, a hand at my hip, a kiss on my breast.

Ours. The word resounded as that pain on my shoulder throbbed.

Ours. I didn't know what that meant.

As the constriction around me turned to the comfort of male bodies, I understood then...understood all too well. It wasn't just the Wolf, Phantom, who wanted me...*it was all of them...the entire pack.*

13

Slow, steady breaths echoed around me. A hand moved on my hip. Thick thighs pushed against mine from behind. But the face pressed between my breasts was the most concerning. The nose was wedged in tight, lips open and humming against my skin with every draw of breath.

I looked down to the dark brown hair of the cocky bouncer. *Arran,* his name came to me. Memories pushed in, faint at first, cloaked in shadows. That smile, dark eyes flashing with pure, sexy wickedness. My pulse raced at the sight, pounding and slamming as I looked over the dark-haired Wolf to the blue-eyed Adonis lying on the other side.

Jesus...*no.*

Ours...

The word surfaced and with it came the throb between my thighs. That ache...that *thick, bulbous knot pushing inside me.* A moan came to life at the back of my throat, and turned into a groan. Ours. That meant more than one of *them.* More than one man...more than one Wolf. More than one lover. Jesus, what the fuck have I done? Heat raced to fill my cheeks, burning until I felt on fire.

I wanted out of this…*now.*

Run, and damn well keep on running.

A sting tore through my shoulder as I moved. I winced and clenched my jaw, turning my head to see the bite mark on my flesh. Fangs and teeth, the indention deep enough to leave a scar. Arms and legs entangled with mine, shifting as I tried to move.

Trapped.

I was trapped here with the…*four of them.*

Like one big Wolfy pile.

Hands and lips and…almost naked bodies. Midnight blue boxers on one, black briefs on another. But one of them…*the Russian,* was bare. A perfect, pale round ass, thick thighs. I couldn't stop looking, following the shift as he moved and stretched. His flaccid cock lay against his thigh.

I slammed my eyes closed and tried to slow that careening train of panic.

Lips and fingers. *Come in her…*the Russian said that.

I closed my eyes and squeezed them shut. This was all just a big fucking mistake.

Four mistakes…

They were there, touching…urging. Heat raced to fill my cheeks as I opened my eyes and slid one foot toward the side of the bed before I froze. Hairs on my arms rose as I became aware of the sounds in the room. Shallow snores…a mumble from one of them. But the deepest draw of breath was quiet now.

"Going somewhere?"

I winced. My heart leaped against the side of my chest as I shoved forward in a rush, digging the back of my heels into the side of the mattress to scoot me forward. I didn't care about who woke who anymore…or my tattered dignity. "I just remembered…" I flashed Phantom a glance, catching that dark, riveting stare following my every move. "I have *ahhhh*…a thing."

"A thing," he repeated.

He was still naked...holy fuck, was he naked. Expansive chest that bulged as he pushed up onto one arm. Silence filled the room. The growing kind of silence that you're suddenly aware of. Their gazes followed me as I scurried like a madwoman, lunging for my clothes, yanking things on one after another, until shit got stuck.

Heat rose, plunging past my cheeks to swallow my entire head. I was burning from their focus. The deafening sound of my heart was the only thing I could hear until Phantom murmured, "Umm, you're trying to yank up your shoulder holster between your legs, Carina. I don't think it's supposed to go there."

I looked down and froze...*horrified.*

The thick black webbing cut between my thighs, pressing against the delicious ache of my sex. What kind of idiot does that? "Fuck." I dropped my holster and gun to the floor once more...and thought I heard a snigger.

I jerked my gaze high, anger and humiliation a dangerous fucking cocktail as I bared my teeth. But not one was grinning...not one was even smiling. "You just...stay right there," I growled. *"All of you."*

Vitold splayed his hands wide and in that gorgeous accent he murmured, "Not moving a muscle, Special Agent."

But he was...his cock twitched and grew *harder.* He looked at me like he was hungry...*no, not hungry...like he was starving, and I was his goddamn meal.*

I stepped out of the holster, yanked the zipper high on my pants, and scanned the floor for my bra. White peeked out from underneath Phantom's black jeans. I kept one eye on them and stepped closer.

My breasts swung as I leaned down, nipples tightening as a growl of desire cut through the room. That ache in my chest flared, burning hotter and colder all at once. I jerked my gaze upwards, all four of them were pushing up now, moving together as one to slip from the bed and stand.

"Carina," Phantom murmured.

Pain flared from the bite mark on my shoulder. I clenched my jaw, and winced as that rolling thunder echoed around the room. It wasn't just one of them now that looked at me with eyes alight with hunger.

"You shouldn't go out there," Phantom warned. "It's not safe."

I hurriedly slipped on my bra and snatched my blouse from the floor. "I'm fine...gotta...go. I gotta get out of here. I'm...*sorry*. I'm sorry, okay? I'm just...sorry."

I slammed my feet into my boots and lunged for the doorway. Desperation burned bitter in the back of my throat as I fumbled with the buttons, missing some and buttoning the others up wrong. But I didn't care now. I was past that point long ago...*sure you were...when you were fucking four men...at once.*

Jesus, what would my father think? Or anyone, for that matter. My face burned hotter than a damn fever as I raced through the Wolf's apartment and back along the hall. What the hell was I thinking, coming here? I should've known. Maybe I need to go to church? Yeah, maybe I need Jesus.

I pounded through the quiet, empty club, dodging around packed up chairs and tables before stumbling up the stairs and pushing through the door.

I blinked in the sunlight, licked my lips, and tried to get my brain working. *Or something to work other than my damn pussy.* Christ, that's brutal. Fingers speared into my pocket as I fished around and yanked the keys to the Jeep free.

I raced for the side of the building, lifted a trembling hand, and stopped dead.

All four of them stood there, barring my way to the four-wheel drive.

"Carina." Phantom lifted his hands, palms turned toward me in a display of surrender. "You can't leave, not now."

I wrenched my gaze to his with the ultimatum. "Listen, buddy. Not sure if you get it now, but you don't *own me*. We fucked, that's all."

"We did more than fuck and you damn well know it." Anger blazed in the Wolf's gaze as he strode forward, cutting me off.

"If you're freaking out about the pack, you never..." he licked his lips.

"We were there, that's all," the gorgeous blonde declared. "Nothing happened."

I let out a hard bark of laughter. "Jesus fucking Christ. I think I just need to wake up now...*yeah,* I just need to wake the hell up."

"But which one is the nightmare?" Arran stepped forward, slow and steady. In another life, I would've dated him, chatted with him. *Kissed him,* if he was normal. "You're alone out there. You're so fucking alone you're stumbling around in the dark. You think we don't feel your loneliness? We all know what that feels like. It's like a track you can't get off of, so you run and run and run. You think you're free, but you're never really free." He moved closer, and with each step his voice grew more soothing. "Phantom is right, you're not like anyone else. You're special, Carina. You're wild and savage. You're mortal, but more like us than we've ever felt before."

"I'm not like you." I shook my head. "I don't want this...any of this."

"Fate." Arran insisted. "Fate brought you to us, don't test her...you won't like what happens when you do."

I won't like what happens? "Is that a threat?" I growled.

"A warning," Vitold denied, and stepped closer. "They will hurt you, sense you're different now."

"Russian," I muttered, "they've been trying my entire fucking life. Ain't *nothing* special about today."

I pressed the button, skirted the wall of Wolf menace, and yanked open the door to the Jeep. A pang of regret ripped through me as I yanked the door closed, started the engine, and drove forward.

I watched them in the rear-view mirror, just standing there, not chasing, not hunting, just fucking barechested and pleading with their eyes. They'll hurt me? What a fucking joke. I winced with the chuckle, then hissed at the sting on my shoulder.

One jerk of the wheel and I was racing back toward the bridge and to the other side of the river. The moment the road straightened out, I reached for the mark on my shoulder. He fucking bit me...fangs and teeth. Goddamnit. What kind of asshole does that?

A Wolf asshole...that's who.

Humiliation and anger at myself drove me harder as I tore across the bridge. I glanced at the clock on the display and winced. Too damn late to go home now...I'd have to shower and change at the office. I fucking hated showering there, but there were just days when you didn't want to track the blood and the shit home with you.

The only difference was this time...I was dragging it to my work. I gripped the wheel, turned off the bridge, and made my way toward the FBI offices. Cars moved slowly today, crawling and moving in my way. I downshifted, turned the Jeep harder, and tore past them all. I wanted...*to move.*

To run and hunt. To be wild and free.

The morning sun was blinding, hurting my damn eyes. I ground my teeth and pulled up at the boom gate. But Beth-Anne wasn't there, with her judgy eyes and her penchant for a smutty sex life. A new guy stood there, scowling, his gaze searching mine, then it dropped lower, to the mismatched buttoning on my shirt. "ID."

I shifted in my seat, dragged my wallet free, and handed it through the open window of the Jeep. "Is Beth-Anne away today?"

There was no answer, not as he scanned my identification

and handed it back. He just stared at me, eyes wandering and not on my face, before he leaned over, hit the button for the boom gate, and let me through.

Cold crept across my skin. I swallowed hard, spun the wheel, and scanned the other cars, finding Murphy's amongst the others. I was too raw to deal with him, too vulnerable and aching. My emotions were scattered and shaken. I needed a hot shower, clean clothes, and to not reek of fucking sex.

I lowered my head as I pulled into a parking space and sniffed. I not only reeked of it, but smelled like I'd bathed in it, as well. *I'm gonna show you just what I think of you waving your fucking gun around.*

The Alpha's words echoed as I killed the engine and climbed out of the four-wheel drive. *I'm gonna punish you for shooting me in the fucking chest. Are you ready, Special Agent?*

There was an ache between my thighs as I walked, a delicious overstretch of muscles and the memory of how that had happened. By the time I reached the elevator, my cheeks were on fire. I pressed the button and waited. Lights shone on the display before the familiar *beep* of opening doors.

I flinched at the sight of another. Crisp shirt, tailored slacks. He was new…and gorgeous. One sweeping gaze and his brow rose. I said nothing as I stepped inside and stabbed the button for my floor.

"Your buttons—" he murmured.

"Thanks, got it." I fumbled and yanked my jacket tighter around me.

The seconds were excruciating as we climbed.

Movement came from the corner of my eye. "You have blood." He touched me, dragging his finger down my neck.

I spun, slammed my spine against the wall, and smacked his damn hand away. "Get the fuck away from me! Don't you fucking touch me. *What the fuck!*"

Surprise filled his gaze as he looked down at his outstretched hand. He shook his head and jerked a panicked gaze to mine. "I'm so sorry...I don't know what came over me. I—"

The elevator shopped with a jerk. I was out of there in an instant, raking him with a savage gaze as I left. I didn't stop, but hauled ass toward the bank of restrooms midway along the hall, my steps resounding on the polished floor.

I punched through the door marked *Ladies* and listened for noise. There wasn't any...thank God. I went to my locker and unbuttoned my jacket before shrugging it free. The shoulder holster was skewed and uncomfortable. Had I really tried to wear it like a goddamn harness between my legs? I shoved the humiliation away with a snarl, grabbed my bodywash and shampoo, and stepped out of my boots.

There was a fresh set of clothes and a pressed jacket, fresh from the dry cleaners, in my locker. I was almost there, back to feeling like myself—I couldn't fucking wait. I locked my gun away in the locker and strode toward the nearest shower stall before closing the door behind me.

Cold water hissed through the shower head as I turned the tap and stepped away hurrying, to shed the rest of my clothes. There was blood on the collar of my shirt. I touched my shoulder at the fresh smear...and looked at the blood on my fingers.

It wasn't healing...why wasn't it healing?

I shoved down my trousers and my panties, grabbed the bodywash and shampoo, and stepped into the spray. A snarl echoed around the shower stall with the sting of heat. That snarl resounded from behind me—I spun, staring at the stark white tiles—no, it was to the side...I scanned the stall, and dropped to the floor, scanning under the gaps in the stalls.

But there was no one. Just me. "What the fuck is going on?" I rose slowly and eased my head back into the water. I squirted shampoo onto my hands and rubbed it through my hair, half listening…senses on fire.

You scared, Special Agent? Phantom's voice echoed in my ears.

I spun, and dropped the bottle of bodywash. It hit the floor with a *thunk,* and the damn lid cracked. But there was that energy around me, that unfamiliar *connection.*

A bond, the Russian called it.

"The fuck it is," I growled, and scanned the empty stall once more.

My heart was hammering as I glanced under the stalls again, and grabbed the busted bodywash, hurrying to wash the rest of me. But the memory of last night rose inside me.

A memory of *more than just sex.*

Darkness and shadows consumed me. The snarl of a warning echoed in my mind…*no, not a warning, a calling.* Power rippled with that call, rising inside me like a tide. Hunger moved inside me, shifting under my skin, and burned like fire in my veins.

I slammed my hand against the cold tiles as that same hunger filled me once more. They were everywhere, those Wolves, claws down my back, fangs sinking deeper than flesh and bone, to the essence of me deep inside.

That hunger was a beast, prowling and predatory. Silver shone from their eyes in the darkness of my mind. They were all there…all *four of them.* Flanking me on each side…and closing in. Only the Alpha came straight for me with sleek, animalistic strides, his mammoth shadow spilling from my head to flow against the wall. The walls trembled under my fingers and the shower stall shook.

My hands slid down the wall as I sank to the floor. The heat of the water beat down on my shoulder, tearing me apart in one instant, and knitting me back together in the next.

Only now, I felt different.

Growls reverberated, growing louder as they neared.

They invaded every part of me, that ache of loneliness in my heart…that desperate need for retribution—they claimed it all. In an instant, my head was filled with images, me *and them*.

Hunting together, fighting together, *fucking…together*.

It was all there…the life I craved.

Pack, the Alpha growled, *until death.*

That call to my soul rose inside me. I knew all I had to do was to reach out…and take it for myself. The bite burned on my shoulder, the mauling was more than a scarring…it was a tethering.

A warning to everyone else…

She is protected.

She is ours.

My breaths were hard and fast as my hand left the shower floor. *Take it.* That desperation roared inside me. *Take it now.* My fingers trembled, dancing in the air, and as that lonely part of me howled *YES*, a door slammed in the toilet stalls, wrenching me from the illusion.

I was slammed back into this moment, cowering and shaking as I sat on the floor of the shower…and the weight of my life came crashing down around me.

The Wolves were gone in an instant, that connection now shattered.

I pushed against the floor and rose on trembling legs. My world blurred and twisted as I switched off the water and dried. But I couldn't shake them. Their claws were in my soul, their fangs on the nape of my neck, *just waiting to bite once more.*

I yanked on my underwear, then my shirt and slacks, before grabbing my shampoo and bodywash and went to my locker. The toilet flushed, and the stall door opened. One of the other agents lifted her gaze and met mine. She looked away before I turned, shoved my stuff into the locker, and hurried to drag a comb through my hair.

Five minutes later and I buttoned my jacket over my holster

and twisted the key, locking my belongings away. Voices were faint down the hall as I yanked open the bathroom door and stepped out. I thought after a shower I'd feel more like myself again. I was wrong.

Jumpy and shaking, I scanned the open doorways of the other agents' offices as I passed and headed for mine. Shouts echoed from Harlan's office. I winced and stepped through the open doors to my own section and hurried to my desk.

Still Harlan's screams spilled out and, as I yanked my chair back and sat down, I caught the words. *"I should have your fucking badge for this, Murphy! Goddamnit, what in the hell were you two thinking?"*

"He's been looking for you." I jerked my gaze to Montey, who just sat at his desk twirling his damn pen. "Seems you two made the headlines."

He leaned forward, grabbed a newspaper from the end of his desk, and cast it toward me. It hit the middle of mine with a *slap*. My gaze was drawn to the titled image in the middle of the paper, grainy at the edges…but it wasn't the edges you cared about.

In the middle was a table…a morgue table and the very dead face of Blane Costello stark, pale, and lifeless filled the image.

"Well done," Montey taunted. "You just put a target on the entire department's back."

14

PHANTOM

"She's vulnerable," Church growled as she tore out of the damn parking area in Arran's Jeep. "She's too damn vulnerable."

"I know."

"We need to protect her."

I turned to the Wolf and held his gaze. "I know."

Vitold rubbed the stubble on his jaw, and even Arran curled his damn lip and bared his teeth. She wasn't the only one exposed here…so were we. With the bond left unsealed, it felt a little too much like rejection.

"She'll be back," I urged. "Next time, she'll stay."

Hunt her, my beast commanded. *Drag her back. Make her one of us.*

I tried to shut out the urgency. Still, it tore through me like the call of the full moon. The beast snarled and bared his teeth. White fangs shimmered in the dark, the tips etched with her blood. I hadn't meant to mark her…hadn't meant to bond with her. *Fuck.* I hadn't meant *any* of this.

But wasn't fate a goddamn bitch.

A real goddamn bitch.

First, she was hunting the Vampires' mate, then she was at the damn warehouse. The one place no mortal should've been—especially a mortal like her.

I tore my gaze away as Church strode toward the open back door and disappeared. Any other woman would be begging to stay...any other woman would pack her shit up in an instant and take over my damn life. But Carina Chase wasn't just any other woman.

She was wild and untamed.

I wanted it to remain that way.

But the woman has a darkness about her. A shadow of terror that clung to her damn soul. I'd scented the taint the moment I laid eyes on her in that warehouse. She might be running from us...but she'd been running her entire life. Running from her purpose...and her damn life. I winced at the memory of the Fae marking. It might be dulled, but it wasn't gone...not anywhere near it.

The darkness clinging to her soul and the Unseelie power would tear her apart. That was a given...the only way she could survive was—

I froze, and sucked in a deep breath.

"What is it?" Arran cocked his head.

White fangs shone from my Wolf, lips curled in a sneer and a smile. "You fucking knew, didn't you?"

Arran stepped closer, silent now. Careful and watching as the pieces all slipped together inside my head. The beast knew. He'd scented it. "You scented a darkness in her. Some kind of curse when she was hit with the Unseelie power. You knew the only way she could survive was if she was part of the pack. We'd bear the brunt of that collision, wouldn't we? If we were bonded."

The beast just slunk backwards, teeth still shining with her blood as he slipped back into the darkness of my mind.

"He bonded her on purpose?" Arran murmured, brows furrowed, dark eyes shining with fear.

"Looks that way," I forced through clenched teeth.

He turned his head and looked in the direction she'd sped away. "Fuck me. She has no idea what's coming, does she?"

I didn't have an answer. If she didn't understand now...then she soon would. "Watch her, Arran." I glanced toward him. "Watch her and protect her with your damn life."

One nod of his head and he was gone, striding toward the open door Church had left behind.

Vitold turned and followed, leaving me staring at the empty goddamn street. My phone gave a *beep,* and for a second, a surge of hope flared as I tugged it from the pocket of my jeans, until I read the text.

Mojin.

We need to meet. Warehouse at 8.

Eight o'clock. Vamp time. I sucked in a harsh breath and strode toward the club. Better not be bad fucking news. My thoughts turned to Justice, and that goddamn tremor in my chest flared to pain.

The male was like a damn brother to me, they all were...an extended part of the pack. And the pack took care of their own.

"What the fuck do you mean, you lost him?" Church snapped. "Then fucking find him, Blaze. I don't give a fuck what you have to do...*just fucking do it.*"

I stepped around the corner of the hallway to find the male leaning against the sink in the kitchen, barechested, his cell in his hand...and a look of fear in his eyes. "They lost him. They lost Finis."

Panic filled me as my mind raced. *He's gone to her.* The fucking piece of shit. If the Wolf of the Inner Circle did that... then maybe her life is over?

"Doesn't mean anything," Church growled.

"The *hell it doesn't,*" I answered. Ice stabbed through my chest as I closed my eyes. *It meant* everything.

"They'll find him. It's what they're bred for."

It was all I had to cling to. I opened my eyes and stared at my second, and gave a nod. "I hope so, brother. I sure hope so, 'cause I can't lose her again. I'll tear this world apart before I do."

15

<hr>

Closed eyes, open mouth…and a missing fucking throat. I stared at the black and white image of Blane Costello as movement came from the end of the hallway.

"*Chase*," Harlan barked, his eyes bright with anger. "About time you decided to turn up to your goddamn job. My office. *Now*."

I swallowed hard and groaned inwardly. *The bastard had it coming.* Was that a reasonable excuse for what had happened? One look at the scowling SAIC and I thought better of it. I lowered my gaze and followed. All eyes were trained on me as I slunk back to Harlan's office like a beaten dog once more.

Just take it. Whatever he has to say. Just don't speak…don't say a goddamn thing, *okay, Chase?* The words raced through my head as I left the others behind and made my way to the SAIC's office.

Tracey watched me over the rim of her glasses. I lifted my hand and flipped her the bird and, in an instant, I was Ruth Costello backing out of the driveway, catching me waiting in the corner of her eye.

The memory was a bucket of water to my senses.

That was the only thing I cared about. Not about Murphy or any of them.

Ruth Costello.

I wanted those files about my father unsealed. I wanted the truth to come out…whatever that truth was. And I wanted her behind bars, for the rest of her miserable fucking life.

I stepped into Harlan's office, took one look at Murphy's lowered gaze, and stepped to the side as Harlan shoved the door closed and stalked to his seat. "Want to give me your version of this goddamn shitshow?"

The paper was open on his desk and Blane stared back at me. I turned my head toward Murphy.

"Don't fucking look at him. Answers…*now*."

I winced at the tone, and swallowed. Heat rose inside me as the memory of that unfolded. "He was just there, sir."

"Just. There," Harlan repeated, and grew still. "He was *just… there?* I ought to have your asses for this. Him for letting the fucking paparazzo walk into the damn morgue, and you for just standing there with your dick in your hand."

"I don't have a dick," I muttered.

Harlan jerked his feral gaze toward me, eyes blazing with fury. I swallowed anything else I was about to say. "I thought for once you two could be professional. That you'd work this case in the background like fucking *professionals*." Then the SAIC dragged his fingers through his thinning hair. "You really fucked me with this," he said, and lifted his gaze, first to Murphy, then to me. "I just want you to know that."

Murphy shook his head. "Boss—"

"You!" Harlan growled. "You should know better. Chase is a fuckup…but you…you were lead on this. You were the one who was to run this investigation tighter than a fish's ass. Now I have…a goddamn mess, that's what I have. I swear to God, either of you step a foot wrong, the only jobs you'll be able to get will be swinging a fucking broom. *Now get the hell out of my office and work that fucking warehouse like your life depends on it."*

I was a fuckup? My face burned as I swallowed his words.

Still Murphy said nothing, just sat there while Harlan burned him with a stare and growled, "Get the fuck out."

Murphy shoved up from his seat in an instant. Cold, dead eyes found mine before he turned and headed to the door. I followed, leaving Harlan behind until he barked, "Not you... Chase, you stay right here."

I swallowed hard and stopped in my tracks, watching Murphy as he turned left, slamming the door behind him as he went.

"I want you with me when we meet with the AD for a briefing."

"Me, sir? The...*fuckup?"*

He scowled and glared at me. "That's not what I meant, and you damn well know it."

"Mean what you say and say what you mean, *sir."* I met his stare with my own.

"You're a damn good agent, Chase. But you're one-tracked, and you give me little room to move."

I stepped closer, hating how I felt so damn raw. "Because busting that one track open will give me all I need."

He sighed, hard and slow, and seemed to shrink an inch in a second. "Your dad is done, Chase. It's time for you to move on. There's no going back for him, no undoing the past."

"I don't want to undo it, Harlan. I just want the goddamn truth. Why is that so hard to understand?"

"There's no such thing as the truth anymore, Chase. There's what you can live with and what you can't. This reckless fucking vendetta you have against the Costellos is gonna see you in a goddamn body bag. For the hundredth goddamn time, I'm telling you to drop it. Work the fucking case, gather the damn evidence, and leave it up to the higher powers to go after those responsible."

"She was there, Harlan."

There was a twitch in the corner of his eye. "I know."

I stepped closer. *"She...was there, Harlan."*

His gaze hardened. I'd push all damn day if that's what it took. A sting carved though my palms. My fists were clenched, nails driving into the flesh. "I'll work the damn case, Harlan. But I'm not giving up taking them down, and I'm not given up on finding the damn truth, either. Even if it's a truth no one wants to hear." I unfurled my fingers. "That's how *I'll sleep at night.*"

He didn't say a word, not even when I spun on my heel and stalked to the door. He could damn well reprimand me all he wanted. Badge or no badge, I'd never stop...not until I knew the truth *and Ruth Costello was exposed.*

I strode toward my overburdened desk, took one look at Murphy's empty chair, and scanned the office.

"Said he'd meet you at the warehouse," Montey muttered without looking up.

I released my breath with a sigh and stopped for a moment. At least I wasn't forced to share a car with the asshole. I grabbed my jacket and shrugged into it as I strode toward the doorway and headed for the elevator.

*You've got blood...*a shiver raced with the memory of the asshole in the elevator before. I listened for the thud of boots around me and glanced toward the stairwell as I frantically stabbed the button for the elevator and waited...

Voices slipped between the doors before they opened. Five agents from the floor above looked at me as the door opened. *Five men.* That hunger in my chest seethed as I shook my head and stepped away. "Sorry, forgot something. You go."

One just gave a shrug. But the biggest of them scowled and lowered his gaze to my chest as the doors closed.

"No, no fucking way," I mumbled to myself. "I'm not doing this."

I strode toward the stairwell door. I'd rather run myself ragged than to be exposed to another goddamn male. A warning snarl tore through my mind as I yanked open the door to the stairs and stepped onto the stairwell.

I gripped the handrail and hurried down one flight, then another before the door to the first floor opened. Heart hammering, I lifted my gaze as the heavy thud of boots rang out. That burn in my side grew bolder, searing down into my hip until it speared taloned fingers across my body.

That ache between my thighs flared, desperate, urgent. I stopped and stepped backwards as the heavy thuds grew louder, ringing inside the stairwell. *No, not now.* I pressed my spine against the stairwell wall. *Don't do this. Please don't do this.*

The agent came into view, head down, hand sliding on the rail as he climbed until he became aware of me. Sweat dripped down the nape of my neck as he lifted his gaze and met mine.

"Sorry," he muttered. "Didn't mean to—" He stopped then, his brow furrowing as a look of confusion filled his gaze.

I didn't wait. Not for him to reach out and touch me, not for another spark in his desperate gaze. "It's fine," I barked, and shoved past, gripping the bannister and hurrying to get away. I made it out to the parking lot before I took a chance to breathe, my hand braced on the hood of the Jeep, my senses on fire.

I can do this. I sucked in a deep breath. *I can do this.*

I waited for the ache in my chest to ease, then strode to the driver's door of the Jeep. I had one last chance here...even I knew when I'd pushed Harlan too far, and this was too far. I climbed in, started the four-wheel drive, and backed out of the space.

The warehouse...my damn pulse sped with the thought. I pushed the panic aside and just focused on driving, past the gate guard and back out into the city streets. Work the case. That's all I had to damn well do...*how fucking hard was that?*

My thoughts turned back to the paparazzo holding his camera like a gun. I'd known in an instant what was going to happen, knew it'd play out this way, with Blane's dead body splashed across the front page. I knew I'd get my ass reamed for it...but Murphy. Holy shit, his face had been fucking burning.

Harlan was right, shit would slide downhill for this. I'd be covered in it before this was done...if it was ever going to be done. *Chase is a fuckup...Chase is a fuckup. Chase is a fuckup.* Harlan's words were on repeat inside my head as I merged with the traffic and sped to the other side of the city.

A fuckup.

That's all I was known for.

Useless. Renegade. *Wild.*

I'd tried my entire damn life to be anything but a fuckup. I'd worked hard and put in the hours, and, granted, my desk was the perfect target for a damn inferno with the stacks of files waiting, but in the field, I was better than most.

I hunted...and I kept on hunting, no matter how many dead ends I hit. It was easy to fight your way out of the darkness when your entire life had been spent stumbling around.

I'd exhausted every avenue when it came to finding out the truth about my father's discharge from the police. But the records gave me nothing, and his so called 'best friends' had nothing more to say.

Drop it, kid. Shubert had demanded. *The case against your dad was airtight.*

"Airtight, my ass," I snarled, turned the wheel, and lifted my gaze to the Jewel.

What was left of it anyway. Three dead, fifteen injured, and one building that now resembled a block of Swiss cheese. I pulled the Jeep over and killed the engine. For a second, I just sat there, remembering that night. It had been the goddamn

Vamps, I just knew it. How could a hundred people just go crazy like that with no trigger?

We'd tested the air. We'd tested the food. We'd tested every damn thing we could get our hands on, and still it came back as nothing. No drugs. No poison. Nothing in the ventilation or in their systems. It was as though the entire club full of people decided one night to kill each other and leave a massacre behind.

Movement came from behind me. Black. Sleek...and *very* expensive, pulled into a parking space about five up from me. The hairs on the back of my neck rose as I caught sight of the dark-haired Wolf behind the wheel. "Not very subtle, are you?"

No, they weren't subtle at all.

Not now...*not last night.*

Pain flared on my shoulder with the memory.

Searing heat welled between my legs. I clamped them tighter...but that only made the desperation worse.

Look down, Carina, Phantom's voice spilled through my mind. *Watch while I fuck you, and when I finish fucking you, then you'll know who you belong to. You'll know whose pack is yours. Pro tip. It's not the one with the shiny badges and the goddamn mortal rules. You belong to us. You are owned by us.*

Owned...by all of them.

The cocky bartender. The towering, drop-dead gorgeous blond. The Russian.

Jesus.

No way...no way was I going back there. I clenched my jaw and shoved the images from my mind as I climbed out. I knew Ruth was in bed with the Vampires...*literally,* and I knew they were somehow tied up with the Vampire Senator that got himself killed. I wanted to make the pieces fit to include my dad in that, but I couldn't see how...*yet.*

The Costellos were more than thugs and bullies. They dealt in drugs, guns, and influence. That I knew for certain. I hadn't given a shit about them before...not until I went looking into Dad's exit from the police and found his records sealed. Then it was that paper that made me look harder. The notepad I'd found in his old study. The one with Cassandra Costello's name pressed into the torn-out piece of paper.

Still everything kept coming back to them...the Costellos, and now I was positive I could add the Vampires in there somewhere. I crossed the street and hurried to the Jewel. The place was locked down, with crime-scene tape stretched across the front. They wouldn't be getting this place back anytime soon.

But the moment I stepped into the alleyway that led to the rear of the Jewel, I stopped. A smashed bottle glinted in the sun, drawing my gaze until a low *thud* came from the building. I looked at the overflowing trashcans, then turned to the closed fire door as it gave a *thud* once more.

This wasn't where I was supposed to meet Murphy, and God knew he was pissed enough as it was. But my instincts blazed to life as I stared into the alley. My pulse sped as I glanced over my shoulder at the flash Camaro and the Wolf parked five spaces down.

*Don't go in there alone...*the words took flight before I weighed them down. This was my job...*this was who I was.* The one who took risks. The one who used everything I had in my arsenal to catch the bad guys.

Thud.

The banging fire door dragged my focus back.

It was open...I scanned the street behind me as my gut clenched tight. No one should be there...not unless they were police. I reached for my holster, dragged my Glock free, and stepped toward the cracked open door.

Everything narrowed to this moment. Every sound, every touch...every thunderous beat of my heart. I hesitated at the door as it thudded closed once more, then grabbed the handle, glanced over my shoulder once more, then opened the door and stepped inside.

Shadows clung to the corners of the hallway as I entered. I scanned the darkness, listening for the slightest sound, and moved further from the door. One fist clenched around the gun, the other around my gun hand, my body was tensed and straining across my shoulders.

My training was all I had, scanning, moving, catching sight of overturned chairs and tables. I hadn't been inside here after the shooting. It wasn't my case and I had my own shit to deal with. But standing in here now, I had no idea how anyone had actually survived.

The walls were peppered with bullet holes, some shots had torn chunks of plaster free, and some had left nothing more than blood splattered holes behind. It had been a massacre here. I had to wonder if this had had anything to do with the warehouse. Two doors away...and two of the biggest crime scenes this city had seen for a very long time.

The warehouse.

The place loomed in the back of my mind as I moved through the bar, sweeping the muzzle of the gun around, and approached the other side of the room. The creak of a hinge came from behind me. I froze, held my breath, and listened.

The bite mark on my shoulder flared with heat. I winced, catching my breath as a tremor coursed through my mind. The same tremor that had found me in the shower—I lowered the gun and moved faster as the bartender's face came roaring back to me—the same tremor that had made me feel them more than I'd ever felt anyone else before.

Wolf, the feeling roared through me. Not just any Wolf. Familiar. *Mine...*the word surfaced before I pushed it away.

I knew who it was now, sensing him like I'd never sensed anyone before. *Arran,* his name swept through my head as the sound of the footsteps grew bolder.

I was already lifting my hand as he came around the corner from the hallway and stopped. Silver shone in his gaze as he swept the bar, and his nostrils flared...*sensing.* There was a hardness in him in that moment. Not so *smile,* and cocky. No, in this second, he was all animal.

"Don't you know the killer always comes back to the scene of the crime, Special Agent?" he teased, and glanced toward me. In an instant, that hardness was gone and the silver shine in his eyes glinted with the curl of his lips.

"You watch too much CSI, Wolf," I complained.

That smile only grew bolder as he glanced at the gun in my hand. A look swept across his face at the sight. Not disappointment. Satisfaction, almost like he was pleased I was armed and not afraid to use it.

"Probably." He glanced away and moved deeper into the bar, giving me a wide berth. "But I do love a strong, powerful woman though. Gets me every time."

"Women like Ruth Costello?" I questioned.

He froze, breath caught, for a second. He was good...I'll give him that, smothering his surprise with the curl of those perfect goddamn lips. "So you know about that, huh?"

"I saw you...the two of you, watched you drive by Costello Head Office then take her out to the water."

That glint wavered, turning from excitement to a cold brush of fear. "And what did you see out at the water, Carina?" The way he said my name sent goosebumps along my skin. He took a step and that smile fell just as quickly as had come. Gone was the sexy bartender grin. He was all Wolf now...all danger and intensity, like a switch had been flipped inside him.

"The two of you," I forced through clenched teeth.

"Anyone else?"

There was no one else. My heart pounded, dragging me back to that night. I was hidden in the bushes, my car parked behind me down the road. I couldn't see them well, sitting in the Jeep, just their outlines, until she climbed out, her voice coming faintly to me in the dark. *Do you see that? Right there.*

I tried to see what she was looking at. But all I saw was darkness. Darkness and shadows and the shimmer of midnight water in the distance. "No," I answered.

He exhaled hard as his shoulders sank. "You need to be careful, Carina. Especially when you follow us."

There it was again...that *threat.* "I can handle myself, Wolf, and you don't scare me."

He closed the distance between us faster than I could track. One minute, he was across the room...and the next, he was pressing against me, making me step backwards until my spine hit the wall.

"I'm not interested in scaring you, Carina..." he lifted his hand and brushed a strand of hair from my face. "But you do need to be more careful."

Jesus, he was perfect. I looked up into his endless midnight eyes. There was intelligence there, sometimes smothered under the cocky swagger of a bartender. Just one second staring into those depths, and I knew he was anything but. He lowered that seductive gaze from my eyes to my lips, then to the open neckline of my shirt, as though he was remembering where his face had nestled only hours ago.

"Careful is my middle name, Wolf," I assured, my cheeks burning as I stepped out from under his hand. "It's about time you understood that."

He just watched as I strode toward the door and pushed through, releasing the lock with a *snap.* I was outside in a heartbeat, breathing in the dank alley air while a shiver raced across my skin as my two worlds collided...one filled with Immortals...and the other filled with guns and badges...and crime scenes.

Power raced across my skin. Arran was coming for me, head down, striding with that sleek hunter's gait. My breath caught as that familiar sensation swept through me like a damn hurricane, making me hurry.

You do need to be careful.

The warning filled me as I tore along the alley and turned the corner. In no time, the warehouse loomed overhead, casting shadows across the ground.

In an instant, I was back there...darkness all around me and the sounds of terrifying howls of rage shattering the night air. My hand trembled, smacking the gun against my thigh as my steps slowed, then stilled. The heady stench of blood filled my nose. Panic found me there at the exit of the alley...panic and terror and as the heavy smack of steps echoed, that tight band across my chest cinched tighter.

Boom...boom...boom.

Darkness splashed across my face, making me turn my head...and stare into Murphy's unflinching gaze. "About time you decided to turn up," he snarled, and stepped into my path. "You and I have unfinished business."

16

"**W**ell?" Murphy just stared at me with that cold, dead stare.

I swallowed hard and took a step, fighting the overwhelming urge to turn tail and run. "Get the hell out of my way," I growled, and stepped to the side.

Panic crowded in. It wasn't just this asshole I was forced to work with.

Or this warehouse.

It was just a crime scene, remember? Nothing I hadn't worked a thousand times before.

My damn hand trembled, the gun still in my grasp as I walked along the towering steel walls to the wide opening. Bright lights blinded me inside my head and the sound of a chopper turned deafening. But it was all a memory, as fragments of that night came rushing back.

Ruth.

The Vampires in the alley…

And the deafening sound of gunfire that had echoed from the steel walls of this space.

Footsteps haunted me as I slipped my Glock back onto my

holster. Murphy was three steps away as I rounded the corner and stared at the open warehouse door. I tried to see the tape and crime scene markings inside. I tried to see the white overalls of the two techs as they photographed and swabbed the floor. I tried to see the weak sunlight as it illuminated the space.

But my mind was a ruthless bitch, ripping away the safety of the present for the terror of the past.

You fight like a warrior. I wonder if you'd fuck as ferociously?

The words cleft through my head as I moved. Two steps and I was inside, spine pressed against the wall, my pulse deafening in my head. The low snarl of Murphy's voice didn't invade this time. Instead I was back there, to the brutal blasts of gunfire and the acrid smell that followed. I shifted my gaze to the concrete floor...to the spot where Jerry Costello lay bleeding from a fatal gunshot to the chest.

"Chase," Murphy growled in my ear.

His chest had been blown open, crimson soaked the front of his crisp white shirt.

"Chase."

I swallowed hard as shadows shifted, reaching from darkened corners with taloned fingers.

Is that all you saw? Arran's voice crowded in.

Shadows and darkness.

Shadows that moved.

Is that all you saw? The question resounded in my head.

Fragments of that night I'd watched him and Ruth flickered, mingling with the terror of what had happened here. This wasn't just any mortal massacre and that wasn't just any moonlight drive. These people were dangerous beings...and not just to themselves.

Two worlds colliding. One of them I shouldn't be in. But here I was, smack bang in the center of it all. A war...that's what this was. A war that spilled through my streets. A war that swept around me like a hurricane.

The ache in my chest grew sharper, making me wince... making me breathless.

Is that all you saw?

The gloom slipped across the blood splattered concrete floor, heading toward the two techs that were working the scene, both with their backs to the danger, a gloom they were oblivious to.

"Are you even listening to me?" Murphy forced through clenched teeth.

"Just give me a *fucking* minute." The words slipped free as I watched the shadows ripple and move, morphing into something so much more. As the shadows grew bigger and darker, rising up to morph into an outline, my heart punched against the side of my chest.

You fight like a warrior.

The image of the Unseelie rose like a nightmare.

Tall.

Dark.

Menacing...

Pain stabbed like the blade of a knife pushing deeper, carving through my chest. I cried out and stumbled.

"What the fuck is wrong with you?" Murphy growled, and grabbed my arm, the tips of his fingers bruising me once more.

"Get off me." I jerked my arm from his hold as the warehouse blurred and swayed. *"I said, get the fuck off me!"* The two crime scene techs lifted their gazes toward us.

"You're out of fucking control, *Chase!*" he barked. "You're fucking *crazy.*"

His face was a mask of rage, his dark eyes glinted with malice, bloodless lips clenched tight. But I couldn't stop this unraveling, not from the memories that slammed into me...or that blinding throb in my chest. I looked down to the green glow pulsing beneath my shirt.

Oh Jesus.

The memory of blood pushed to the surface, driving acid into the back of my throat. Blane Costello's blood as the Vampire ripped his neck open in front of me. My eyes watered, and I shoved Murphy to the side as I staggered for the warehouse door. I was out of there in an instant, scrambling to the side as I dropped to my knees.

Hot liquid shot from between my lips and splashed against the ground. I shoved my hand against the edge of the concrete, hearing the crunch a second before the sting across my palm. Glass slivers shimmered in the sunlight as I heaved and retched. Blood, darkness. Death. It was all around me.

I tried to breathe, tried to narrow my world to the sharp pinch in my hand and the rough concrete under my knees, tried to focus on all the things I could control and none of the ones that controlled me.

"Hey, you okay?" An unfamiliar voice came from above.

Blood ran down my wrist as I wiped my mouth and lifted my gaze. The crime scene tech yanked the white plastic hood from his head and glanced at my hand, his eyes widening. "Oh shit, you're bleeding." He drove his hand into the pocket of his overalls and pulled out a folded white cotton handkerchief. "It's clean, I promise." He stepped closer and held it out.

Rage lashed through the air, standing the hairs on the back of my neck.

I could feel Murphy behind me, feel his rage building.

"Thank you," I murmured, and pushed to stand.

Blood sank into the white cotton as I took it from his hand. Crimson so bright against the white.

"We're just packing up," the tech muttered. "You gonna be okay here?"

I lifted my gaze from the blood-oaked handkerchief and met his. Brows were furrowed on a kind and chubby face. He looked tender and nice. One of the good guys. I forced a smile and nodded. "Sure, thanks, just being a klutz is all," I answered and lifted the mess in my hand.

"Keep it." He waved the motion away and looked at the cut on my hand instead. "You better get someone to look at that. Looks like it might need a stitch or two."

I closed my eyes as he moved away. It was all too much. Murphy...the Wolf, the warehouse haunting me. Agony roared through the flesh of my palm as I clenched the handkerchief tight. Pain did things to you, made you act...and with the action came blinding clarity.

"You heard Harlan." Murphy was waiting, arms crossed. "You think I won't hesitate to have you removed from this case and from the department. I'm the senior agent here, so you'd better learn your goddamn place."

"And where is that?" I forced the words through gritted teeth.

"Under me," he sneered, and took a step closer.

But he didn't reach for me, not while the techs loaded their gear into the back of a white minivan. But they wouldn't be here forever. Shadows grew bolder from the open warehouse doors, reaching out as the sun moved lower. Night was coming, barreling down on me like a runaway train. With it came the loneliness and the panic. With it came the Wolves.

I didn't even need to shift my gaze to feel him...Arran watched me from the corner of the Jewel. He'd never leave, never give up. He could become a pure predator in the blink of an eye. They wanted me...wanted me back there at the damn club, wanted me where they could control me. I took a step backwards toward the street. No one controlled me but me.

"Where the fuck are you going?" Murphy strode forward as the van's door slid closed with a *bang*.

I turned at the last moment, used the cover of the crime scene van as it started with a roar and a splutter, and in a second, I was heading across the road. If the Wolf thought I was going back for the Jeep, then he was mistaken. I gripped the bloody handkerchief and hurried down the street, heading for the busy mall a block away.

"Get the fuck back here, Chase!" Murphy roared.

"Fuck you." I lengthened my stride. "Fuck all of you."

The world was too small, too closed in, choking me like a hand around my throat. I lifted the bloody handkerchief in my palm, blotting the blood on my skin as I hurried. With every step I lost control of myself…*and I'd never felt more alive.*

I picked up the pace until I was jogging. Christ, I hadn't jogged since Quantico. But the memory came roaring back to me making me drive my heels harder into the pavement as I tore across the street once more toward the mall parking lot.

Still, I could feel him, stalking me like I was prey. I risked a glance over my shoulder as I rounded the back of a massive pickup. Arran was head down, long legs striding out, moving faster and sleeker than I could. There was no way I was getting away from him…no way I could outrun…

A woman ran toward me, just a blur in black. She had her headphones on and pushed one of those active mom's strollers. She was fast, I'd give her that, built for way more speed than I was.

My heart hammered as a thought slipped in and I looked at the bloodied handkerchief in my hand. *Blood.* Lots of blood. I jerked my gaze high as she raced toward me and stumbled forward, moving directly into her path.

She scowled and slowed, her eyes drifting to my chest as my jacket blew open and revealed my gun. In a heartbeat, fear moved in, making her slow even more.

"Sorry," I murmured and knelt to the ground on the other side of the stroller as she passed. The movement was quick, one small flick of the wrist as I tossed the bloodsoaked cloth into the bottom of her stroller before I shoved upwards and hurried for the end of a large U-Haul truck. She was gone before I had a chance to look again. I shoved my hand under my arm and clenched my fist tight. "Come on…come on, Wolf, follow the blood…" Arran came around the end of a four-wheel drive and slowed.

Confusion flared in his eyes for a second as he scanned the packed parking lot. His nostrils flared with a tilt of his head, scenting the wind. My heart boomed as he turned his gaze my way. I shoved backwards and flattened myself against the truck and tried to remember how to breathe. Seconds…they felt like hours as I waited.

And waited.

…and waited.

My muscles twitched as that green glow in my chest shone brighter. I clamped my arm down on my hand, driving the pain all the way into the bones. *"Please,"* I whispered. *"Just this once."*

Still that burn ebbed and pulsed, burning like the acid in the back of my throat. I trembled and took a step forward, edging toward the corner of the truck as voices cut through the air behind me.

"Hey, what the hell are you doing at my truck?" a man growled.

One more inch…just one more inch. I pressed against the hot metal and peeked around the edge. He was gone…*gone.* I scanned the vehicles around where he'd been.

"Hey." The man grabbed me from behind.

I spun, threw my hand out, and shoved him backwards. "FBI, *get your fucking hands off me."*

His eyes widened as he let me go and splayed his fingers wide. "Whoa, sorry about that."

Goddamnit. I stepped away and turned back to the corner of the truck. But he was gone…like gone, *gone.* I risked a step out, scanning the cars and trucks. "Don't tell me it actually worked."

I was betting the panic of losing me would trigger his Wolf.

He'd follow the scent of my blood, especially if he thought I was hurt.

I took another step and glanced at the steady flow of shoppers through the mall, my heart pounding. I didn't have long, minutes…that was all I needed. One glance at the taxi rank and I lunged forward. I needed to get out of here…get this hand stitched…and find out once and for all if there was anything I could do about this shit in my chest.

There was only one person I trusted.

One person that wouldn't go running to the damn authorities.

One person who wouldn't attack me no matter how much this shit burned.

Unless it affected women as well…

17

PHANTOM

"There's blood in the water," I murmured and focused on the voice on the other end of the phone. "And now the goddamn sharks are circling."

"It's bad," my contact said. "There's talk of an uprising. First Caedes and now Finis."

Just the sound of his name made me clench the phone tighter. "Have they found him yet?"

"Not a damn whisper."

My lips curled as I stared at the first glint of stars in the twilight sky. "He has to be there somewhere. I want you to keep searching. I want every fucking rock shattered, Galaxy. I don't care what it costs, money, blood...I want that motherfucker found."

"You and me both, brother. You and me both. And Forllen?"

*Forllen...*the fucking bloodsucker who'd come here for betrayal and found loyalty instead. I fought the twinge of regret. I should've trusted Elithien, should've known the Vampire would've rather torn out Forllen's throat than throw us to the Inner Circle's dogs. But I hadn't, and I'd let that fear take hold ... we all had, me and the damn Fae.

That night was a blur, the first half filled with horror at what we'd done. We'd turned our backs on the Vampires, pushed them out into the open for Caedes and his men to slaughter. And the second half was buried under the blood and carnage… *and her…the one goddamn piece of this puzzle I couldn't yet work out, Special Agent Carina Chase.*

It had been a violent and bloody battle, one we'd barely made it away from.

But I had…and I'd taken Carina with me.

Hunger shifted under my skin. The kind of hunger that set my teeth on edge. It was savage and dangerous.

I wanted her, more than I'd ever wanted anyone else in my miserable fucking life. I wanted her alive, and safe, and away from this treacherous battleground.

The rogue Vampire, Forllen, hadn't been the start of this war. I knew that now. But he's almost been the end. And the end for us could've been very different indeed.

There was more than the war with the Inner Circle at play here. With Caedes's seat on the Circle now vacant, it threw open the door for every Immortal with bloodlust in their veins and power in their eyes to make a move.

Looked like for Forllen, that move was about to be swift and brutal.

Should I tell the Vampires? Would they even care?

Forllen wasn't one of us. He was a shark…swimming amongst bigger, more dangerous sharks. He just didn't know it. He and his coven were nothing more than one bad move away from being taken out. Greed. Lust. Power. If he thought things were bad before…he was about to find out how wrong he was.

"Leave him," I answered. "Let him feel the fucking cold."

Honor. That's what kept us Immortals in Crown City together.

"They'll come after him," Galaxy commented. "They'll see him as weak."

Maybe that's what he deserved. "So be it," I answered.

The call ended in silence.

I felt that silence like a hole in my fucking chest. The Inner Circle was now shattered, and after all these fucking years under their goddamn control I was still here, still frozen, unable to do a damn thing until Finis was found.

He *had* to be found and he had to be found *alive*.

I refused to consider anything else.

The faint sound of thunder drifted to me. I'd know the sound of the Camaro anywhere. Midnight black, sleek, and powerful. I lifted my gaze to Arran as he pulled into the parking lot and killed the engine. As soon as he opened the door I caught the bitter whiff of anger.

Head down, he turned and slammed the car door behind him with a *bang!* I winced at the sound, the goddamn thing had cost me a fortune. But it was the Wolf I looked at. I'd never seen Arran so *pissed.*

"What's eating you?" I muttered as he strode past.

He didn't answer, just stalked toward the door. I narrowed my gaze. This wasn't my smiling assassin. He didn't get rocked like the rest of us, just rolled with the punches...*until now.*

He lifted his hand to the handle of the back door, and stopped. His gaze didn't meet mine as he muttered, "I lost her."

"You *lost her?*"

One deep breath and the beta met my gaze. "You got a problem with that?"

"Seems to me, *brother,* you're the one with the problem."

"I fucking had her. One minute she was with that asshole partner of hers at the warehouse, then she just...*flipped.* She ran and I did like you said. I followed her until I caught the scent of blood."

I froze...blood...she was with her partner and then there was...*blood?* "Did he hurt her?"

Arran shook his head. "I couldn't tell. I chased her to find out if she was okay, but found this instead." He shoved his fingers into his pocket and pulled out a piece of cloth stained crimson with her blood.

My nostrils flared. The beast growled, drawing lungfuls of her scent inside.

Her blood…

I took a step closer and reached out, taking the handkerchief from his hand. Not a mortal wound. Not anywhere near the kind of flow that could be dangerous, but still the sight of it… and the smell. I lifted my hand and pressed the fabric to my nose.

The beast shifted under my skin, writhing like something dangerous…like something *savage.*

"Where did you find this?"

"In some woman's stroller. Scared the shit out of her when I stepped into her path. Didn't have to say a word, just walked up, knelt, and grabbed it from under the kid."

"She used your own senses against you." I shook my head. "Knowing you'd be triggered by her blood."

Arran sneered and muttered a choice word under his breath. But I couldn't help but smile. The woman was smart…and goddamn ruthless, and every time she bucked and fought it only made me want her more. My smile turned to a grin.

"What's so fucking funny?" Arran snarled.

"She's playing hard to get…*and I fucking love it,"* I answered, and left with that euphoria, striding toward the Harley. Night was settling, faint lights sparkled from the front of the club as I started the bike and turned the wheel toward the bridge.

She made me want to run, this damn woman. She made me want to throw my head back and howl at the damn moon. She made me want to hunt…like I'd never hunted before.

I goosed the engine and felt the tire slip before it caught the asphalt and all but threw me toward the bridge. I was at the corner before I knew it, loving that heavy growl between my thighs.

Find her, the beast in me growled. *Find our mate.*

I didn't even wince now at the word, didn't fight that cornered goddamn feeling as that dark desire rose. *Our mate.* It was more than the Unseelie mark in her breast, more than the bullet she'd put in my chest, and more than just fucking. I wanted to own the woman...and I wanted her to own me.

Cars seemed to stand still on the bridge. I opened the bike up and tore between them, moving faster and faster until the world was nothing more than a blur. I cut across the off-ramp as the cool night wind whipped along the river.

Something deeper than instinct made me turn the wheel toward the Jewel. But it wasn't the wreck of the bar that filled my mind. It was the warehouse...the bloody ruin we'd left behind. I turned the bike and let the headlight sweep through the darkness. The place was closed up now, the warehouse doors pulled down and secured. Crime scene tape stretched all the way across the front and even wrapped around the power pole at the corner.

Kill that fucking thing, for Christ's sake.

Her roar filled my head. I'd come to this place for retribution. I'd come to defend, and I'd left with her...that chill from the water danced across me as I stopped the bike. Hairs on the nape of my neck stood on end. I turned my head and inhaled, scenting the wind. Blood. Death. *Rage.* The shit was choking, even days later.

The beast inside let out a low, warning snarl. There was something in the wind tonight. Something that made the hackles rise along his shoulders. Something that made him pace across the darkness of my mind. "What is it?" I whispered.

He inhaled, scenting, searching...and found nothing. I took one last look at the warehouse before I kicked the bike into gear and pulled away. Downtown streets blurred. But it wasn't downtown I wanted. I lifted my gaze to the moon. I had a little over an hour until I needed to be across the bridge to the other side of the city to meet the Fae and the Vampires.

A little over an hour to track her down.

Arran's pissed off expression filled my mind, making me smile.

Hunt and seek.

I twisted the throttle and tore through Crown City's downtown streets, heading back once more to the grittier suburbs where she lived. Something nagged me about where she lived, something that had wormed its way inside my head and refused to let go.

It was a rough neighborhood, not somewhere you'd expect a cop to live, let alone an FBI agent like Carina. I'd expected a modest house in a quiet neighborhood. Red and blue lights shimmered in the distance now, growing brighter the closer they came.

The cop car tore past me with its flashing lights as I kept on riding, making my way to River Heights. The flickers of TVs danced behind flimsy curtains as I turned into her street. I slowed the bike, watching those curtains move and small beady eyes peer out. They didn't like strangers here, liked Wolves even less, especially Wolves like me.

I scanned the clapboard houses, some with holes punched into the front doors, others with steel grates as locked doors, and looked at hers. Faded bottle green, weeds and cracked pavement, the windows too grimy to even see out of.

Still, this was her…that man…this place.

I needed to know her, needed to unlock her secrets and bare her soul to mine. I needed to scent her, to touch her, to get her down on her back and bury my nose into the most private places of her.

That desperation rode me as I killed the engine and pushed out the kickstand. I climbed off the Harley and took a step toward the house where she lived. Two steps and I was striding out, drawn by something deeper than instinct and more savage than love.

The filthy car was still in the same place under the carport. Two flat tires at the back told me it didn't venture out much. I drew in the faint scent of her and kept on walking, following the trail through the knee-high grass to the fallen fence at the back, then climbed.

My boots thudded against the stairs, booming in the night. But I didn't need to worry. My little prey wasn't home...and hadn't been, as far as I could tell. The flowery fragrance of her shampoo lingered, but faintly. I gripped the handle of her door and twisted.

Only this time it was locked.

"Well, well...now you're learning," I muttered, and reached for my wallet.

Two seconds later, the lock pic found the pins and the lock snapped open. I pushed the door and stepped inside. It was just the same. Bare. *Fucking lonely.* The place didn't feel like her. It felt like a safe house. One designed to harbor and not to provide, and Christ if I didn't want to provide.

I wasn't as rich as the damn Vampires but I wasn't dirt poor either. I had enough to protect her, enough to comfort her...but somehow, I knew she wouldn't take a damn thing from me. She'd have to earn it, have to want it...all I had to do now was to figure out how.

I walked through her house, taking my time, and knelt at the worn mattress on the floor. It was almost like she blamed herself...denied herself. *Almost like she hated herself.* I traced the rumpled sheets and grabbed the pillow, lift it to my face. That sight of her came back to me, naked, content, her bare breasts rising with her breaths...and Vitold looking down at her with the kind of expression that made me both jealous and proud.

She needs to be protected, the Wolf's words sounded. I placed the pillow back and rose. The meeting with the Vampires wouldn't wait, so I made my way back outside, flipping the lock as I went.

The faint wail of sirens was the backdrop as I made my way down the stairs and through the grass. The foul stench of sweat and methylated spirits wafted toward me on the air. I knew the mortal was there, caught the sway of shadows and that faint whiff of someone resigned to their fate.

"The fuck doju want here, Wolf?" The slur came from the corner of the building.

Steel glinted in the darkness as the muzzle danced far too wide. Hate bristled, standing the hair on my arms. I clenched my jaw and reminded myself this was her kin...*her father.* Even if he was a poor excuse for one. "To make sure she's safe, that's all."

"When is anyone safe around you bastards." Those words came out clear as a fucking bell. He had a beef with Immortals. Figures.

"Your problems are not hers. I want to protect—"

"The hell it is...tell that to the fucking Costellos...*if there's any left.*"

Costellos? "You know them?"

He barked a laugh and belched. "Yeah." Those unfocused eyes hardened to stone. "You could say that. Which is why I'm warning you. Stay the fuck away from *my* kid. Come near her again and I'll shoot you with a gut full of silver...see how you like her then."

The warning pissed me off. Fucking silver.

I wanted to close the distance, wanted to grip that pathetic excuse for a father by his fucking throat and haul him into the air. I wanted to say...*and I'd gut you before you even lifted the fucking gun, old man...*

He flinched as that bestial image took hold. I let it all play out in my gaze...every terrifying instant, before I stepped forward. The bastard actually whimpered and stumbled backwards as I moved to press my chest to the end of the shotgun. "You reek of death, old man. Death and fucking regret. Threaten me again and you'll find out just how much of a *bastard* I can be. I…" the words stuck in the back of my throat. "I care about her. More than you ever could. Do her a favor and clean yourself up. You smell disgusting."

I left then, giving the drunken failure my back and made my way to my Harley. I still felt him watching me from the darkness, that stench of rage now turning bitter and sour. He knew the Costellos all right…knew them enough to hate them.

I climbed onto the bike and started the engine as that nagging feeling took hold once more. There was something connecting them, something that hadn't yet revealed itself. Why else would Carina have been at the warehouse that night? The answers eluded me…*for now.*

I pushed off and eased the throttle, scanning the swaying shadow at the corner of the house before I turned the bike around and left the place. An urgency filled me as I tore my way out of River Heights and headed back toward the bridge. Lights sparkled along the waterfront. Towering ships still crowded the space. Costello Corporation was no more, but the shipping industry in Crown City was thriving. There were more cargo carriers than ever, more cranes working from the docks…and more money flowing. The only problem was, it wasn't flowing to the Costellos, not anymore.

I made my way across the bridge. The traffic was moving faster this time. Still, I wove the bike between the other cars until I was on familiar ground once more.

The club was in full swing as I tore past, the engine of the bike screaming, rattling windows and doors as I headed to the darker part of this side of the river, where abandoned buildings meant nothing to the Fae. If anything, it was a warning to those not Unseelie—*stay the fuck away.*

Most heeded that warning.

Unless you paid their price.

Magic singed my skin, the sting brutal as I slowed at the massive gate and lifted my gaze to the Explorer outside the warehouse. The Vampires were here already...something must be urgent. That damn thud in my chest boomed a little louder as I rode the bike through the opening gate and parked beside the gleaming four-wheel drive.

Justice...the damn Vamp filled my head. The last time I saw him, he was being carried toward the chopper...barely alive. Word was, even the Breeds were reluctant to help him, maybe he was too far gone for their synthetic DNA to help. I only hoped the brother had survived.

I climbed off the bike and strode toward the side entrance. Weak light from inside spilled through the open door. I stepped in, scanned the space, and stilled at the sight of E and Shrike before I closed the door behind me.

"About time you decided to show up," Mojin growled from the shadows at my right.

"Eat it, Unseelie," I responded, and glanced at the brutal male as he stepped closer.

He was wary this time...much warier than usual as he reached out a hand, waiting for mine. "Haven't seen you around," he commented. "That Special Agent keeping you busy?"

It was a careful prod. Was the male worried for her? Or did she intrigue him...

My beast curled his lips and bared his teeth.

"Easy, Wolf," Mojin muttered, and lowered his waiting hand. "Just making sure the female's still alive is all."

"Alive and *mine*, Unseelie."

One nod and the male backed away, slinking into the shadows once more. There was something strange about the way he was acting toward Carina. He'd never cared about the females that had caught my eye before. Then again, none were like her. My pain-in-the-ass Special Agent.

I strode toward the others who waited. A nod to Shrike, and I met Elithien's haunted gaze. Christ, I'd never seen the bloodsucker so lifeless...not even when he was fucking dead. "Everything okay, E?"

"I've been better," he answered, meeting my gaze.

"J?"

He winced, his pale lips curling as a flash of rage tore through his gaze. "He's alive if that's what you're asking."

"Just alive, then?"

"There's been...a complication," he said. "But we're working through it."

That's all the Vampire wanted to say. The rage hardened in his gaze, turning to that same icy look he always wore. A look that said *'don't push it'.* I gave him a nod and turned to the Unseelie. "You wanted me here...so I'm here."

Shrike shifted uneasily and looked to E. "Apparently the fallout from the warehouse has ruffled mortal feathers. They want assurances our shit won't spill across the river again, and part of those assurances is a detailed breakdown on what actually occurred that night."

"Surely we're not going to give it to them," I protested. The Fae was quiet...and so was the damn Vamp. *"We're not giving them information about us..."* I pushed the point. "They could use it against us."

"They could," Elithien agreed. "But I think that's a chance we have to take. To deny them now would put a target on our backs, more than we have already."

"Elithien's right." Shrike rubbed the stubble on his chin.

"What exactly are we supposed to say?" I growled, hating this idea.

"A condensed version, a rogue Vampire led an attack on the

Jewel, then ambushed us when we went to peacefully end this call to arms."

I barked a laugh. "That's fucking absurd. They're not going to buy that shit."

"They will if we make them," Shrike growled.

"And who are these so called *'mortals'* that demand we expose ourselves like this."

"The FBI," Elithien answered. "I received a call from Special Agent in Charge Harlan and he wants one of us to sit down with him and his lead investigator in front of the Deputy Assistant."

"Harlan?" I repeated. The name...that fucking name meant something. I searched my mind and, as always, Carina was there. "When?"

"Tomorrow. It's the only day they could do it," Elithien explained.

"Fine. I'll do it." I offered.

Both heads turned my way. I scowled and met their gazes. "Why the fuck are you looking at me like I have a goddamn bomb in my hand?"

"You feeling alright, brother?" Shrike searched my gaze.

"Maybe he's sick?" E questioned.

"Fuck the both of you," I growled. "I can be nice when I have to."

"As nice as an atomic bomb..." Shrike glanced at Elithien.

"Sweet as arsenic," Elithien added with the hint of a smile. It looked awkward on the Vamp.

"With a side of laxatives," Shrike said, and chuckled.

I flipped them the bird...*both of them.* "Fuck you. Text me the time and place. I'll show you how fucking charming I can be."

"Just don't...kill anyone," Shrike added.

My phone gave a buzz, vibrating in my pocket. I glanced at E and Shrike. Both Immortals gave a nod, it looked like they'd said all they wanted to say…to me that is. "I'll leave you to your mothers' meeting then."

A middle finger from Shrike was the response. I chuckled and walked away, yanked my phone out, and swiped the call. "Phantom."

"It's Path," the Alpha muttered. "We have a situation here."

"What is it?" I glanced at the shadows as I headed to the door. But the Unseelie was gone, lost to the darkness…though it was where he always belonged.

"Something's come up and we gotta bounce."

"Fuck, *now?*" I growled.

"Afraid so, brother, call if you want us to double back in a day or two, but we got a lead on the Ferryman…and I gotta take it."

"I understand," I forced the words through clenched teeth.

"Besides, it's boring as fucking hell here. I dunno how much more titty I can stand."

I forced a chuckle and climbed onto the bike. "Yeah, real tough gig."

"Your young Wolf didn't turn up for work. Which is why I'm giving you a heads-up, otherwise I'd already be on the road."

I snapped to attention in an instant. "Wry didn't turn up?"

"Cocky fucker must've had a big day. Not a peep from him. Your bartender, Jace, said not to worry, though, it's a slow night. Not a lot going on anyway. So, look. I gotta haul ass. Call if we can babysit the booty later, okay?"

"Sure…no problem," I muttered, not even listening to him anymore.

I started the bike and rolled backwards. The gate was already opening as I kicked the Harley into gear and eased on through. Wry had never taken a night off since I'd hired him over three years ago. Not once had he let me down. He was young and eager, especially with the mortal women. But who wasn't at that age?

I cruised around the streets and made my way to The Hunting Ground, killing the light before I turned into the parking lot. I parked at the back, killed the engine, and climbed off the bike.

The faint throb of music from inside was barely background music. I was too used to the sound, dulling it from my senses. The wind picked up as I punched in the code for the back door and grabbed the handle. The pungent scent of blood made me freeze...*a lot of blood...*

Wolf's blood...

I'd know that scent anywhere.

I turned my head and inhaled. Shadows spilled across the girls' cars in the parking lot. I scanned each one...and stopped at the Camaro.

Movement came against the rear tire...the shift subtle...*so very fucking subtle.*

Then a moan spilled out.

"Jesus *Christ!*" I yelled, and lunged for the glistening black car. "Church!" I roared. *"Church, get out here NOW!"*

18

"You've got to be shitting me," mumbled the mess of a person behind the cracked open door. At least I thought it was a person. Sunken black eyes, food stains on the shirt, cracked lips curled into a sneer. "Fuck off, Chase."

"You love me," I protested. "And you'd never leave me stranded."

She left the door opened as she turned, still dressed in green scrubs and an old threadbare yellow t-shirt. "That's where you're wrong. One, I don't love you. Never have. And two..." she stopped suddenly in the middle of the hallway. "Two," she muttered, sleep slurring her words. "Oh, who gives a shit about two. Coffee's in the kitchen. I need at least two more hours of sleep before I can even stomach your damn face. Lucky for you I'm on days off. Food, coffee. And a damn good explanation on why you're standing in my door with a slashed hand better be ready when I wake up. Wait," she grunted, stumbling, then turned to peer at me with bloodshot eyes. "That's all you have, right? Nothing else that's serious...like a gunshot or anything?"

See, she did love me. "Nothing that can't wait for a few more hours," I answered. "Now, go, sleep. I'll be here touching all your shit when you get up."

"Fucking figures," she groaned, and staggered for the bedroom.

The door closed with a tired *slam.* I stood in the hallway of the large two-bedroom loft in downtown Crown City and felt the world close in around me. Bedsprings moaned, drawing my gaze to the closed door. Walker was the only person I could trust, with *any* of this.

I left her to sleep, no doubt she'd been on one helluva stretch of work with no end in sight. Lucky for me this was her time off. For the next few days, her life would be food, sleeping, sex, and outdoors. Add to that patching me up and hopefully getting rid of this shit in my breast—*once and for all.*

I went into the kitchen as that thought took hold. With it, this dangerous need for the damn Wolves would be gone, too. It had to be. I refused to accept anything else. There was a picture of Ebony stuck to the refrigerator. A new one, taken recently. Wide smile, perfect eyes shining and that innocent looking face familiar with someone with Downs Syndrome. Walker loved her sister fiercely. Loved her more than she loved air she breathed. Ebony was her little sister by three years and Christ if she wasn't as protective of her as a momma bear.

Walker told me Ebony had struggled to communicate, born deaf was hard until they learned sign language, now Walker said she couldn't shut her sister up. They video-chatted every Sunday, and met up every few weeks for a 'girls night out'. I'd been on one of those nights out. Movies, bowling, heavy frosted cupcakes sitting beside the river and laughter was on agenda. Always laughter.

I was envious of their love.

Envious of their acceptance.

If only I had a sister like that.

I guess family was what you made it. Mine might not be perfect, but it was all I had.

I yanked open her refrigerator and stilled at the shelves packed with food.

That's right. Days off. Walker had her cleaning lady shop for her and fill her fridge and cupboards before she stayed away for the few days or the week Walker was off from work. I looked at all the food and realized how pathetic my existence was. My refrigerator was bare, my cupboards much the same…as was my damn bank account.

I pulled out food, taking my time to make two ham, cheese, and pickle sandwiches, then plonked myself in front of her TV. One click of the remote, and that sinking feeling took hold once more. Blane Costello's face was splashed across the screen as the newswoman spoke of the grisly death. I pressed the volume, turning it all the way down and glanced at the closed bedroom door across the hallway.

Walker would sleep like the dead. Still, I made sure I was quiet and turned back to the news to find an older image of Ruth Costello splashed across the screen. They still thought she was dead, But still tried to crank up the ratings by posting news stories of the sudden and spectacular fall of one of the richest families in Crown City.

The Costellos were over.

Good as dead.

One day closer to being forgotten.

The longer Ruth hid under a damn rock, the better. Until I was ready, that was. I sat back against the soft sofa, chewing on my sandwich as I flicked through channels and watched the world darken outside. I tried to watch anything, but my mind was stolen by the night…and the memory of them…*the Wolves*.

I felt bad I'd given the sexy bartender the slip. That twinge of regret was soon smothered by the need of my own safety. *Life fucking altering.* Weren't those the words that had slipped through the crack of the door the night after the attack? That's what the male had said…that growl still resounded in my head.

I knew that growl…knew it from the warehouse. That dark beast of a male, striding toward me. *Unseelie,* Phantom had called him. Whatever he was, he'd said the words that now filled me with terror.

There was no room for *life fucking altering* here. No room for anything other than trying like hell to survive and keep my damn job—if that was still able to be saved.

I spent the next two and a half hours flicking through channel after channel, and finally switch the TV off. Walker's loft was on the sixth floor of a fairly new apartment building, with views of the city stretching all the way across the river.

I rose from the sofa, placed my plate in the sink, and grabbed a beer from the fridge before making my way to the floor-to-ceiling windows. Across the river. Where the Wolves in their seedy sex club waited. How the fuck had I gotten tangled up in this?

"Pretty, huh?" Walker muttered behind me with a yawn. "Gets me every time, that view. See you helped yourself to the fridge." She padded barefoot across the space and into the kitchen. "Want another beer?"

She grabbed two out before I could answer, cranked the top off one, and took a long swallow before she placed the half empty bottle down. "Feel like a fucking zombie," she groaned, and motioned me forward with a jerk of her head. "Right, let me get my kit and I'll take care of that hand, okay?"

"Thanks, Walker. I really—"

She lifted her hand, stopping me cold. "First pain, then explanation."

I couldn't help but smile watching her trudge her way to the red duffel bag plopped inside her bedroom door. She bent, grabbed the handles, and hauled it with her. "On the counter, Chase, and I want you to know you are the single biggest pain the ass I've ever met for interrupting my first goddamn day off in over a month."

"I'm sorry." I headed for the counter and held out my hand.

"Lucky I fucking love you," she finished. "And I miss your ugly face. Jesus, just look at you. I bet you don't work out, do you? Bet you don't even use cream for your face, or the thousand other things I do to try and look somewhat non-terrifying. You suck, you really do."

I opened my mouth, then thought better of it.

"Figures," she growled as she reached in and splayed a plastic-lined mat on the counter. "Hand."

I placed it on the mat, palm up, and turned my head. I didn't want to see the mess from the sliver of glass. Cold hit my palm with a hiss. The spray was wet and tingling, then smooth wipes followed, until they stopped.

"Okay, I give up. What the hell am I supposed to be stitching here?"

I flinched at the words and jerked my gaze to my hand. The blood was gone...and so was the gash. "That's not right," I muttered. "There was a gash, a decent sized one. It was bleeding and everything." Walker just leaned back and looked at me like I was high. "I'm not high. The cut was right there."

"Well, it's not there now," she insisted, and stared at me, searching my eyes...and scanning my body. "But there is something going on with you. You're standing all wrong, scrunched up, spine bowed...like you're in pain. You in pain, Chase?"

I swallowed hard. *Tell her,* that desperate voice inside my head urged.

It's why I came here, right? I mean, I'd had barbed wire scratches worse than that cut on my palm. That's not why I was here, not why I'd needed a friend, someone I could trust. God knows I didn't have many anymore.

"I need to tell you something." I lowered my voice, choosing my words carefully. "I want you to promise not to freak out."

"Chase," Walker muttered, and grabbed her beer before draining the last of the contents. "I'm like the least freaking out person I know. I work in the Emergency Room, for Christ's sake, and you don't want to know the kind of shit I deal with on a daily basis."

I swallowed hard and lifted my hands to the top button of my shirt. I'd known Walker for almost five years. We'd become friends by accident at some gala event run by the Costellos. I was there for any kind of dirt I could on them and she was just there for the free drinks…and food.

I loved that about her. Honest. Solid. The kinda friend you needed when shit got real…

It was about to get very fucking real.

I opened the top button, watching her as her gaze followed my fingers until she muttered, "Now this is either the unsexiest striptease I've ever seen, or you're fucking scared." Walker pushed off the counter, her eyes alert now and darkening as she came toward me.

I tried to manage, but my hands were shaking, yanking the button instead of opening it.

She rounded the counter and clasped her hands over mine, staring into my eyes. "Easy now. Let me do it. Let me see, Chase."

I dropped my hands, letting her work the buttons of my shirt one by one until my breasts and stomach were bare. The savage hiss from her lips was brutal. She jerked her eyes to mine as they flew wide.

"What the fuck is this, Chase?" She reached out, touching the sparkling jewels embedded in my skin, and the hot flare of pain followed. I winced and hissed, making her wrench her hand back.

"Magic," I answered. "At least, that's what I was told."

"*Magic?*" she repeated, and reached out once more.

"Wait." I grasped her wrist and gripped tight, stopping her cold. "There's something you should know."

Her brows narrowed before she lowered her gaze to my hold. I eased up, not wanting to hurt her. "It's Unseelie magic, dark magic. *Sex magic.*"

The ghost of a smile cut across her lips before it was gone. "What do you mean *'sex magic'*?"

"Exactly what it says," I said, easing back. "Makes men fucking crazy, makes them…want me."

"Chase." She shook her head. "I hate to tell you this, but of course men want you. You're fucking gorgeous."

"No," I forced the words. "Not like that. Not a smile, or a wink. I mean grab me and push me against a wall. I mean come after me like I was their favorite meal and they're fucking starving. The Wolves warned me, but this…this shit is out of control."

"*The Wolves warned you?*" she repeated carefully, then took a step backwards, turned to the fridge, and pulled out another beer. "I think we need to sit, Chase…and you need to tell me everything that happened."

She handed me my beer from the counter and twisted the top of hers with a hiss. She was right. I think I needed this more than I needed her to try and save me. I needed to unravel, to make sense of everything that had happened to me.

Because the truth was…*I couldn't make sense of it myself.*

I opened my beer as she rounded the end of the counter and motioned to the sofa. "Sit, relax. I only care about you in whatever this is, so I'm on your side here. I don't give a shit about anything else."

My shoulders sank and my feet grew heavy as I made my way to the sofa once more and sat. She perched on the leather ottoman, elbows resting on her knees, with a look of concern.

"You know how I've been shadowing Ruth Costello," I started.

She took a swallow. "The endless path to self-destruction, yeah. I know it well, go on."

"I followed her a couple of nights ago."

She scowled with surprise. "Isn't she supposed to be…"

"Dead. Yeah, funny about that. She's very much alive, and in hiding with the Vampires across the river."

"The Hidden?" She sat up and nodded slowly. "Wow, wasn't expecting that."

"Neither was I, but the other night I followed her to some meeting with a coven of other Vampires, they looked like they weren't friends. One hit her and knocked her to the ground, anyway. They grabbed her and hauled her into the Jewel."

"Carina…" she moaned my name. "Don't tell me you followed them."

I didn't have to. Walker knew me too damn well.

"Idiot," she growled. "You're gonna get yourself killed one day."

I closed my eyes and lifted a shaking hand. "I almost did. I followed them to the warehouse two doors down."

"The one from the massacre?"

I nodded.

"Jesus H. Christ, Chase. I saw some of those poor fuckers. Tried to patch two of them up, but there was nothing *to* patch up. They were mauled, teeth and claws and bullets holes everywhere. You were there?"

"I was there." The words came out on a tremble. "I got cornered, saw Blane Costello get his damn throat torn out by a Vampire. Almost became a Vampire meal myself."

"No…oh, Chase." Sympathy raged in her eyes.

But I didn't want it, not yet. Not when I had so much left to tell. "A beast came after me, wanted to hurt me, or fuck me, I don't know. He did something to me, Walker. Pressed this." I looked down to my open shirt and the sparkling green embedded in my breast. "Whatever *this* is, inside me. He would've killed me, if not for the Wolf."

"What Wolf?"

I licked my lips. Even before I said his name, my heart started thundering. "They call him Phantom."

"Not *the* Phantom?" she queried, stunned. "The Alpha who owns the strip clubs and the girls?"

I felt myself nodding. "Yeah, that one. Saved my fucking life. Guess I saved his, too. He carried me out of there and took me across the river. See, this shit." I brushed my fingers across my chest. "It doesn't just cause me pain."

"Sex magic," she exclaimed. "Jesus, Chase, you didn't…"

"I didn't have much of a choice, Walker. It was either that or fucking die, and no matter how much I wanted that, it never came. Just waves of lust and agony, wave after wave after wave."

"You fucked a Wolf." She leaned back and shook her head, throwing her hand into the air. "*No.* You fucked an Alpha, *the* goddamn Alpha."

Desire sparkled in her eyes. I only needed one look to know *exactly* what she was thinking. "No fucking way, Walker."

"Chase."

I shook my head. "No."

"Chase, come on."

"I'm not telling you *that.*"

"Dude. You told me about the first time you got laid. You even told me about the first time you went to a rave and took an E."

I flinched. "You were *never* supposed to mention that again."

"Yeah? Well, I just did. Now, you *have* to tell me. Was it good? Please tell me it was good."

My cheeks blazed to life. My mouth became dry. I couldn't tell her anything. *I couldn't fucking speak.*

"Oh my God. It *was* good, *wasn't* it?" She took a big swallow of her beer. "You fucking tramp."

I fought the smile. "The fifth time was better," I added in a mumble. "Until I woke up in the morning with all four of them in bed with me."

She fell off the leather ottoman, spilling her beer on her shirt as she hit the floor with a thud.

"Fuck, Walker!" I jumped up and lunged toward her. "You okay?"

"*What the fuck?*" she howled, and scrambled upwards. "Four of them. Four fucking Wolves? You slept with *the entire pack?*"

I straightened as she tried to right herself. "It wasn't like I intended to."

"But you had intended to sleep with the Alpha, didn't you?"

I didn't answer, just felt that hunger inside me. That urgency to be seen by him…to be touched and wanted by him. But the more I imagined him, the more they were there. All of them. The blonde, the Russian…and Arran. "I can feel myself slipping, Walker. Feel it all just running through my fingers like sand. This world…*their world.*" I met her gaze. "I don't know where I am anymore."

"Where do you want to be?"

I knew she'd ask me that. Knew she'd find the part that was painful and drive a needle into its heart. She was brutally honest and she made me brutally raw. "I…" I swallowed hard.

"That's what I thought," she answered. "You like them, the Wolves. You have a connection to them, a lot more of a connection than you ever had before, even with your own family. Face it, Chase, you never really belonged in this world, anyway. You're more a Wolf than you are a mortal, on the inside, at least."

She was right. This skin, this fragile existence, made me feel caged. Dangerous. *Cornered.*

"So you want me to what?" Walker stepped closer and

lowered her gaze to the glow in my breast. "You want me to try and dig this out, knowing it's going to hurt and may potentially kill you? Tell me what you want here, Chase. Tell me what you need."

"I need to understand it all, that's what I need. I need to breathe, need to think without this shit driving me constantly. I need to get it under control."

"You said it yourself, it's sex magic." She reached out and took my hand. "And honey, I love you and all...but I just don't swing that way."

Laughter erupted, tearing along my throat with a hard bark. "Thank fuck for that."

Still she gripped my hand and held my stare. "I love you. I know you're going to figure this out. You need more than I can give you. If it came from an Immortal, then it has to end there as well. But maybe, just maybe...it's in you for a reason. You said yourself the cut on your hand is healed. Maybe it's protecting you more than you know."

Her gaze dropped to my shoulder and there it stopped. One swift move and she'd opened the collar of my shirt wider, exposing the bite mark on my shoulder. "Jesus, Chase. They bit you?"

"Yeah."

She leaned closer, fingers probing around the teeth marks. "Does it hurt?"

"A little," I admitted. "Seems everything hurts at the moment."

"You want a place to crash for a while?" She pulled me closer and wrapped her arms around me. It felt good...felt honest and safe. Felt almost as comforting as lying in bed with the Wolves. I could still feel them pressed against my back, Arran's nose wedged between my breasts.

I swallowed hard as my throat tightened.

That moment felt more like home than anything I'd ever felt before.

"I'll make up the sofa," Walker declared as she still hugged me. "Right after I shower, 'cause I freaking stink."

She made me chuckle as she pulled away. I fixed my shirt, managing the buttons all right, and watched her rise and slowly walk toward the bedroom before she stopped and looked at me over her shoulder. "Do you like him, that Wolf? Like, I know what they say, they're beasts and they're dangerous, and all that. But *do you actually like him?*"

That damn thunder boomed in the middle of my chest.

Did I like him?

In my mind, callused fingers brushed against my skin…and that look of savage hunger filled my mind. "Yeah, I do."

"Then you have your answer," she responded. "Forget about Ruth Costello and chasing damn ghosts. Your father resigned himself to his fate long ago. He made his own decision, made his own life. It's about time you did the same."

She left me then, slipped into the bedroom, and closed the door. Barely a minute later, and the faint hiss of the shower drifted through the closed door.

He made his own decisions…it's about time you did the same.

Her words filled me, smothered me. Made me feel…scared. That's what I felt. Fucking terrified.

I rose from the sofa, listening to the spray of the shower as that fear turned into something else.

Something solid…something *true.*

I left my beer on the floor beside the sofa. Left my best friend too, and made my way to the front door of her apartment. Walker had told me the brutal truth. Even if it was a truth I wasn't yet ready to face. Still, it stayed with me as I rode the elevator to the first floor, and walked the three blocks back to the warehouse.

Faces blurred as I tried to slowly unravel this mess in my life.

The truth was, it wasn't really a mess, not *my* mess, anyway.

Do you like him...

The question stayed with me, haunting every step as I strode past the warehouse and then the Jewel. The Jeep was still there, still exactly where I'd left it. One glance at the line of cars parked behind it and I knew Arran was gone. A pang of regret consumed me as I reached into my pocket for the keys.

I'm not interested in scaring you, Carina...

Those words lingered as I unlocked the Jeep and climbed in. Minutes later, I was pulling into the steady stream of traffic and wincing at the blinding glare of the oncoming traffic.

Walker's cutting clarity stayed with me.

That shit in my chest was a damn battleground. Something I couldn't ignore...maybe that was the reason? Maybe the hunger it made me feel was making me face my own demons? I worked my way home, to the volatile streets of River Heights, and tried to understand whose battle was I actually fighting, and who I was trying to save?

Was it Dad?

Was it Mom?

It sure wasn't myself.

I pulled the Jeep up alongside the forgotten family home. I almost laughed. Family. I didn't have one, not if I was honest. A call from Mom every three months just to check if I was still alive. The calls were longer at first, gushing tears and words of *I'm sorry but I had to leave.* Now they were filled with discussions of the weather. That's what my *'family'* had been reduced to.

I turned off the engine, my gaze finding the flicker of the TV through the windows. I climbed out of the four-wheel drive and closed the door behind me. Each step was agonizing. I tried to fight that sinking feeling in my chest as I walked to the rear.

I fucking hated myself for the resentment at being his daughter. Hated myself for wishing my life was anything but checking on a drunk every day for almost my entire life and fighting for him to survive. Because the truth was, he didn't care, not about surviving…and not about me.

I opened the screen door and stepped inside, made my way to the fridge, and stopped with my hand on the handle. Tears slipped down my cheeks, hot and slick. A stray bead lingered at the edge of my jaw before it fell.

"You brought that *thing* to my home?"

I flinched at his voice, swiped at the tears, and jerked my gaze to my father as he swayed and clutched the wall. "Dad. You're up."

"You brought that filthy fucking dog to MY house?"

I blinked at the sting and straightened. "What are you talking about, Dad?"

He shoved away from the wall, took three steps, and slammed into me, the neckline of my shirt bunched in his fist. "You *fucking liar.*"

I winced and fought the need to retch from the stench of his breath. "You're fucking drunk." I swatted his hand away and tried to straightened. "What the fuck is wrong with you?"

But there was no stopping him, no shoving him away…no ignoring the burning rage in his eyes. "You fucking whore."

There was no slur in those words. No, they were clear as a damn bell. "What did you call me?"

"You heard me," he snarled, stumbling backwards a few steps. Hate raged in his eyes. "You're *not my daughter. No blood of mine would be anywhere near those fucking monsters.*"

"You mean I should just stay on this side of the river with monsters like you?" I spat.

I regretted the words as soon as I said them, stunned cold by the savagery in the truth.

Dad's lips curled back from yellowed teeth. "Get out," he said finally. "Get the fuck out of my house and never come back. *You are dead to me. You are fucking dead.*"

Pain plunged deep into my chest.

He'd said cruel things before. But *never* this.

I forced myself to swallow, but all I managed to do was take that poison deep inside as I headed for the door.

"Don't *EVER* come back here! *DON'T YOU EVER STEP A FOOT INSIDE MY DOOR!*"

The tears came as I punched through the busted screen door. My steps were a blur, everything was a blur.

Everything but the pain, that was.

No, that found me just fine as I scrambled through the fallen fence and lunged for the safety of my home. But there was no safety here. There never really was. It was a shell. A hollow fucking shell.

Just like my heart…and my life.

19

PHANTOM

The stench of blood was sickening, crammed in the back of my throat like a filthy rag.

"Church!" I screamed and dropped beside the male. He was dead...*he had to be.* No one could survive...not this. "Church, get out here *NOW!*"

One splutter, and droplets of blood smacked my face. Even in the shadows I knew who it was. "I got you, buddy," I muttered, then slid one arm under his knees and the other behind his back as he moaned. "I got you, Wry."

His head lolled backwards as I lifted him into the air. I stared at the sickening gash across his throat. Bone glinted an eerie white in the night. The back door to the club slammed open. Church was a blur in the corner of my eye as he lunged toward me. "What the fuck happened?"

"He was just here." I lifted my gaze. "Call Mojin."

"Phantom..." fear flickered in his gaze.

"Call Mojin!" I roared.

He sucked in harsh breaths, lifted his gaze to the young Wolf's blood-smeared face, and yanked his phone from his pocket. I didn't listen to what he screamed into the phone, all I cared about was Wry.

"I got you." I stumbled toward Church's Hummer. "Hold on, buddy, I got you."

The Wolf's eyes were wide in the darkness. the black shimmering with fear. Immortal or not, this was a fatal wound. *Who did this?* The question roared as Church lunged, yanked the back door's handle, and barked into the phone, "We'll be there in five."

Five…

Five…

I climbed up into the beast of a four-wheel drive as the door slammed behind me. The world seemed to blur as I cradled the Wolf in my arms. The hiss of breath through the gash was sickening. Blood splattered my arms with each labored exhale as the Hummer started with a roar and lunged forward.

"Stay with me," I commanded. "You hear me? Stay with me. We're gonna get you fixed up, buddy. We're gonna get you good as new."

The brush on my arm made me flinch. I looked down as he smacked my arm, fingers clawing, trying to draw me closer.

"You're gonna be—"

Eyes wide, choking with panic, he clawed my arm, nails carving through the skin as he tried to drag me closer. I leaned closer, watching his pale, bloodless lips move without a sound.

"We're here," Church barked, and yanked the wheel, spearing us through the gate.

"What is it?" I growled.

His lips moved, over and over. Even in the dark, I knew the words. *He's coming…he's coming. HE'S COMING.*

The Hummer stopped with a jolt. The rear door opened. Darkness swept in, lifting the Wolf from my arms.

"We got him, brother" Mojin growled. "We'll try our best."

Try their best? The words filled me as Mojin carried Wry from the back seat of the car and that same terrified gaze from the young Wolf fixed on mine. He was gone in an instant, carried by honor as Mojin pressed his hand to the Wolf's chest and that green emerald glow pulsed.

They were gone in an instant, disappearing around the corner of the warehouse, leaving me staring after them from the back seat of the Hummer.

"What the fuck happened?" Church turned my way from the driver's seat.

"He was just there." I didn't turn my head, didn't look away from the corner of the building. "I didn't see him…not at first. Then the smell of blood hit me."

"Jesus, and you didn't see anyone else?"

He's coming. HE'S COMING! A shiver raced along my arms at the memory. "I should go in there," I mumbled and practically fell through the open door. Church followed, leaving the Hummer behind.

An unprovoked attack like this had little to do with the victim and *everything* to do with the recipient. It was a message…one they were determined to deliver, and I got the message alright. My lips curled. I got the goddamn message. Loud and fucking clear.

The warehouse was quiet. Our shipment was due to arrive at midnight. Hurrow would soon follow, and the Unseelie, Ruin, would come after that. Money would be stored away in the vault for…we didn't know who yet.

The Inner Circle was falling and with it, our obligation to send them the money we made from our trades. I hadn't really thought about that, not until now.

The thought grew thorns now and dug in deep. That deep green Unseelie glow from behind the bank of windows grew brighter, pulsing with the kind of magic the Fae commanded.

Dark magic.

Death magic.

Sex magic.

"You want to go up there?" Church enquired behind me, wrenching me from the thought. The glow pulsed and shadows moved. I'd seen what Fae magic did...seen what had become of the bodyguard, Russell. I didn't want to see what would become of the Wolf. I shook my head.

"The Breeds, did they see any—"

"They're gone," I cut him off with a snarl.

"When?"

"About five minutes before I found him."

"That's a little convenient."

I met Church's gaze. His dark blue eyes sparkled with the same questions that gnawed at me. We were the same in many ways. In different circumstances, he might've been Alpha...but if our fates hadn't collided, he'd be dead...still buried in that old ice chest in the middle of nowhere and left to rot.

"Do we still trust them?" he asked.

"I don't know," I answered. "I honestly don't know."

The Breeds were supposed to be unaligned with the Circle, loyal to no one but their own cause. If they were responsible for this, then their entire reputation was at risk. Would they do that? I just didn't know...not after everything that had happened.

I splayed my fingers, then clenched my fist, turning to pace across the warehouse floor. It was quiet up there, *too damn quiet.* The image of Wry's wide eyes lingered, his bloodless lips moving without sound. "He tried to tell me something, but he couldn't speak. *He's coming.* That's what he tried to tell me, I'm sure of it."

"He's coming?" Church repeated. "And he didn't say who 'he' was?"

I shook my head. "It's all unraveling, brother." My beast paced and sniffed, growing dangerously quiet in my head. "I can't seem to keep it all locked down."

A strike of a claw here.

A bite at the back of the neck there.

Teeth sinking deep.

Danger was coming at us from all directions and I couldn't keep my pack safe. I needed them close...*all of them.* I needed them where I could see them. Where I could *defend* them. Carina filled my head and that burn inside me blazed to life. Where I could touch them...scent them, smother them with desire.

I was done with waiting. I was done with being patient...*this Wolf wasn't patient anymore.* "Stay here," I commanded. "Call me the moment anything changes, and I'm taking the Hummer."

Church gave a nod. "I'll make some calls. Get someone else around to Wild."

I was already turning, striding toward the open door of the Hummer, even as that emerald glow dulled once more. Only silence remained up there in the rooms above the money. Only silence and the threat of death. I left them behind, part of me hating myself for being a fucking coward and the other part barely holding myself from breaking into a run.

I climbed into the Hummer. The keys glinted, still in the ignition. I knew where I wanted to be. Knew who I wanted to be with. I started the engine, backed around, and nosed the four-wheel drive out of the parking lot as the gates closed behind me.

It felt like I'd spent my entire day chasing her—that *Special Agent with the FBI.*

Chasing her. Thinking about her. *Wanting her.*

I gripped the wheel, and headed for the bridge once more. All I could hear was those gasps of breath as Wry tried to stay alive...and all I could see was the moonlight reflected in his wide, terrified eyes.

My phone vibrated just an instant before I yanked it free and swiped to answer. "Yeah?"

"He's alive, for now," Church said as he sucked in a deep

breath. "But it's going to be touch and go. They can't risk moving him, can't risk a damn thing."

"Thank fuck," I moaned.

"But the kid will never speak again, it severed his voice box straight through."

I winced at the words. A mute, for the rest of his damn life. Unable to speak, unable to howl. Christ, that'd be rough. I turned back onto the bridge, taking the drive slower this time as I envisioned myself in his shoes.

With death, there was no revenge.

With survival, there was honor.

We'd find who did this…and make them pay with blood and pain.

I melted into the traffic. making my way back along the back streets to River Heights again. But it wasn't the old man's house I wanted anymore. It was hers. I kept driving past the turnoff I'd taken previously and took the next left. My headlights splashed against the houses. I slowed the Hummer and pulled up outside her house. If she wasn't here, then she was bound to come back.

I'd wait…all damn night if I had to.

One way or another, the mortal was coming with me.

I killed the engine and slowly climbed out.

The place was quiet…a little *too* quiet.

Gone was the soundtrack of sirens. Gone were the blaring sounds of TV's. But the flickers still came from behind the drawn curtains as I closed the driver's door of the Hummer and slowly made my way to her house.

No sounds came from inside the house and Arran's Jeep was nowhere to be seen…that's if she'd gone back for it. I strode along the front of the wraparound verandah and glanced at the uncut grass and the backyard of the old man's house, and caught the lingering scent of her.

She was here…or had been recently.

I glanced around me, strode to the door, gripped the handle, and turned. It gave way this time, letting me push into the darkened space. "Carina?" I called, my voice resounding. "Carina, it's me, Phantom."

Silence filled the space. I drew in her scent and sensed the space was changed somehow. It was larger...*emptier.* I flicked on the light in the kitchen and stared at open, empty cupboards. Something didn't feel right. I marched to her bedroom, strode in, and flicked on that light. The bed was the same...but the open closet wasn't. Gone were the few cheap suits she'd had hanging there. I let out a snarl and hurried for the bathroom. That too was empty. Drawers were open, her shampoo, conditioner, and toothbrush were all gone.

Like she was running.

But running where? "Fuck!" I snapped.

I left, flicking off the lights as I went. Frustration burned like acid in my gut. She might've left the pathetic excuse of a house, but there was no damn way a woman like that would leave her job. Not like this. I yanked the Hummer's door closed with a *bang.*

I still had a chance to find her. Tomorrow was the meeting with the head of the FBI division. Tomorrow I'd force her to face me...and leave with me, whether she liked it or not.

20

"You look like hell," Beth-Anne muttered as she bent and peered into the Jeep. "What happened, you sleep in your car or something?"

"Something," I answered, and left it at that.

One nod of her head and she pressed the button to lift the boom gate. I was rolling the Jeep through a heartbeat later, pulling into the closest parking space to the elevators, not even bothering to look for Murphy's car anymore.

You're *not my daughter. No blood of mine would be anywhere near those fucking monsters.*

I didn't even wince this time when the words rose like an aftershock. Didn't even feel that choking pain plunge through my chest. I just felt *numb.* I felt betrayed…more than anything, I felt fucking stupid.

Tears blurred the parking lot as I pulled in and killed the engine. First rule of the FBI, don't bring your personal life to work with you. Second rule, don't take it home. I guess I'd been fucked from the get-go. I'd lived and breathed my work and my retribution. I'd fought for him, fought even when he no longer wanted to fight for himself.

And for what?

To be disowned? To be threatened? I exhaled hard. Still that ache pulsed in my chest, mingling with the bitter taste of desperation. I looked at the thin blanket I'd yanked from the closet, now tossed on the floor of the passenger side, then at the bag of my clothes tossed on the back seat. I'd left, just like that... I'd left.

I didn't care about the house. Rent would come due and I wouldn't pay. They'd get someone in to live there soon enough, someone who actually filled the place with energy, rather than a vacuum.

That's exactly what I was...a fucking vacuum. A *black hole of disappointment.*

I yanked the keys from the ignition and climbed out, rounding the rear of the four-wheel drive to grab my clothes before I hurried to the elevator.

Voices drifted through the parking lot. I didn't bother to lift my head, just punched the button and waited. A flicker of relief swept through me as the doors opened and no one was inside. I rode the elevator to the upper floor and hurried to the locker rooms. The floor was a flurry of activity. Agents were already hard at it, brows furrowed, shirt sleeves rolled up, some looking panicked. What the hell was going on?

I shoved the bag into my locker, pulled out a clean, although wrinkled suit, and rushed to the showers. Five minutes later I was scrubbed clean, my still-dry hair piled on top of my head. I hurried to dry, dress, comb through the tangles, and slide my jacket on.

By the time I walked along the hallway and headed for my desk, the entire floor was in an uproar.

"Where the *fuck* have you been?" Harlan demanded, pacing the floor in front of my desk, his hair disheveled. *Was he sweating?* "You know what? Never mind, I don't have time to listen to your pathetic excuse. Cromwell will be here any minute, Chase, and you'd better have a damn good report to give to him."

Report?

FUCK!

"Yep," I lied. "Got it right here, Harlan." I tried to keep the fear from my voice. "Just give me five."

He stilled, raking his fingers through his thinning hair as I yanked out my chair and wiggled my mouse, bringing the screen to life.

"You *do* have a report to give him, right, Chase?"

"Yes, sir." I lied again. "I have it right here, just need to put the final touches on it and a good edit."

"You have ten minutes, Chase. Don't make me look bad in front of Cromwell and the Immortal delegate."

Immortal delegate? What the hell?

"Ten minutes, Chase." Harlan leaned across my desk. "It better be good. Your career is riding on this."

"Yes, sir," I acknowledged, and logged into the computer.

My face grew hot, and that rush of heat reached around the back of my neck. One lift of my gaze caught the stares of everyone around the room, and the cool touch of a bead of sweat slipped down my collar.

I swallowed hard and brought up the half attempt of a report I'd started. The words were a blur as I yanked the files from the warehouse close to me. Seventy unread messages in my inbox made me wince as I scanned the subject line and opened the Crime Scene report from the warehouse.

The two techs had done a good job, detailing the blood splatter, as well as matching the blood to the bodies at the morgue. My pulse stuttered at the names *Jerry and Blane Costello.* I licked arid lips and turned to the report, starting to type, outlining the bodies and the fatal wounds at the scene before digging into the locations of the bodies and the types of ammunition recovered at the scene.

Ten minutes turned into twenty. I felt Harlan hovering in the hallway, his dark stare stabbing, until he strode toward me. "He's here. Print it out, bring anything else that doesn't make us look fucking incompetent, and I'll meet you in the main boardroom."

He left then, muttering under his breath. Beads of sweat were trickling down my spine as I typed the last sentence, gave it a final check, and pressed print. I leaped from my desk, buttoned my jacket, and caught the musky scent of sweat.

"Good luck," someone muttered behind me as I snatched the report from the printer and raced for the door. "You're gonna need it."

Just don't let them rock you. I sucked in deep breaths and practically sprinted for the boardroom on the second floor. I was shaking by the time I stepped into the elevator, goddamn petrified by the time the doors opened to the executive offices. The boardroom door was open at the end of the hallway, and voices spilled out. I glanced at the glass doors of the executive suites reserved for the ASAC and Deputy Assistant when they came to Crown City.

My hands shook as I slowed outside the boardroom. I closed my eyes for a second and tried to remember my damn name. I could do this...I could *do this.* I opened my eyes, lowered my gaze, and stepped inside the expansive room.

I'd met Cromwell twice before, but neither time had been particularly pleasant. Kiss-ass Harlan was doing all the talking as I turned, closed the door behind me, and strode to the vacant seat on one side of the table.

"Chase, nice of you to grace us with your presence." Cromwell's snooty tone grated on me already.

"Sorry, s—" I lifted my head and froze.

"Chase?" Harlan muttered.

No...no fucking way. Phantom sat on the other side of the table, opposite me. Dark unflinching eyes that sparkled with amusement and savagery. Perfect lips curling slightly as Harlan continued to blabber.

"I'd like you to meet the representative of the Immortals, Mr. Phantom."

The sonofabitch had the gall to smile at me and rise as he extended his hand. "Special Agent," he murmured.

I just stared at him, panicked, pissed off more than anything.

"Well, are you going to just stand there and gape, Chase?" Harlan snapped. "Shake the man's hand and let's get on with it."

My body moved on its own. My hand extended and was swallowed by his in an instant. Heat burned through me at his touch.

"Nice to meet you, Special Agent," Phantom performed, and stared into my eyes.

"Mr. Phantom is here to explain the different factions that rose during this unwarranted and unmerciful attack," Harlan broke in as he glanced at my hand still smothered by the Alpha's.

All I could feel was him. His heat. His power...swirling inside me like a tornado.

Until Cromwell cleared his throat.

I flinched, snapped back to reality, and dragged my hand from his before taking a seat.

"Let's just start by clearing the air." Cromwell turned to Phantom. "We don't hold you personally responsible for the attack in Crown City. But we want to make sure nothing like that happens again."

"I can't promise that," Phantom answered, still staring at me.

"And why not?" Cromwell snapped.

The silence turned chilling as Phantom finally shifted his gaze from mine to the ones of the area heads of the FBI. They didn't understand who they were dealing with. That was obvious. They had no idea who and *what* Phantom was.

To men like these, Immortals were a blight on our

existence…an *inconvenience* no one wanted to acknowledge, let alone deal with. They were outcasts, unwanted and unwelcome. That feeling resounded inside me. I felt a connection to him in this moment, one so blinding I couldn't look away.

Pain rose inside me, bitter and cruel, twisting a knife in my heart. My own father disowned me last night. He hated me, threatened me…all because someone like Phantom showed up on his doorstep. All because Phantom cared.

And he did care, one look in his eyes was all I needed to realize the truth.

"Because we're beasts," Phantom answered, his tone deepening. "And if you thought that night was bad, just imagine what it'd be like if we weren't here to defend your precious city."

Carnage.

"What did you say?" Harlan jerked his gaze to me.

I swallowed, not realizing I spoke out loud. "It'd be carnage. This is his territory." I muttered not strong enough to meet the Alpha's gaze. But his focus bored into me, clinging to every word I said. My heart clenched as forced my head upwards, finding his connection. *"We are his territory."*

Not *we,* his eyes raged. *You. You are my territory.*

A flash cut through my head…a memory.

In his bed. The sheets tangled around my feet, his head lifting from between my legs. "I licked it, so it's mine."

The memory was brutal. I grasped the armrests, my nails digging into the stitching as a wave of desire hit me. Merciless. That's how Phantom looked as he glanced at me once more.

Merciless.

Unforgiving. ·

"It's just sex." His growl bloomed in my head and with it came the memory as he loomed over me, naked and raw, his cock pushing into me, making me whimper.

That sound carried, dragged up from the past to slip from my lips as I sat in the boardroom.

"Special Agent, are you okay?" Cromwell asked, concern furrowing his brow.

I dug my nails in harder as that delicious heat rolled through me. The memory of his thrusts as relentless as his damn gaze. I clamped my thighs together, fighting the heat that bloomed in my core, and whispered, "Fine...*sir.*"

"The report, Chase," Harlan growled.

I tried to focus, tried to see the damn files in front of me...until.

"Look down, Carina." His voice surrounded me in stereo. *"Watch while I fuck you, and when I finish fucking you, then you'll know who you belong to. You'll know whose pack is yours. Pro tip. It's not the one with the shiny badges and the goddamn mortal rules. You belong to us. You are owned by us."*

I cried out as I reached for the file. The damn thing slipped, casting pages of the report from inside the cardboard sheath to flutter from the table and fall to the floor.

"Goddamn it!" Harlan barked, and shoved up from his chair.

He hurried to help me, bending down while my hands shook and my mind blurred.

My ass clenched with the memory of his thumb pressing against that tight muscle.

I tried to hold my thighs together, but it was useless. I was slick and hot. My body pulsing and aching, desperate for him...

I lifted my gaze as I straightened, the neat pile of reports now a crinkled mess in my fist. That smug bastard just watched me from across the table with depraved hunger in his eyes.

He knew what was happening to me.

He knew it all.

Because he was doing this to me.

Flooding my mind with memories.

That wretched hunger rose inside me like the beast it was. I didn't have to look down to feel that pulse in my chest. That malevolent desire rippled through me. That depravity that only wanted one man…*the Alpha sitting in front of me.*

His nostrils flared. That glint in his eyes was now dangerous. I shoved upwards, casting what was left of my report across the table.

"What the fuck is wrong with you?" Harlan snarled.

Phantom wrenched his gaze Harlan's way. Rage curled his lips. The threatening stare was all kind so possessive. I clenched my jaw as desperation roared to the surface. One more word from Harland and he'd find out just how brutal Phantom was.

"I…" I whimpered as Phantom crossed his hand in front of his body. "I'm sorry…I think I forgot something."

My knees trembled as that hunger licked deep between my thighs. An orgasm barreled toward me. The onslaught unstoppable. I staggered to the door, wrenched it open, and ran as fast as I could…

21

PHANTOM

She ran like a scalded cat, yanking the handle of the door so hard she almost tore the damn thing off its hinges. I straightened in the seat as the thunder of her steps resounded, tearing along the hallway as she ran from me. But she wouldn't run far...*I'd make sure of it.*

And my beast growled in hunger.

"Where the fuck do you think you're going?" Harlan snapped, jerking his gaze to mine.

I rose, looming over the pissant that spoke to her like she was *nothing,* and felt the savage part of my nature rise. I closed the distance, watching the pathetic excuse of a male cower, his spine bowing backwards as he leaned back against his chair. "To remind her exactly what she forgot," I snarled.

"Hold on a second," Cromwell spluttered, but I was already striding through the open door, ready for this hunt to be done.

Orders were barked behind me, but I was no longer listening...*and I no longer cared.*

I wasn't here for them. I'd come for one reason, and one reason alone.

Her.

She was mine.

The stairwell door just out of view gave a *boom* as it closed, and the sound carried. I breathed in the delicious scent of her excitement as it lingered. She was close to release, so damn close I could almost taste it.

I wanted to taste it more than I wanted anything else.

One quick scan and I found the stairwell door. I yanked the handle and stepped through. The sound of panicked steps echoed from down below, boots hitting hard as she took the stairs two and three at a time. I lengthened my stride, pacing myself. I'd hunted her this long.

Down…*down…down…*

Until the *slam* of the door ripped through the narrow space.

A smile twitched at the corner of my lips as I drew in the musky scent of her desire. Soft and delicious, the tang filled my nose and rolled down the back of my throat.

My beast panted, desperate to run…desperate for her.

I yanked open the door marked 2BL. We'd gone down three flights. 2BL. Second basement level. I smiled as I stepped out into the faded yellow light and winced as the choking scent of dust and stale air filled the space.

Hinges gave a howl further along the empty hallway. I passed open doors to rooms stacked high with furniture and old servers, then kept going. Her heart was thundering, filling my ears with the delicious sound as I strode along the hallway and slowed outside the door to the ladies' bathroom.

It was quiet down here…*empty.*

No one to interrupt us.

I pushed the door inwards and was slammed with her terrifying carnal need as she came into view. "I can almost taste your release, Special Agent."

She whimpered, head down, gripping the edge of the basin until her knuckles were white.

Fuck me, I wanted her.

"No," she moaned.

"No?" I strode closer.

She lifted her head, her gaze meeting mine in the mirror.

"You're prepared to stay here?" I asked. "Let those assholes upstairs treat you like that? You deserve better." I caught the flinch in her eye, a nerve exposed. The sickly scent of her pain washed over me, hitting me like a sledgehammer in the center of my chest. "You deserve to be listened to, cared for...honored."

"You don't know a damn thing about me," she warned.

Rage lashed the air, cutting and cruel. She was cruel in that moment, all fangs and claws, hackles raised. Her beast was backed against the wall...and there was only one way out. But she wasn't ready to give in yet. Oh no, my little fighter would howl and rage before she yielded. Clarity and change had a way of bringing out the beast in all of us.

Hers was here, lifting her gaze, her eyes wild and raw meeting mine in the mirror.

I stepped behind her, watching as I splayed my hand against her collarbone before sliding it up her throat, until I cupped her jaw, forcing her to meet my gaze in the mirror. "You don't belong with them."

"You think I belong with you?" Her fists curled as she turned. "Think I'm gonna give into you because we fucked, *Wolf?*" She closed her eyes, her words were cutting. "You did this to me. You turn up at my work...you turn up in my *goddamn life.* I was fine before you showed up. I was..."

"Lonely. Empty. Adrift."

Her fist lashed out, slamming against my chest. "I had *purpose!*"

I didn't lift my hand, just let her unravel in front of me. *Use me,* I pleaded. *Let me take your pain. Let me take everything.* "You've always had purpose, Carina. But not here, not where they don't see how incredible you are. Not here where they ridicule you, push you down, hold you back. You are caged here. You're shackled."

Her lips curled. "Fuck you.," she growled, her tone gravelly and raw. "Fuck you for making me feel this."

Her breath caught and that sickeningly sweet scent of heart pain washed over me. She was hurting today, a different kind of hurting. I lowered my head to the base of her neck, kissing the thready throb of her vein. Her heart was pounding, pressing against my tongue as I licked her neck.

A moan echoed from her chest as she sank against me. "You don't have to fight anymore," I murmured and kissed, working my way slowly up until I forced her head to turn and her lips to meet mine. "Let me fight for you. Let me protect you, let me stand at your side. Together, we could be unstoppable. Together, we'd be a force."

She trembled with the words…for a second at least, until I kissed her *hard*.

She fought me, her mouth hard and unmoving, her body rigid even as that heat rose inside her, delicious and decadent. She gave it her all, even as her body betrayed her, softening to me, her breasts rising to mash against my chest as she moaned.

My grip was unforgiving, her mouth was mine to claim. That hunger burned inside her, seething and snarling, savage in its own right. It wanted sex…and it didn't care who gave it. But my bite mark on her shoulder claimed her. No Wolf would dare touch her…not while I lived.

Carina

His hold was cruel, ferocious, but his lips, *dear god, his lips.*

My mouth felt swollen and bruised as he broke away to stare

into my eyes. "They don't deserve you, Carina. *We* do. The pack wants you. I think you want us, too."

Agony let out a howl from the vast pit inside me.

No...I can't do this. I can't betray everything I was.

"Let us show you." He took a step, pushing me against the cold tiles of the bathroom wall, his massive body a cage around me. "Let us teach you all the ways we want you right now."

He lowered his head and nuzzled the part of my neck that made me whimper and shake. "I don't need you to take care of me," I protested, forcing the words. "I'm not weak."

"Never," he answered. "But you *are* alone." He lifted his arm to brace against the cool wall. "I can feel your loneliness, like a cage around your heart. Steel bars trapping you in, protecting yourself from pain. You don't need that, not where we're concerned."

He lowered his hand from my jaw, the back of his bare knuckles trailing down my neck to the open neckline of my shirt. "Let me show you how it could be," he murmured, "with us."

He worked the buttons of my shirt with barely a movement, fingers sliding down lower and *lower*...until he opened my shirt, the bottom buttons still trapped by the waistband of my pants. I closed my eyes as his lips met my collarbone. He sank, his hands moving to my waist before he lifted me and turned.

My ass hit the sink, the ceramic cold and hard against my thigh. But I didn't care, not when he dragged the straps of my bra down my shoulders and not when he pushed against me, lowering his head until he found the peak of my breast.

The warmth of his mouth closed around my nipple. I shuddered and lifted my hand to the back of his neck. He lifted his gaze, his hand cupping my breast to his lips. But he pierced me with that gaze...with that ravenous, predatory gaze.

I knew what he wanted.

Flesh.

Blood.

The beast inside my heart.

He wanted it all…every terrifying and damaged part of me.

"Let me in, Carina," he murmured, and rose to claim my lips before whispering against my mouth. "Let us prove how much we want you. I won't leave without you. I can't…not again."

My breath caught as the silver shone brighter in his eyes. Something moved there. Something deeper than his soul. This was more than sex, more than just *fucking*. This was real. Jesus…*this was really real*. I cupped his cheek as his hands went to my belt. There was no denying this…not anymore. We'd been here too many times to deny whatever this was.

Call it fate.

Call it desperation.

My world cracked as that power rippled through my chest and that heat followed.

The green glow flared and faded against his body. My thighs widened, my core aching, desperate to feel him slide all the way deep inside. I lost myself with him. I lost everything and became someone else, someone who threw her head back and howled.

He saw me. Saw me more clearly than anyone had ever seen me before.

Those feral eyes shone with his beast.

I felt myself slipping, unable to cling to the edge anymore. Now I fell, tumbling into that bottomless chasm. He was there, his touch drawing my focus. His desire all I could feel, until it claimed me. That bite mark on my shoulder ached, throbbing with both need and pain.

I didn't give a fuck, not anymore. I slipped my curled finger under the point of his chin, pulling him closer with the lightest of pressure. He was more than eager to please, kissing me until I pushed backwards. I touched him, yanking his shirt from his pants. His growl of desire spilled into my mouth and plunged down my throat. I'd never felt anything so bestial and wild. So consuming…and he *was* consuming…*all consuming.*

"Yes," I whispered.

He froze, his eyes widening. "What did you say?"

My stomach muscles trembled with the balancing as I uncinched his belt. "I said yes."

I wanted to feel joy or elation, but instead I felt relief…the feeling so powerful it was like my soul sighed. "I need time with the others first. I can't just…be like that."

He swallowed hard, the silver in his gaze glinting brighter as he smiled. "Take all the time you need." He kissed me, and the curl of his lips felt different against mine as he smiled.

"But I can't leave my job, Phantom. I can't just pack up and walk away from my entire life."

Ruth Costello tore through my mind. Her face was the last thing I needed to see in this moment, but there she was all in her bitchy fucking glory. She brought out the worst in me, and the best. Whatever happened between me and the Wolves, I wouldn't give up bringing her to justice.

He gripped my hips and pulled me forward, sliding me from the edge of the vanity until my feet hit the floor. One flick of his fingers and the button of my pants opened. His hand slipped down my body, sliding under the elastic of my panties.

He was down my pants in an instant, forcing my thighs wider as his finger slipped inside. I was wet, so fucking wet. My nails dug into his massive shoulders, and I clung to him as my orgasm roared to the surface once more.

He lowered his head and growled into my ear. "Let us take care of you." His finger slipped in and out until that ache burned. "I promise you on my fucking life we'll protect you."

I drove my hips forward, pushing his fingers deeper, and moaned. I lifted my gaze to his, tightening my hold, staring into his eyes. I hadn't seen him before, not the real him. I'd seen a beast, a *Wolf.* I'd seen the danger and the savagery. But right here…right now, he was so much more.

I splayed my fingers, cupping the back of his neck, and pressed against him. "No more fucking," I whispered. "Not anymore."

I moved my hand to the open belt of his pants and lowered the zipper. His finger slipped from me, leaving an ache behind until he turned me, shoving my pants low. My ass was bare, exposed, as I lowered my chest to the sink. He pushed his pants down, and that thick, hard cock slid down the crack of my ass to find the place I needed him.

With a brutal growl, he thrust deep, and my orgasm blinded me. His thick, callused fingers slid under my shirt and along my back. His other arm wrapped across my hips like a steel bar.

"Look at me," he commanded. I was helpless to resist, lifting my gaze to his as he bucked his hips. "Now come."

Lightning tore through my core, shuddering and burning. I clawed the sink, holding his stare in the mirror as my body tightened and clenched. The carnal onslaught was punishing as he smiled, sliding his hands to my hips and thrust deep. "No more fucking, Carina," he growled. "It's all love…all desire. All hunger…for you." He roared, gripping my hips in his vise-like grip, and stilled.

I pushed back against him, forcing him deeper as he released.

I wanted this…god, I wanted this.

I wanted him.

Even more than I wanted revenge.

I let him see that, dropping my guard, as his grip eased and he slid his hand over the curve of my ass. He wouldn't ask me to give it up, though. I knew that now. He'd never force me to change, never force me to do anything I didn't want to do.

He was patient.

A Wolf waiting.

22

An ache bloomed as he slid from my body. The panicked flutterings in my heart followed...turning into rumblings of thunder as I watched him in the mirror.

Past and present collided. I was back with him in his shower on that first night, my hands splayed against the cold tile wall as the water beat down on my body. He washed me, cared for me...made love to me.

It's just fucking, my own words resounded.

Just fucking? I could still hear the distaste in his voice as he answered. *I'm offering myself here.* The memory of that night was blinding. *You can use me. It's just sex, isn't that what you said?*

I *had* used him. I'd let him ride me, let him take me over and over again. He had, but never once did he make me feel anything other than safe with him. *And every time after that...even now.*

Was it ever just fucking to him? Was it ever just a physical thing, no emotion...no feelings involved?

No...I didn't think it was.

Jesus. I reached out and grabbed the edge of the vanity.

Unseelie spell or not, this was beyond need now, beyond

hunger, beyond the physical. I closed my eyes for a heartbeat as resignation rose. This was love, the faint beginnings of it, at least.

That scared the hell out of me.

"You okay?" he asked.

I opened my eyes, meeting his in the mirror. Confusion furrowed his forehead as he bent and grabbed his pants with one hand and helped me with my panties with the other. Heat rose in my face as I swallowed and nodded. Could he see what was rising inside me? See how damn panicked I was?

"You'll stay with us?" He looked into my eyes as I turned.

"Tonight," I agreed as I yanked my pants up and zipped them. "After I finish here. If I still have a job that is."

"Fuck them if they don't value you."

The ghost of a smile danced across my lips. I wanted more time for us...I wanted to be bold enough to ask what this was. He dragged the back of a curled finger down the top of my breast before he slid it under the strap of my bra and righted my clothing.

He was more considerate with me, more in tune somehow. Touching, covering, more attentive than I'd ever had before. That panicked beat in my chest turned thready and out of control.

"Tell me what you need," he commanded as I buttoned my shirt and tucked it in. "You want me to sit in that boardroom with those fuckers? You want me to sugarcoat how fucking feeble their hold is over this city? You want me to play to their damn egos and let them think they're the ones who keep these streets safe? Because you and I know it's not them who defends this territory from outsiders. It's us."

He was right. I knew he was right. I'd seen it with my own eyes. There were always going to be attacks from other Immortals and there was always going to be death. "No," I sighed. "It'd do no good. They won't listen, not even when it slaps them in the face. Let me talk to Harlan. Let me try to get him to listen to me. We don't need damn reports about what's already happened, we need a plan for the next time it does."

"And there will be a next time." He reached up and curled my hair behind my ear, the movement so fucking sweet. "There will *always* be a next time."

Was that why he was so desperate for me to stay? "Is there something you're not telling me?"

He straightened, letting his hand fall. "No. Not yet."

And just like that, the magic of the moment faded and the real world pressed in. "What happened?"

I could see him fighting to be truthful, to not hide the danger in his world from me. "There was an attack last night at Wild."

"The club this side of the river?"

He gave a nod. "The young Wolf I had managing the place was mauled."

My gut clenched as the memory of that night in the warehouse returned. "Is he dead?"

"No. He's alive...barely." He winced as his voice deepened. "But he's lost the ability to speak."

Jesus. I dropped my hands to the edge of the vanity behind me and leaned backwards. "Do you know who did it?"

One shake of his head, and fear crowded in. "That's the reason you want me with you."

"One of them, yes."

I held his gaze and the truth shone bright in his eyes as he murmured, "Tell me what I have to do to keep you safe and I'll do it."

It was my turn to reach for him. I cupped his cheek, feeling the hard, chiseled edge of his jaw move against my palm as he turned his head and kissed my palm. "I'll be there," I answered. "I'll come tonight, okay?"

"Let me go and speak to those stuffy assholes upstairs," he suggested. "I'll make sure they get the full fucking report."

Danger sparkled in his eyes as he cupped my hand against his face, then stepped away.

"Don't ruin this for me, Phantom," I growled, my hand falling, and was rewarded by a cocky grin.

"Trust me," he ordered, and turned.

I groaned, knowing exactly what that glint in his eyes meant. His chuckle echoed through the bathroom until the door swung shut behind him...and I was left alone.

I turned slowly, meeting my own gaze. What the fuck just happened? The panicked beating of my heart answered for me. I gave in...*no, not gave.* More like dragged kicking and screaming. Enticed by more than the lustful desire of his body, I wanted to be with him...with all of them. *Friends at first,* I cautioned myself, and then I guess we'd figure it out.

Phantom.

Church.

Arran and Vitold.

Five of us all living under the one roof. I sighed. Things were about to get interesting...interesting indeed. I leaned forward, ran the tap, and splashed water on my face before turning to use the toilet. A few minutes later and I was rinsing my hands and flicking water from my fingers as I strode to the door.

Lower basement? What an idiot. Who ran to the one level that had no way out to escape their own desire? I did, that's who. My boots resounded along the hall as I headed for the elevators, until something made the hair on the back of my neck rise.

I slowed my steps as the cold touch of instinct raged, turning to glance over my shoulder. The hallway was empty, only dust and forgotten furniture was down here. I kept going, still feeling that caress of danger as I passed the closed doors, hurrying to the elevator and pressing the button.

That sinister feeling stayed with me, making my heart pound inside my chest, until the elevator gave a *ding* and the doors opened. I all but lunged inside and stabbed the button for the first floor, but my mind drifted to the closed doors I'd just passed. I was almost sure they'd been open when I'd raced for the bathroom. *Almost sure.*

The elevator doors closed, ending that trembling feeling, and it carried me the three flights up to the executive offices on the first floor. I winced at the low snarl of anger as Phantom's voice hit me like a blow.

"My fault. She wasn't prepared. You want promises? They're the same as wishing, pull your head out of your ass and look at what's really happening. You need us. And you need her."

"Promise me, huh?" I muttered, suddenly remembering the bloodstain report from my emails. *"Shit!"* I jerked my gaze to the receptionist in the Deputy Assistant's office, and rushed for the door.

It opened with a squeal, making the pretty brunette lift her head from behind the desk. I searched her face as she gave me a warm smile. "You okay, Special Agent? The meeting is in the boardroom."

"Yeah, I umm…forgot a report that's attached to my emails. Do you think I can borrow your computer for just two seconds?"

"Sure," she answered with another smile, then reached over, logged out of the FBI's mainframe, and rose from her chair.

It took me three seconds to log in, but by the time I pressed print, Phantom was already striding past the glass wall of the executive offices. He turned his head and held my stare. He was pissed…really pissed. That cold glare of a predator raged, until he gave me a wink and left.

The resounding thud of his boots still echoed behind him as I pushed open the door again, swallowed hard, and stepped back into the boardroom. Harlan and Cromwell were silent, sitting there staring at the table as I closed the door behind me.

Cromwell looked up as I entered. He looked at me, confused for a moment, then spoke, "Yes, Chase?"

Harlan followed, glancing at the report in my hand. "Just leave it on the table and go, Chase."

Go...as in clean out your locker.

My pulse was pounding as I came closer. "Sir, I need you to look at something." I tried to keep the tremor from my voice, even as my face grew hot.

I'd known something was strange when I'd glanced at the damn thing. I knew the blood typing from the scene were all wrong. The Vampires and Werewolves were grouped in one... and the mortals in another. I slid the report onto the table in front of them, letting them see the highlighted red marker beside the one blood type they couldn't match. Ruth Costello.

Her blood had all the markings of a Vampire but one. "Fucking figures." I glared at the report. "Always knew you were a cold, undead bitch."

"You want to know the reason for the attack on our city? You want someone to blame, I get that." I pushed my luck as that thunder in my head became defeating. "You have that someone right here, the one blood type they couldn't narrow. The one who you refuse to accept is responsible for all of this. Not mortal...but not Immortal either, a hybrid. A *disease.* Ruth Costello."

They stared at the report with its markers and numbers... stopped at the words *UNKNOWN TYPE,* and lifted their gazes to me. I got it now, I truly got it. They wanted someone to blame, someone they could splash all over the media and announce as the bad guy. They wanted someone they could direct their focus to hunting...and I was giving them that focus...right here.

"Leave the report," Harlan directed.

What? I straightened slowly. "But, sir—"

"I said, *leave the damn report, Chase,*" Harlan snapped, and jerked his glare to me.

His eyes shimmered, cold and glassy as they held mine. I was giving him the solution right here, a way he could save face from the mortals in the city, as well as Cromwell. I shifted my gaze to my boss's boss, and flinched. He had the same look... that same, *my mind is already made up* look.

I swallowed hard and took a step backwards. "Yes, sir." Anger rose like a wave inside me, white hot and alive. "You do know this is going to happen again if we don't do something." I was out of line here...and I didn't care. "The Wolf is right, *they* protect us. They are the packs that run the city. But Ruth Costello isn't one of *them*...nor is she one of *us*. She's dangerous."

"That will be all, Chase," Harlan answered without meeting my gaze.

Something was happening here. Something unseen, something dangerous. The dark, spiced scent of the Alpha still lingered in the air, as did his words in my head. *You need us. And you need her.*

But they weren't acting like they did.

No, they weren't acting that way at all.

I left the boardroom and made my way to my desk. Phones rang and the constant clatter of keyboards turned into a background drone. I scanned the space as I stepped in, my gaze finding Murphy's empty desk before I exhaled with relief as I yanked out my chair and sat down to open the report still on my screen.

That icy feeling breathed against the back of my neck. I lifted my gaze to the stares of everyone else in the damn room. *"What?"* I barked. *"What's so fucking interesting?"*

Montey just turned red and looked away, but the rest of them stared until I couldn't fucking stand the attention any longer. I shoved up from the desk, hit the button on my desktop, and logged out. Fuck them...fuck them all.

They didn't want my damn report. They didn't want any

fucking report, not even the one marked in red from the lab. They weren't interested in anything anyone had to say.

Their minds were already made up.

Those words filled me as I made my way to the locker room. Fucking assholes. I punched through the swinging door and heard the toilet flush further along the cubicles, so I turned and headed for my locker instead. They wanted the damn report and I gave them the damn report. They wanted Murphy on my fucking case and I dealt with that too.

I yanked open my locker door and tried to quell the fire in my belly. There was an envelope sitting on top of my clothes from this morning. Yellow, and it looked new. I glanced over my shoulder as one of the agents from another department walked out with her gaze down.

Hinges squealed as the door was opened and closed once more, leaving me to turn back to that envelope. I reached up and lifted it free. The top was unsealed and open, suspicious as hell from the start. I looked inside before reaching in. You couldn't trust anything nowadays, there could've been any kind of drug or virulent disease just waiting for that one idiot to touch, tilt, or tamper. I didn't want to be that idiot.

But there was nothing inside but a 6x9 grainy black and white image, a photograph printed from a computer. I pulled it out, and taped to the front was a message. *If you want more information meet me at 1254 Bledsoe Way 7pm and come alone.*

More information?

I peeled off the note and stared at the photo. It was a man, tied to a chair, with another face-down on the floor in front of him. The pool of blood under the downed man's head gleamed black in the picture. It wasn't until I stared at the dying man's face turned toward the camera that I understood. *I'd know that face anywhere.* "Lenny," I hissed.

I jerked my focus to the man in the chair, the one with tape across his mouth and his hands bound to the armrests. *Jesus Christ, that was Dad...that was...my dad.*

Tied.

Gagged.

There was no way he could've shot his partner. The more I stared at the picture, the more I understood. That wasn't just a cop killing, *this was a set-up.*

Want more information meet me at 1254 BledsoeWay 7pm and come alone. Whose handwriting was that? It seemed too neat to be a guy's, too clear. I glanced around at the empty bathroom, then turned back to my locker. Someone with access. It had to be another agent, a female.

My gut clenched and my heart raced. My damn hand shook, rattling the paper I held. I stuffed the sheet back into the envelope as my phone gave a beep.

Murphy

Where the fuck are you? No excuses, Chase. Get your ass to the warehouse and work the damn scene.

Work the scene. Panic mingled with desperation. Work the damn scene. I shoved the envelope into my open bag and hauled it from my locker. I didn't plan on coming back to the office, not today at least. My steps mirrored the frantic beating of my heart as I raced for the elevator once more.

Someone out there had information about my father.

I was betting it was all I needed to go after Ruth Costello once and for all.

23

PHANTOM

The FBI was going to be a problem. *A big fucking problem.* I could feel it. My lips curled as I climbed into the Camaro and drove out of the parking lot, slipped into the traffic, and headed for Wild. I rolled my neck and rubbed my shoulder. The sting was still there, biting and sharp, a reminder of how it had been with Carina. Fuck me, I wanted more.

My damn heart clenched as I turned the wheel. She was coming to the club tonight, I'd make damn sure of that. That heavy ache inside my chest intensified. She'd stay...she *had* to stay with us. There, we could protect her. There, we'd make sure she was safe.

I tightened my grip on the wheel and worked the gears, making my way from one busy side of the city to the other. She filled my thoughts as I drove. The ache from her fists slamming against my chest was a reminder of who I was dealing with. She was all animal, all white-hot fire and tenacious as fuck.

Mine, the beast growled inside my head. "Ours," I corrected. *The pack's,* he finished.

"The pack's," I agreed. Church, Arran, and Vitold. It all played out in my mind.

The four of us.

Like it'd been before.

My damn cock twitched at the memory. I'd watched her with them, watched them kiss her, caress her, welcome her. We had to be careful, not come on too strong. I didn't want to scare her away.

But I had a feeling Carina didn't scare…not easily anyway.

I hit the turning signal and pulled into the parking lot beside Wild. That savagery seethed inside me, anger and rage, with some matching desperation. I'd kept a lid on the shit, forcing myself to focus first on Wry surviving, and then Carina.

But now…now it was time.

I climbed out of the car and closed the door behind me. One car remained in the otherwise empty parking lot. It was too early. The girls would be home sleeping, the clients would be clawing through another fucking day, nursing a hangover and a lighter wallet. And then we'd do it all again. *Every fucking night.*

I scanned the dirt lot and inhaled. The stench of blood still stained the air, mingling with the choking stench of fear. There was a darker patch of dirt toward the edge of the lot. The ground was no longer splashed with red, now it was brown, the blood had soaked into the earth.

Flashbacks filled my head, and terror rose.

Screams followed, piecing screams.

And with it came the panic. I jerked my gaze from the bloodstained ground and headed for the back door of the club. My hands trembled as sweat broke out on my scalp. This was more than just an attack, this had been premeditated, they'd waited until the Breeds were out of the way.

I felt exposed.

I felt *vulnerable.*

And that was never a good thing.

The place was quiet as I strode in, leaving the door to slam shut behind me. Perfume and sex lingered in the air. I winced as

I drew in the fetid taste of the scents. The taste was nothing like Carina, nothing like that taste of darkness on her skin… darkness that now was part of her body, and part of her.

I hadn't had the heart to tell her this was how it was going to be for her.

To hunger. To be…*dangerous.*

The fever in her was over, but still that Unseelie sickness remained. It was part of her now, part of who she was. Vitold was right, she was vulnerable…but then, so was everyone else around her. She needed the pack…*she needed* me.

I made my way past the darkened back rooms, each with its own dancer's pole, and strode along the hallway, turning at the end to the door marked *Private.* One shove of the handle and I entered another hall. The girls' changing rooms were further back, but it was the manager's office I wanted, the one which held the CCTV camera. Wry was alive. I had to remind myself of that as I pushed through the door and flicked on the light. That was all that was important. The kid was alive. He'd just never fucking speak again for the rest of his fucking life.

My lips curled in a snarl as I yanked out the chair and sat in front of the monitor. I grabbed the mouse and waited for the computer to wake. A second is all it took before I was logging into the CCTV recorder and searching the date.

Black and white images flickered on the display. Cars filled the parking lot, one reversed fast and took off as another drove in. I fast forwarded the recording, running the minutes by, until the big black Hummer pulled up and the Breeds piled in. That damn Wolf, Path, said Wry hadn't turned up, so the attack must've happened after they left. Path would've smelled his blood otherwise. It was too much of a damn coincidence. The day they leave and my manager is attacked.

Can we trust them? Church's voice rang inside my head.

I didn't have an answer.

Something in the corner of the monitor made me stop. I pressed rewind, and went back to before I'd caught the frantic scuffle in the far corner of the screen, then I hit play. Wry's car came into view, the midnight blue European sports car taking it slow as it left the pavement behind and turned into the dirt parking lot.

I glanced at the time and then checked the call log on my phone. Fifteen minutes. That's all it'd been since the call from Path. Fifteen fucking minutes. I watched the young Wolf get out and close the door behind him, then he turned.

There was someone out of range of the camera, someone who made him turn. I caught the movement of his lips and the furrow of his brow. "Who the fuck is it?" I muttered, and leaned closer.

Wry left the car behind, stepping toward the edge of the screen, then stepped out of view, leaving his shadow behind. In an instant, there was a scuffle. His legs flailed into view and, as a growl rose in the back of my throat, I realized that was it. Blood splashed on the dirt...before the Wolf hit the ground.

He jerked and spluttered, lifting his hands to his torn-open throat, until hands reached for him and wrenched him from view. He was gone...just like that. Slashed, mauled, and then dragged from the place where he should've been safe.

"Fuck!" I roared as I clenched my fist and drove it into the monitor.

Sparks flew inside before they died, and bits of plastic went flying across the room to hit the wall behind me. But I was already rising, already punching the power button on the recorder and turning away.

He should've been safe.

He should've been watched.

They *all* should've been.

Can we trust them? Those same fucking words resounded

inside my head. Trust. Such a fickle fucking thing. There was no such thing as trust in the animal kingdom, it was survive or perish, and you aligned yourself with those who wanted to survive as much as you did.

It wasn't just the Vampires in danger now. It was us, too...

I checked the logs for the night before, left instructions for Hale, the assistant manager, to take care of next week's dancers, and left the office and shattered monitor behind. The sun was low overhead by the time I climbed into the Camaro again. The day was getting away from me.

The throaty growl of the engine usually exhilarated me, but not today. Today, my skin felt far too thin and strained. Today, my beast writhed close to the surface. Today, he wanted blood...

I drove over the bridge, my mind too occupied by the images on the camera to care about the flow of traffic. Instead, I gripped the wheel, my gaze fixed on the cars ahead. First it was Caedes and the Vampires...and now Finis was gone. I tensed my shoulders and tried to piece it all together. I needed a bead on the Ancient Alpha's location. I wanted the bastard right where I could keep track of him. But so far, I had nothing, no sightings and no information.

It all felt bad...*very fucking bad.*

I hit the turning signal and exited onto the off-ramp, heading past the Hunting Ground to the Fae's warehouse once more. Darkness moved in, choking out the sun as gray clouds filled the sky overhead.

A storm was coming, vicious and electrical, standing the hairs on my arms as it barreled down on us. The bitter stench of ozone was already in the air, slipping through the vents in the car to plunge down my throat.

I felt that danger...felt it deeper than I had in a long time. I waited for the gate to roll open before I eased the Camaro forward. Church's Hummer was gone, he'd be at the other clubs we had in the city, patrolling our grounds, beefing up security, and watching for anything out of place. I rolled the car through and parked outside the massive doors before I killed the engine and climbed out.

The wind picked up, howling through the abandoned buildings where the Fae played and hunted, and carried with it the stench of savage darkness. A shudder tore along my spine as I headed for the small side door.

The place was quiet. Too quiet.

I yanked open the door and stepped inside as the door to the offices upstairs opened and Ruin stepped out. In an instant, my Wolf let out a warning growl. He didn't like the Unseelie, and sure as hell didn't trust him.

"Wolf," The male snarled acknowledgement, and kept walking. But the air rippled around him, shuddering the bannister and shaking the huge walls of the warehouse. Word was he was a direct descendant of Banrion Medh, the infernal dark queen herself.

But that's all it was…just words.

The Unseelie refused to speak about his bloodline…*to anyone.*

"Unseelie," I returned as the male kept walking, the sound of his boots ringing out as he left. I climbed the stairs, the metal humming under my hand like a damn tuning fork.

I'd never felt the air like this, never so *volatile.* What the fuck was going on here? I opened the door at the top of the stairs and stepped inside and, as always, that shadowed power slipped over my skin, tasting me…allowing me to enter. I'd hate to be unwelcome here. I had a feeling this place would be very different to an outsider.

"Phantom." Shrike headed toward me. "You came for the Wolf?"

"How is he?"

The Fae Master winced. "Alive."

"Still no…"

A shake of his head was all I needed. Somewhere here there was a young male who could hear every damn word I said…and feel every emotion. I steeled my spine. "Can he come home?"

"He doesn't want to," Shrike said. "Physically he's weak, and needs rest, food, and comfort. But he doesn't need *us*, not anymore."

"Then why doesn't he want to leave?" I turned my gaze to the darkness and inhaled the foul taste of someone's broken soul, a scent I'd smelled before…and that shit still stayed with me.

"You'd better ask him that yourself," Shrike said, jerking his head toward the hallway.

He was my Wolf…one of my pack, and that call as Alpha rose inside me as I left the Unseelie behind and made my way along the hallway. I didn't need a light to illuminate my way, I tracked him down on instinct alone to an open door toward the end of the hallway.

The room was empty…at first glance. The small cot along the wall was freshly made but unoccupied. I winced at the sight, my gaze finding the shadow clinging to the corner of the room. A shadow that moved.

I stepped inside the dim room. This place was always in darkness, no matter how bright the sun was outside. But today, threatening clouds rumbled and snarled overhead, threatening to unleash fury, making it even more oppressive.

"Wry," I tried his name. "It's me, Phantom."

The murky darkness shifted, silver eyes glinting as the young male watched me.

"I'm not going to hurt you." I stopped in the center of the room, hands out, nonthreatening.

Still, he made no move toward me, just clung to the shadows like that was where he belonged. Fuck.

"I saw the security footage." I carefully kept my tone neutral. Strength was what he needed from me now, not my rage. "I'm going to hunt that bastard down. I won't rest, not until I find him."

Still, he didn't move. He barely blinked, just watched me.

"Tell me what you need. Tell me how I can help you get past this."

The shadow flinched before it slowly rose. He came toward me, stepping out of the gloom and into the dim light. Those unflinching eyes were cold and lifeless as they met mine. Instinct made me lower my gaze to his throat, finding the raised red claw marks that savaged his throat. He punched his chest, the dull feeble sound hollow as his lips moved soundlessly.

He was just a kid…a fucking kid, barely eighteen. He hadn't yet started to fill out, hadn't yet begun his transformation. But this would change him. This would *harden him.*

For a second I couldn't speak either. All I could do was stare and bear witness to his agony. "I understand," I sympathized.

The shake of his head was violent as his lips peeled back, exposing thick fangs that lengthened with rage. He didn't need a voice in this moment. He needed the pack.

I stepped closer and wrapped my arms around him as he shuddered and quaked. "I will find him," I promised.

His fists smacked my arms, the blows nothing compared to his pain.

Smack!

Smack!

I tightened my hold. "I will find him."

I held him until his blows became weak. I held him until he stilled and that empty stare found me again before he drew away, turned, and made his way back to that darkened corner of the room once more.

We failed him, my beast moaned, lowering his savage gaze. *We. Failed. Him.*

I turned from the kid, leaving him in the shadows, and strode from the room. Pain and anguish filled me until I could barely breathe. I stalked from the hallway and through the offices and was racing down the stairs before I knew it.

Thunder roared overhead, the sound deafening inside the building.

Not an Alpha.

Failed him.

Failed your pack.

I yanked the door and charged outside as the first heavy drops smacked against the ground and, as the storm finally fell, I threw back my head and howled my rage. The air trembled and shuddered.

This was no unleashing of fury.

This was an Alpha's call.

The wild, bestial sound echoed from every Wolf in my pack. They responded, heartbeats pounding, echoing like thunder in my head, hunters instantly aware of the hunt. We had a predator in our midst, a vile, unwelcome invader. One I wanted on his knees in front of me...one I wanted dead. In the wake of that consuming call came a flare of pain, one so piercing I caught my breath.

Agony ripped through my chest, tearing me from the connection with my pack. The stabbing sensation dulled, blending with the deep, resounding throb of my heart. My jaw ached and my fangs throbbed, desperate to lengthen. My beast was here, pushing against me, searching for that hunger in my veins and the desperation in my body.

She was there. Blindingly real. The scent of her consuming me.

My mark on her burned brighter than any howling response from my pack. I didn't just remember her...*I felt her.* Pain. Confusion. *Love.*

Love? I sucked in hard breaths as my beast calmed. Panicked

love, the kind you backed away from, the kind that hunted you down like a predator. My beast's focus shifted to that feeling, ears pricked, lips unfurled from his teeth, his eyes bright and clear, glinting with urgency.

Mine, he insisted. *Mine...*

24

I spent the next six hours avoiding Murphy, hiding on the other side of the warehouse as the techs cataloged and took even more photos of bullet holes and blood splatter. A storm descended midafternoon. The thunder was savage, and lightning unmercifully illuminated the warehouse with blinding flashes of neon-white light. By the end of the day when the storm lessened, leaving only the rain behind, I was exhausted… and preoccupied.

My mind was on the envelope and the black and white picture of my father and Lenny the night he was shot. With the right kind of evidence, it'd be enough to reopen the case against my father and expose all their dirty secrets once and for all.

Secrets I knew they were all hiding. Then maybe I'd finally be able to rest.

"You going to stay here all day?"

My heart sped at the sound of his voice. I swallowed hard as my throat turned arid, and rose from the floor, tucking my evidence folder under my arm. In an instant flashbacks roared back to me. His hands crushing my arm, as he drove me against the stainless steel morgue table. I tried to fight the panic and forced the words. "No," I answered. "I'll clear the rest, if you want."

"Don't tell me you're actually offering to do *real work?*" He snarled, feigning surprise. "I'm shocked."

"It'd be better if you were dead," I answered.

The crime scene tech lifted his gaze. It was the same guy from the other day, the one whose handkerchief was still dirty in the bottom of my bag of washing. I looked away, waiting for Murphy to get the hint.

"You know, you can be a real bitch, Chase," the asshole muttered, then turned on his heel and left.

I kept my focus as his steps faded before his car started and pulled away. The night moved in, darkening the already brooding sky as I stretched the cramped muscles in the small of my back. My body still hummed from the encounter with Phantom. I felt hot and feverish, too hot. My muscles twitched, aching for his damn hands once more. But it wasn't just lust that gripped me. Something else rubbed me raw. I glanced over my shoulder and scanned the darkened corners. It was this place. This *fucking* place.

Terror still lingered in this place in flashes of my haunting memories of that night. My gaze drifted to the spot further inside the doorway, a spot I'd tried hard not to go near. In my mind, it was still drenched with blood and stained with terror.

You fight like a warrior.

The memory rose as that dark beast filled my mind. His haunting infernal eyes, that sickening curl of his lips as he'd fixed on me. I licked my lips, my fingers rising to my throat. I could still feel his grip around my neck, still feel the hunger of his desire. A dark hunger. *An Unseelie hunger.* Shadows shifted in the corners of the warehouse, rippling almost. And in the belly of that darkness came a sense of something else, something that watched me, something that *sensed me...*like a beast.

I swallowed hard and tore my gaze away. Nope. I wasn't

going there, wasn't letting this shit in my chest affect me any more than it already had. Because of it, my life had been turned upside down—*or maybe the right way up?*

The words came out of nowhere. I tried to shove them aside, and I tried not to think about him, tried not to get carried away by my nervousness about seeing him and the Wolves again. The techs were shedding their white coveralls. I kept myself busy and helped carry their equipment to the van before climbing into the Jeep.

I started the engine and glanced at the clock. It was still early, too early to head to the meet with whoever had left me the picture. My belly let out a rumble, then a full snarl. Food. The shit had slipped from my mind. I pulled out and made my way toward that side of the city.

BledsoeWay was on the rural side, open stretches of road and small farming lots. A place I hadn't been for a long time. What in the hell was all the way out there? *Because they don't want to be seen.*

Had to be an agent, female, I was guessing. Maybe she came into contact with old information working a current case and wanted to do the right thing? I prayed that was the case as I pulled into a small burger place that looked busy enough to know they served decent food but not so busy that I'd have to wait in line for a damn hour.

That *unnatural* feeling lingered as I climbed out of the Jeep and strode to the to-go window. I waited, watching those around me, and ordered a sandwich to go. Food had never been a priority for me, but this festering shit in my chest needed more than just sex.

Just sex? Phantom's voice lingered. *Just fucking, right?*

I strode to the Jeep and climbed back in with the sandwich and a drink. No, not just sex. Not anymore. I ate, watching people come and go from the busy restaurant, and watched the damn clock. Phantom and the others were waiting for me. But if I could just meet this agent, exchange information, and leave, then I'd have plenty of time. It wasn't like the damn strip club was closing anytime soon.

Wolves.

Strippers.

Sex.

Fuck me. I scrunched up my trash, started the Jeep, and pulled up alongside the trash before tossing the remnants of my dinner out. The truth was, they were starting to feel a little too familiar. I pulled out onto the street and made my way toward the outskirts of the city. The Russian, the gorgeous blond, and Arran…the bartender's cocky smile still made my heart flutter.

One on one was bad enough. I could almost deal with them protecting me at the damn morgue, almost handle them one on one when they cornered me in a dark, deserted crime scene. But all together? All four of them standing there, watching me like I was their last damn meal?

That shit made me sweat.

Headlights from the oncoming cars were nearly blinding, but the more I drove, the less there were, until I left the sparkling lights of the city behind. There was only darkness out here, only the quiet…only freedom. I reached into my pocket, grabbed my phone, and pulled up the maps.

BledsoeWay was off an unsealed road up ahead. I winced, dragged my gaze from the screen to the safety of the city lights fading in the rear-view mirror, and hit the turning signal. I wanted answers, and this was my only real opportunity. Whoever it was wanted this quiet and away from prying eyes. So that meant they valued keeping their identity a secret… enough to force me out here.

Jutting rocks jolted the Jeep, and I was lucky it was this rather than my piece of shit sedan. I gripped the wheel, letting the compact four-wheel drive do its thing. Fuck, I loved this car. Trees blocked in the view from all sides of the road, leaving me to slow as a break in the road came up ahead. My headlights splashed against the street sign *BledsoeWay.*

I didn't even bother with signaling, just turned the wheel and followed the narrower trail down a deep gully before climbing back up again. The further I drove, the more this felt like a very bad idea, until I slowed and stopped the car at a small leaning mail box, *1254 BledsoeWay.*

I was here.

My pulse sped at the thought. I scanned the trees, catching lights in the distance. It looked like some kind of farm. A family farm, maybe? I bit my lip, glanced at the eerie red glow from the Jeep's brake lights in the rear-view mirror, and tried to think. It was almost seven…almost time to make the meet. Could I risk blowing this? "No," I answered myself. "Turn up and be a goddamn hero. You're trained for this, Chase."

I *was* trained for this, trained to follow my hunches, trained to take risks others wouldn't…or couldn't. I shoved the Jeep into gear and turned the wheel, found the driveway, and headed for the farmhouse through the trees.

The deeply rutted driveway made fighting the wheel a goddamn workout, but the closer I came to the farmhouse, the more I realized it wasn't a house I was looking at. Instead, it was a bank of stables. Stacked hay bales loomed a distance from the buildings. I tried to rack my brain for any female agent that had mentioned horses, but came up empty. The truth was, I didn't really talk to them, nothing personal anyway.

Shit. I hadn't realized what a cold-hearted bitch I truly was.

Need to be a bitch to catch a bitch, though.

That thought stuck, until I dislodged it with…*hunt someone long enough, you start to think like them…act like them…hell, you could almost sympathize with them.* "Fuck that" I chastised myself. "That will *never* happen."

I pulled the Jeep up under the only light blaring yellow against the darkness. There was a gap between the stables with the roof still covered, more hay stacked high on one side. I waited, the engine running, and scanned the area.

There was no car.

Why wasn't there another car?

Panic flared as I killed the engine and listened. Maybe they'd left already? I glanced into the rear-view mirror, then the side mirrors. Maybe they hadn't turned up yet? If they weren't here, it gave me a chance to comb the grounds, find any kind of information I could. I glanced at my side mirrors once more, then cracked open the door. My jacket was off, thrown across the passenger seat, and my entire goddamn life was in a duffel bag in the back seat.

I was, to all intents and purposes, homeless...*and I'd never felt so damn free.* I closed the door to the Jeep and hit the button on the remote to lock it before stopping at the front wheel, reaching underneath, and balancing the key on top of the tire.

The bite mark on my shoulder flared to life, the ache making me wince and rub it. Goddamn Wolf. I still felt his fangs sinking deep and leaving his mark behind. It was that mark that lingered, that mark that consumed me as I made my way to the open area in front of the stables. Something shifted. I jerked my gaze toward the sound until a low nicker slipped free.

Just a horse...just a damn horse.

My hand rose to the grip of my gun before I pulled it free. I stepped through the opening to the other side where the harsh yellow light didn't reach. In the distance was a house, small, low-set, dark. No life there that I could see.

I lifted my phone: *7:05.*

There were no cars around, no lights on except for at the damn stables. My belly sank like a goddamn stone. I'd been stood up. I lowered my gun and turned back to the gap in the stables as something came at me from the darkness. Something bestial…something with a terrifying green glow.

You fight like a warrior…

I jerked my gun upwards, taking aim. But there was nothing there, no blur of movement, *nothing.* My heart slammed against my ribs as I stumbled backwards, my gaze fixed on the trees in front of me.

"Should've listened to me, Carina." Murphy's voice came from behind me. "I tried to play nice."

The blow was a whistle, slamming into the back of my head with a dull *crack!* Blinding pain followed as my head snapped forward and I staggered to the side. My knees trembled, barely holding as the movement blurred again. The hard steel smacked the back of my knees, sending me crashing to the ground.

I hit the ground hard, my head bounced and stilled. A low sound ripped free.

"Should've *fucking* listened." He growled.

Agony boomed through my back as the blow came at my side. I screamed, howling with pain and rage and clawed the ground, shoving myself upwards as a blast tore through my mind.

Hard breaths blended with the pain. I stumbled, my knees weak and shaking as Murphy hunted me. "Now you've left me no goddamn choice."

"Fuck you," my words were whimper as I slowly lifted my gun, took a trembling aim at the shifting shadows…and pulled the trigger.

Crack!

Murphy was a blur as the bullet hit, his head down, rushing me. I tried to brace for the impact, tried to lift the gun before it was too late. A *crack* tore from my gun again, and this time it was followed with a roar of agony before I was hit and lifted.

Air buffeted my face until I hit the ground hard.

Carina? Phantom's growl cracked like thunder through my head as I tried to roll and shove to stand. Murphy was hit, blood blooming on his shoulder.

Carina! the Wolf raged as a moan tore from Murphy and he opened his eyes. *CARINA, RUN!*

25

CARINA, RUN!

Phantom's voice detonated like a blast in my head. I clung to that resounding boom, and it spurred me to move. That desperation, that *rage* rippled through me as I tried to draw in a breath, and the darkness blurred. My gun...*my gun.*

"Fucking bitch!" Murphy howled, and lifted a hand to his shoulder. His fingers came away bloody before those rage-filled eyes lifted to mine. "You fucking shot me."

A whimper tore free as I blinked, wrenched my gaze from him, and scanned the ground. The black blur was nestled near the hay. *There!*

I lifted my gaze to Murphy at the same time he caught my focus. Desperation punched through me as I drove my body forward and lunged. But he was already moving, already scrambling forward.

"No, you fucking don't!" he roared.

We collided and scrambled, shoving and clawing. Bits of hay scattered as I fought for my gun. Terror ripped free, and a shrill sound tore free, burning along my throat. I punched, driving my left fist into his face, and drove my boots into the ground, blocking him with my body.

Fight, Carina! Phantom howled. *We're coming! Hold on...we're coming!*

"Get the fuck off me!" Murphy howled, and shoved me forward, slamming me face-first into the ground, on top of the gun. Steel edges pressed against my breast. I prayed his finger wasn't on the trigger.

Fight...

Fight...

I lowered my head and opened my mouth. In that moment I was more beast than human. More fighter. More *Wolf.* I snapped my head forward and with everything I had, bit down, my teeth sinking deep into his arm.

He roared with agony, bucking and thrashing. His fist was a blur in the corner of my eye before it hit me, slamming into my cheek and tearing my hold free.

"Fucking cunt."

I lay there, dazed, my head pounding as he wrenched his hand out from under me...and with it my gun. Harsh breaths shook me, and his cruel fingers dug into my shoulder as he yanked me over until I lay on my back.

"I tried to be nice to you," he panted, and dragged his leg over my thighs, straddling my hips. "Tried to keep this fucking...*clean.*"

Agony throbbed in my cheek as stars danced in my vision. "Fuck you," I spat.

"Fuck me?" he snarled, and those cruel eyes rose to mine as he lifted my gun. "You don't like my kind, remember? You like those filthy beasts. You like to rut like a goddamn animal in the bathroom where you work."

I stilled and tried to think. Memories danced behind the brutal pulsing in my cheek. Memories of that feeling...that clench of my gut as I'd walked from the bathroom to the elevator. "You were there?"

"You and your fucking boyfriend were a little too busy to care," he gloated, and pressed the muzzle of my own gun against my chest, then looked down. "Was he good?" The muzzle scraped against my chest, opening my shirt to the swell of my breast. "Like that Wolf cock, do you?"

Panic filled me as that look of hunger raged in his eyes. I knew where this was going...and where it'd end. Naked. Bleeding. *Dead? Stop this...you can stop this,* the panicked sound of my own voice filled me. "The photo," I forced the words through my terror. "Where did you get it?"

He smiled then, and jerked his gaze back to mine. "Wouldn't you like to know?"

Keep him talking, Phantom growled in my head. His rage was chilling, making me whimper. *Keep him busy...we're on our way.*

"Tell me," I demanded. "Where the fuck did you get it?"

"They traffic, did you know that?" He spat wincing as he pressed his fingers to the blood in his shoulder. One guttural moan and he swayed, sucked in a deep breath and shoved his hand over my breast. There was a hardness in his eyes, pain turned to cruel determination.

My heart jackhammered in my chest. "What?"

"The Wolves. They traffic their women. Didn't they tell you?" Murphy leaned close, digging the muzzle of my gun against my breastbone. "I bet he didn't. Bet he didn't tell you a lot of things. It's only a matter of time until you'll be in some filthy fucking motel with track marks in your arms and five guys lined up to have their turn with you."

A memory slipped in. The man from the office parking lot, the one screaming and hollering about his wife. *They kidnapped her!* His words surfaced. *They fucking sold her. Do you care more about the fucking monsters than you do about us?*

Cruel cold plunged deep as I whispered, "No."

*Carina...*Phantom called. *Carina, what is it?*

"Yes," Murphy insisted, opening the top button of my blouse, then the next. "I can give you the name and address of one of their husbands. He can tell you exactly the kind of *monsters* those men are. You fell for the wrong monster, Carina..." He bent lower, his lips parted and ready. "You fucked the wrong beast."

"No!" I screamed and bucked, not caring about the gun pressed to my chest anymore. "Get off me!"

I jerked my head to the side, evading his mouth. Desperation drove me as I punched and slapped, fighting like a wildcat until I knocked the gun away. He tried to reach for it, stretching his arm over my head to the ground, his bloody shoulder right in front of my face. I grabbed his wound, digging my fingers into the flesh until he screamed and fell away.

I was up in an instant, scrambling to my feet and lunging through the trees.

The house...just get to the house.

Twigs snapped under my boots as I stumbled and ran.

"Get the fuck back here!" Murphy bellowed.

I kept on running, kept on focusing on those darkened windows until the unmistakable snarl of a Wolf echoed around me. I stopped, skidded, and whipped my gaze to the trees. My pulse was deafening, smothering the sound. "Phantom?" I called.

Darkness shifted at my right, a midnight blur moved, low, slinking...silver eyes shining in the night making the hairs on the back of my neck stand on end. I knew in an instant it wasn't Phantom.

Knew immediately it wasn't any Wolf I knew at all.

A howl cracked through the air like a gunshot and the midnight Wolf jerked his gaze toward the sound. His black lips peeled back from stark white fangs. I stepped backwards, smacking into the wall of the house as Murphy came belting from the trees.

Boom! The gunshot shattered the air.

But the bullet wasn't for me. Movement came from the trees behind him as Murphy ran and tried to fire behind him at Wolves bigger than any I'd seen before...and Phantom.

He was savage, sleek, and predatory, his gaze fixed on the bastard who'd tried to hurt me.

"Carina!" he roared in my mind.

I stumbled out from the side of the house, tearing my gaze from the sight of him to that hulking lone midnight beast. But it wasn't there now. The beast was gone. I lifted my head to the rustling in the trees in the distance.

"I'm here!" I stumbled into view. "Phantom, I'm here!"

All four sets of eyes glinted as they found me. I should've been terrified as the beasts in front of me flanked me on all sides...and closed in.

I should've been running for my life.

But I didn't.

Instead, I was mesmerized as the smaller beast slowed and stopped in front of me. Dark eyes glinted as its hackles rose. It was magnificent, massive shoulders rolling as it took a step closer, nostrils flaring wide as it panted. *Arran...*the sexy Wolf's face filled my head. *It's me...Arran.*

I wobbled on my feet, reaching out before stumbling toward him and fell. He was there in an instant, thick fur pressing against me as a drag from a cold nose slid down my neck. Hard breaths, that's all I heard...it's what I clung to.

I turned my gaze to the others, to the enormous sandy coat of a Wolf even bigger than Arran's beast. *Church,* I realized, as the beast stalked forward, moved to Phantom's side, and glanced my way. He scented me, nostrils flaring as those silver eyes darted over my body.

Fingers sank into Arran's fur. Sleek muscles tensed underneath as he drove himself against me in a pillar of power and strength.

I found the other beast, *Vitold.* His head lowered, lips curled, his gaze fixed on his prey...and that prey stumbled backwards, his gaze tearing from beast to beast until he stopped on the most powerful hunter of them all...

My heart thundered as Phantom turned his head. That silver gaze found mine, then dropped to my torn shirt hanging open. Cold air licked the swell of my exposed breast as thunder slipped from the Alpha, the growl so deep and threatening, it trembled against my skin as he slowly shifted his gaze to the pathetic piece of shit who'd lured me here.

"Stop right there!" Murphy commanded, taking aim once more. "I said *stop right fucking there or I'll shoot!"*

He was wasting his time...I could've told him that. I'd shot the Alpha myself and still he was here, striding toward the mortal until he grabbed him by the throat. "Carina," Phantom growled, his voice deep and raw. "Are you okay?"

"Yes." I sucked in a deep breath as the sleek midnight Wolf came closer. Arran moved like the ocean, rushing toward me with barely a movement or a sound.

Cold and wet pressed against my neck as the beast nuzzled my skin. The blast of his breath was like a furnace as he nudged me, sliding his muzzle from my neck, to my breast, then lower.

A dangerous sound slipped from him, rumbling in the back of his throat. I lifted my hand slowly, fingers splayed, inching closer to him. He lifted his gaze as I touched him, my fingers sinking into the thick fur.

"Give me one reason not to tear out your fucking throat?" Phantom wrenched Murphy higher.

I caught the movement in the corner of my eye, but my focus was on him...the Wolf who'd slept with his face pressed between my breasts, the Wolf who'd followed me...*protected me.*

They'd all protected me.

"Thank you," the words trembled and I hated how weak they sounded.

My body shook, and it wasn't just from the cold. Movement came from the side as Vitold came forward, his rich coat glinting like burnt umber as he moved.

"You l-lay one fucking hand on me and I'll have the whole department hunting you down," Murphy choked out as Phantom tightened his hold.

"He's not worth it," I snarled, turning my gaze to the vile fucking scum.

Tremors coursed through me. I hated them, hated how my body said one thing…and my violent soul screamed another. I dropped my hand from Arran's neck and turned. I forced myself to move, if only to tear myself free from terror's hold. No man would make me his victim…and no *man* would claim me as a prize. Now I had my own pack…and my own *Alpha*.

I crossed the distance between us, stumbling over tufts of grass and sunken hollows to where Phantom still the piece of shit by his throat. "I'd really like to knock your fucking teeth out," I winced with the stab of pain in my head. "Lucky for you I'm not my full potential. But Phantom here," I glanced at the Alpha catching a glint of amusement in his eyes. "I bet the Alpha could do some real damage. So I'm going to ask you once, the photograph. Where did you get it?"

Even with his gun still in his hand, he was weak. His vile lips curled in a sneer and that spark of hate echoed from deep inside him…an untapped well of cruelty and anger. I knew in that moment he wouldn't tell me, just because I was desperate…and I *was* desperate.

But it was a different desperation now. I was in control of this, in control of it all. "Let him go," I said, and shifted my gaze to Phantom. "He's not worth it."

The Alpha's lips curled, baring long fangs. One word from me, and Murphy's life would be over. Two simple words. But Phantom waited and watched. His strength was all I needed. *All of their strength.* Twigs snapped as the rest of the pack closed in, flanking us, their rage directed at one man...and one man alone.

"You know what? Don't tell me." I swept my gaze to Murphy once more. One step, and Phantom released him, letting the bastard stumble, gasping and choking. I moved before he realized it, grabbed him by the shoulders, and drove my knee between his legs.

He buckled...like I knew he would, falling to his knees as he grabbed his cock...that he wouldn't be using anytime soon. "Come near me again, Murphy, and I'll do more than knee you in the balls. I'll hang you out to dry, then I'll fucking shoot you again. Next time, my aim will be better."

I turned as agony now roared to the surface leaving the pathetic excuse for a man to whimper and moan. "Can we please get out of here?" I whispered.

The world blurred as the sickening *snap* of bones filled the air. Phantom's arms were around me in an instant, holding me against him as Arran's Wolf dropped to the ground. *He's hurt. Arran's hurt.* I took a panicked stumble forward as the beast whimpered, stopping in an instant as his body shattered and shifted, morphing from beast to man until the thick midnight fur of his beast drew inwards and sank under his skin.

His chest rose under deep breaths, and his arms trembled as he pushed his torso from the ground and pierced me with that electric gaze. "Only if I can drive my goddamn car."

"Deal." I fought a smile, until he pushed himself upright, standing in front of me as naked as the day he was born.

"Touch her again and see what happens...there won't be enough mortals in this fucking world to stop me from tearing you apart," Phantom promised Murphy as he stalked closer, watching the whimpering piece of shit cower and raise his hands in defense. "Arran," the Alpha growled, and the cocky, *very* naked Wolf snapped to attention. "Take her home...*our home*, where she belongs."

Arran's grin grew wider, showing his perfect white teeth. "About fucking time," he cheered, and held out his hand. "Special Agent, if you'll allow me…"

Warmth closed around me as I took his hand. He drew me close, nuzzling my neck once more, only this time the sound that came from his chest was comforting and safe. *You are safe,* his voice bloomed in my head. *You're safe with us.*

I glanced over my shoulder at Phantom, who still stood over Murphy.

They traffic, did you know that? Murphy's words roared into my head. *I bet he didn't. Bet he didn't tell you a lot of things.*

I let Arran lead me away, let him wrap his arm around my shoulders and draw me against his chest. But I wasn't stupid… nor was I weak. The beasts had come to save me…*only who would save me from them?*

26

"You're quiet." Arran glanced my way as we hurtled along the road heading for the sparkling city lights. "It's my driving, isn't it? Ruth prayed the first time," he chuckled, "funniest fucking thing I've seen."

He scowled then, glanced at the speed, and tapped the brakes. "With you it's different. I'll go slower, do better."

"It's not your driving, Arran." I reached out on instinct and touched his arm. He wore sweat pants now and a gray t-shirt that'd been hidden in a compartment in the back of the Jeep.

"Then it's something else. What is it?"

I searched his face. Those sparkling eyes and perfect fucking lips. Still, Murphy's remarks lingered, worming their way deeper into that glimmer of happiness. "He said something to me...said *the Wolves traffic their women.*'" I watched him flinch, then swallow. "That's a lie, though, isn't it?"

He tried to hide the reaction, but the quick smile didn't quite warm him, not like it had before. "That's ridic—"

"Lie to me and we're done," I warned. "I'll walk away. I'll do this on my own."

The words died, as did the hint of a grin. Instead, he swallowed *hard.* "It's not what you think."

I leaned closer, rage driving to the surface once more. I'd found my gun and found my courage, as well. "Then tell me."

We tore past the service station at the entrance to the city and Arran slowed the Jeep. "I can't," he growled. "It's not my place."

"Then whose fucking place is it?"

"You want the truth? Talk to Phantom...he'll tell you the truth."

Just like that, he changed in front of me. These...*Wolves* weren't any fucking different from every other asshole with an agenda up their sleeve. I closed my eyes and pushed myself back in the seat. "How could I be so fucking stupid?"

"Give him a chance, Carina." I'd never heard the Wolf so serious. "It's not what you think."

We spent the rest of the drive in silence. I wrapped my arms around my body as shock slowly wore off and pain moved in. My damn head was bleeding and my lip was split and swollen. I pressed my tongue to the split and licked the blood.

By the time we were across the bridge, I was feeling nauseous, my stomach rolling with every corner. I yanked the door open as Arran pulled the Jeep into the parking lot beside the Hunting Ground. He was out of the car in an instant, striding around to lift me in his arms.

"You've got a concussion," he murmured, clutching me to his chest.

"Wait, I can walk..." I muttered as the world spun.

"Jesus Christ, you're stubborn," he groaned, and kicked my door closed. "Sexy as fuck...but a solid ten on the pain-in-my-ass scale."

"Fuck your scale." I wrapped my arms around his neck, and held on tight.

The scent of blood and earth filled me. Like freedom. Like *a beast.* God, he smelled good. I pressed my face deeper into the allure and dragged my lips along his neck.

"Carina," he said carefully, his tone deep with hunger. But it was fear that pushed into my head. Fear with the taste of his Wolf. Fear that bloomed like a dark desire. Here was the hidden male…*here was what I wanted.* "Don't…don't make me want you, not more than I already do."

Pain echoed in the darkness. Rejection. Suffering…

I saw it all before he tore his raw gaze away, punched in the code for the back door, and yanked the handle. Darkness waited for us. Tiny white lights shining from the floor were all we had to see.

"What happened to you?" The words ripped free before I could stop them.

He carried me toward the private entrance as the heavy beat of music echoed from the nightclub. Sex filled this place, spilling from the cracks and crevices until it found that Unseelie hunger and pushed my pain aside.

I held onto that desire and dragged it closer to the surface as Arran stopped walking. He turned his head, and a wave of lust hit me like a savage blow.

"Tell me, Wolf." I whispered.

His nostrils flared as he slowly lowered my feet to the floor. We were outside the door, still in the hallway that connected to the club, but I was past the point of caring. I opened myself to that unfathomable desire, and saw that same ache in him.

"I was rejected by my mate," he murmured with a smile. "She didn't want me. I wasn't *Alpha enough for her.*"

"Not Alpha enough?" I repeated, and lifted my hand. "Is she fucking blind?"

The tiny bark of laughter did nothing to hide the truth.

"And Ruth?" I snapped, agony blending into jealousy. "Was she *the right fit?*"

"Ruth," he shook his head and sighed. "I thought I'd protect her, thought I'd be what she needed, even if was just for a while. But I wasn't, story of my fucking life really."

My heart thrummed at the sorrow in his voice. I lifted my hand as that sickening wave of hunger ripped through me. *Sex and blood and death and hunger.* That's all this desire was…and it fueled me now, forcing that screaming need to be careful, to not become attached aside. As that foul green from my chest brightened the space around us, I sank my fingers into the thick curls of his hair as I whispered, "Thank god for that."

Surprise flared in his eyes for a second before I slid my hand around behind his neck and pulled him closer. I shouldn't want him like this, shouldn't want any of them. "Otherwise you would've never met me."

His lips met mine. I winced at the flare of pain from my lip before he broke away. "Christ, I can't do this again. I can't…"

I tightened my hold as the soft green glow brightened against his chest. Need roared, pushing everything else aside. "Shut the fuck up and kiss me."

He did, his lips claiming mine, tasting my mouth.

"Nice to see you two are home in one piece," the Russian murmured behind us.

We broke apart as the door opened at the end of the hallway and Phantom strode through. He took one look at me, then cut a glare toward Arran. "You okay, Carina?"

"I'll heal," I answered, finding that flicker of anger. The Russian slipped past, shoving open the door to the Wolves' den. "But we have things to discuss, you and I."

"We do?" One brow rose on the Alpha as he glanced at Arran once more.

"She knows," the Wolf muttered beside me. "That piece of shit…"

Phantom tried to smother the flinch, tried to mask the flicker in his gaze. But I could feel him…feel him more clearly than I'd ever felt anyone before. Panic hit me…follow by a heavy throb of loss.

"Inside," he jerked his gaze through the doorway. "I'll tell you what you want to know."

I followed the Russian into the living quarters as the TV was switched on and he disappeared, yanking his shirt over his head. Muscles flexed and strained, and the image of his Wolf rose once more, with the perfect amber-colored fur, a powerful predator, before he turned at the hallway and disappeared.

The door closed behind me as Church strode in, stopping for a second to capture my chin and look at my face. I lifted my gaze to meet his.

"This hurt?" He brushed his thumb across my swollen lip.

"A little," I answered. "Not as much as my head."

He lifted his hand to the back of my head, his careful fingers finding the painful bump. I moaned, fighting a wave of nausea. "What the fuck did he hit you with?"

"Tire iron," I replied, closing my eyes. "Right before I shot him."

Savage silence filled the space. A harsh rush of breath followed, then a threatening growl, one that made me open my eyes.

"Should've killed the bastard," Phantom lamented, watching me from the kitchen. "Should've gutted him on the spot and left him alive."

A chill raced along my spine with his words as Church pressed and worked his fingers around the knot on my skull. I glanced at the blond Adonis in front of me. These were dangerous men…and he was the most dangerous of them all. A savage. A predator. *A Wolf.*

"He told me the Wolves traffic their women, said I'd be next." There was a tremble in my voice, a weakness I hated.

Phantom glanced at Church, who stilled, then dropped his

hands from the back of my head. "She's all yours," he announced with a careful glance at his Alpha before he turned and left.

A chill settled in the air. Beyond the doors, the grinding music from the nightclub could still be heard. But it was only background noise, making me aware it was just us again.

"Come with me," Phantom murmured, and lowered his arms. "I want to show you something."

I didn't move right away, searching my instincts. I wanted to believe him, wanted it more than anything right now.

It's not what you think. Arran's words made me step forward and it was those words that lingered in my mind as I followed the Alpha, turning right where the Russian had disappeared and striding along the hall.

Phantom stopped at a closed door at the end of the hallway, waiting for me before he turned the handle and pushed the door wide. Bright lights flickered, then illuminated the space as I entered…and for a second, I thought I'd stepped onto the homicide floor of Crown City PD. The walls were covered with images and connections, and three photos sat at the top. Two had names and some information connected to them. But it was the middle one that held my gaze, a male with long, pitch-black hair that cascaded down his shoulders. He had the look of a killer. The look of a Wolf.

I turned my focus to the first image. Cold dead eyes stared back from the Vampire I'd seen in the warehouse, the one torn apart by Ruth's Vampires. "I saw him that night."

"Caedes." Phantom stepped closer. "This is the Inner Circle."

I looked his way as that pain in my head dulled. "Are they some group of mercenaries?"

"They are the head of our lines, the ones who set our laws and govern them., the ones we work for."

Surprise filled me. "Work for?"

"We send them the lion's share of our profits, the Vampires

manage the money, we take care of the women, and the Fae the magic."

Take care of the women... "So you *do* traffic! You sell them...*sonofabitch.*"

"*No!*" he roared, and closed the distance between us in an instant, grabbing my arm as anger seethed in his eyes. "I offer them opportunities. *I* offer them *safety.*"

"In the back of a truck until they're sold like cattle to a man or men who'll rape them until they cease to exist."

He flinched as though I'd slapped him. His voice was as cold as stone. "After all we've been through, you honestly believe I'm that kind of man?"

Rape you? You're sick, female. I'm offering you a way out of this. Use me. The Alpha's words filled me, words he'd said that night. But it hadn't been just words, had it?

He'd taken care of me.

Washed me.

Fucked me.

Rode my body over and over again until that Unseelie glow in my chest dulled. He'd protected me, he'd watched over me. Instinct raged to the surface, but it wasn't because of what Murphy had said, or the mass of evidence taped to the wall in front of me. "No." I met his gaze. "No, I don't think you are."

"I'm not a perfect man." He pinned me with his stare. "Nor am I fair. I'm cruel at times. I'm savage. But I protect those girls." He swallowed hard, his voice cracking. "Like they're my sisters."

That was the truth here.

That was the heart of it all.

I knew it in the sorrow that darkened his eyes and cracked his tone. "The center man you see there is Finis, the leader of the Wolves. I served him for a while, like an enforcer of a kind, until I found out he was murdering innocents, selling them exactly like you said. Most of them were women...to be used for breeding or for sport. I tried to stop him, found enough Wolves to support me to take him out." He closed his eyes then. Throat muscles worked as he tried to swallow. "He found out and sent men to infiltrate my camp. So much bloodshed…so much death. He killed them all while I was out finding more men to stand with me…and he took my sister."

Oh no…no…

Phantom opened his eyes then, and the pain that raged inside them swallowed me whole. "She was just a kid…no more than thirteen."

Agony plunged like a knife in my chest. "He sold her?"

"No," he answered. "He hid her."

That agony in my heart beat a thousand drums. "She's ransom, isn't she?"

It was the only thing that made sense. The only thing that'd keep a man like Phantom in line. *It's not what you think.* Arran had tried to tell me. He'd tried to warn me this was more than what it seemed. This was all connected…every single piece of it.

"I've had men watching his every move since. They'd been able to track him…until a few days ago."

My blood ran cold. "A few days ago."

"Just before the attack at the warehouse." He turned and glared at the wall of information. "They haven't found him since."

A tremor raced through me like something icy slithered up my spine. "And the girls who work for you, the ones who disappear?"

"You mean the ones beaten by their husbands or boyfriends? The ones whose bodies are sold at private functions to earn that Lamborghini or shiny new Tesla? They come to me desperate, bruised, and in pain. I take their pain…I take *all* their fucking pain and I give them new identities. I give them money…I give them a way out."

Relief swept through me in a torrid rush. "Oh, Jesus." I stumbled backwards, turning to find a desk and a chair. I flopped into the chair, letting that heady emotion carry me away. "You fucking give them protection?"

"If I can't save Marian," he answered, meeting my gaze, "then I'll save those I can. *Including you.*"

My breath caught in my chest. I was trapped by his desperation, driven harder and further than I'd ever dared before. He'd saved me that night, saved me in the warehouse and again when he'd brought me here. I pushed up from the seat and strode toward him.

There was no tremble in my body now.

No flicker of distrust.

Only desire...only hunger.

...that's what kind of man he was.

A protector. A savior. *An Alpha.*

"I would never hurt you," he murmured, holding my gaze. "Never betray you, never deny you."

Jesus. "Never deny me?" I whispered, and reached for him. "Deny me what?"

"Us," Church answered from the doorway. "He'd never deny you *us.*"

The massive blond stepped forward, and the others followed, the Russian next, then Arran.

"We are yours," Arran murmured. "If you want us."

Hope danced in his eyes, hope and longing.

"You can take your time," Vitold reassured with his Russian accent. "Touch us," he held out his hand as he came to me. "Kiss us. Get to know us."

I glanced at Phantom, who watched as I took Vitold's hand in mine. "You want this?" I questioned as that powerful wave of hunger rose in me. "Tell me the truth before feelings are involved."

Phantom took a step closer and flanked my side to lower his head and murmur into my ear. "Feelings are already involved here, Carina. I thought you understood that by now. You're healing faster now, this…" he lowered his gaze to that throbbing green glow in my chest. "Unseelie power is making you stronger."

Vitold released my hand and trailed his fingers up my arm until they wrapped gently around my neck. He moved behind me, pulling me back against his hard body.

"So the only question left is," Phantom asked as my head fell to the shoulder at my back, the powerful muscles rippling at my contact. "Do *you* want this?"

Arran moved closer, leaving Church behind to watch.

"Answer the Alpha," Vitold urged, his hand tightening just a little as he moved against me. I could feel his cock, hard… straining against the confines of his jeans.

"Yes," I growled as that green glow blazed to life in my chest again. "Yes, I want this."

Phantom's lips curled in a satisfied smile. "Do you want to kiss him?"

Panic pushed to the surface. "Which one?"

"All of us," the Russian behind me declared, then turned my head with a thumb against my jaw.

He kissed me, his soft lips taking mine with smooth strength. I lost myself to the feeling of him, to the way he dragged his teeth gently across my lip and claimed my mouth with his own, until in an instant, he drew away.

My lips throbbed as Arran stepped closer, lifting his hand to cup my cheek. "Do you really want me?"

Desire was untamable inside me, wild and free. "Yes, I want you, Arran. Christ, I want you." He lowered his hand to the torn remnants of my shirt. "Touch me," I demanded. "I want the memory of Murphy's touch gone."

Arran winced at the words and slowly lifted his hands, which trembled as he parted the torn halves of my shirt. I should be terrified being like this with all of them. I should be frozen with fear. "Arran," I whispered, drawing the cocky bartender's gaze.

"I just don't want to fuck this up," he muttered with a smile that was more of a wince.

"I want you," I whispered. "I want you to touch me, to kiss me. I want you..."

Vitold pressed his body against my back again and moaned, his splayed fingers stroking my throat. "Say it," the Russian murmured in my ear. "Put the poor bastard out of his misery. Put us all out of our fucking misery."

"Make love to me," I instructed.

"Jesus fucking Christ," Arran choked, his eyes filled with so much need. His fingers didn't tremble now as he slid my shirt down my arms.

One drag of my bra strap and my breast bounced free.

"Fuck me, you're beautiful," the Russian sighed.

I lifted my hand to Vitold's cheek as Arran moved closer. The warmth of his tongue made me shiver as he licked my nipple and took me in his mouth. "Mine," he growled as I turned my head over my shoulder to Vitold.

"Mine," the Russian echoed and kissed me again.

The soft beep of a phone never broke their focus. Mouths, lips. *Insatiable need.*

"What did you say?" Church snarled. "Fire? What the fuck...*a body?*"

Arran snapped his head upwards as I broke Vitold's kiss.

The air changed in an instant. Gone was the urgency of need as Church's panicked gaze found Phantom's and he barked into the phone. "We're on our way...*we're on our goddamn way!*"

27

The Camaro roared as we hurtled toward the other side of the city, heading for the nightclub Wild. Smoke billowed into the sky, blending into the storm clouds above. The sight only made Phantom drive faster. Arran, Church, and Vitold followed in a Hummer, taking every turn just as fast as we did. Red and blue lights streamed toward the blaze...as well as unmarked sedans, unmarked sedans that didn't normally respond to a callout like this.

"Something's wrong," I worried, watching as car after car tore past us.

"Yeah, my fucking business is burning to the ground," he snarled, downshifted into the turn, and punched the accelerator.

"No, Phantom. *Something is wrong here,*" I repeated, my hand going to the empty pocket of my pants. "Shit, my phone."

We turned the corner with a squeal and hurtled toward the towering flames as they lashed and raged. Firetrucks lined the streets, but it was the unmarked FBI cars that concerned me, especially when I caught sight of Harlan standing in the middle of the darkened lot behind the club. "What the fuck is Harlan here for?"

Phantom snarled, yanked the wheel hard, and pulled us over to the far side of the street away from the blaze. I was out of the car in an instant, striding toward Harlan as he barked orders.

"What the hell is going on?" I called over the roar of the fire.

Harlan whipped his gaze to mine, rage curling his lips as he charged toward me. *"Where the fuck have you been? I've been calling you for half a fucking hour."* Harlan was fiery at the best of times, but never like this…he looked manic, *unrestrained.*

"I lost my phone," I answered, and glanced at the crime scene guys at the back of the blaze. They were handling a body.

The skin was blistered and shriveled, and a white shirt gaped open. But it was the entrails that dangled from the sides as they moved him…and as the tech moved, I caught sight of the deceased male's face.

"No," I whimpered. *"Is that?"*

"Murphy's dead, gutted like a goddamn fish. But we have an eyewitness." Harlan's voice was savage as he turned that deadly gaze to Phantom. "Said it was the Wolfe who owned the nightclub, the one who drives a Camaro. The one they call Phantom."

"No," the Alpha growled behind me, and shook his head. "There's been a misunderstanding…"

Agents and police moved behind Harlan, like a wall of law enforcement. Guns were drawn as Phantom let out a savage growl. "I did *not* do this."

"Harlan, wait," I barked, and stepped in front of my Alpha. "This wasn't Phantom. It wasn't any of them. Murphy lured me out to a damn farmhouse. He tried to rape me and he almost succeeded but Phantom saved me. They *all* fucking saved me."

Harlan's cold, unmerciful gaze found mine. "Why the fuck should I believe you? You've had it in for Murphy from day one.

Are you *one of them, Chase?* Is that what this is? Kill a goddamn agent and stake your claim with the Wolves?"

"No," I cried and shook my head. "You know me better than that."

Harlan's gaze slipped behind me to all four of the Wolves at my back. "Take them," he ordered. "Take them all."

The wall of enforcement lunged toward us, gun muzzles aimed at me…and the Wolves.

"Get the fuck down!"

"Get on the ground! I said, GET ON THE GROUND!"

Screams mingled with the roar of the fire as my world became surreal as I was grabbed, lifted, and carried away.

All I could hear was Harlan as he roared, *"I WANT THEM HUNTED DOWN!"*

Gunshots blasted the night. Behind me, Phantom roared with pain. I was practically smothered by all four of the Wolves as they closed around me, protecting me with their bodies as we ran for our lives…

Crown City is divided.
Mortals on one side of the river and the beasts on the other.
Only I'm a woman caught in the middle, and now I'm forced to choose a side. Return to the FBI who's hunting us, or run with the Wolves?

Get ready for Wolf's Hunger!

I will fight. I will hunt. *I will love.*

Wolf's Hunger out now.

www.ingramcontent.com/pod-product-compliance
Lightning Source LLC
Chambersburg PA
CBHW071139180726
48291CB00007B/2261